Suto

THE LOVE GODDESS'
COOKING SCHOOL

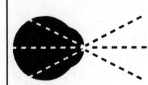

**This Large Print Book carries the
Seal of Approval of N.A.V.H.**

THE LOVE GODDESS' COOKING SCHOOL

MELISSA SENATE

WHEELER PUBLISHING
A part of Gale, Cengage Learning

GALE
CENGAGE Learning

Detroit • New York • San Francisco • New Haven, Conn • Waterville, Maine • London

GALE
CENGAGE Learning™

Copyright © 2010 by Melissa Senate.
Wheeler Publishing, a part of Gale, Cengage Learning.

LIBRARY OF CONGRESS CATALOGING-IN-PUBLICATION DATA

Senate, Melissa.
    The love goddess' cooking school / by Melissa Senate.
        p. cm.
    ISBN-13: 978-1-4104-3579-8 (hardcover)
    ISBN-10: 1-4104-3579-2 (hardcover)
    1. Single women—Fiction. 2. Cooking schools—Fiction. 3.
Maine—Fiction. 4. Chick lit. 5. Large type books. I. Title.
    PS3619.E658L68 2011
    813'.6—dc22   2010049605

Published in 2011 by arrangement with Gallery Books, a division of Simon & Schuster, Inc.

Printed in the United States of America
1 2 3 4 5 6 7 15 14 13 12 11

In memory of my grandparents,
Ann and Abe Steinberg

ACKNOWLEDGMENTS

Many thanks to my agent, Alexis Hurley, whose insight, especially at the idea stage, was invaluable; my editor, Jennifer Heddle, for yet another brilliant, thoughtful revision letter; my family and friends (Lee Nichols Naftali, I am particularly talking to you) for their cheery support; and my dear son, Max, who turned me from the takeout queen into a cook in constant training. (Note: Max is proof that the recipes at the back of the book are kid-friendly.)

I was thirty-two when I started cooking; up
until then, I just ate.

— Julia Child

ONE

According to Holly Maguire's late grand-mother, revered on Blue Crab Island, Maine, for her fortune-telling as much as her cooking, the great love of Holly's life would be one of the few people on earth to like *sa cordula,* an Italian delicacy. It was made of lamb intestines and stewed with onions, tomatoes, and peas in a savory but-ter sauce that did little to hide the fact that it looked exactly like what it was.

"So I'll know if someone is 'the one' if he likes stewed lamb guts?" Holly had asked repeatedly over the years. "That's it? That's my entire fortune?" She'd kept hoping her grandmother would say, *Just kidding! Of course that's not it, bella. Your true fortune is this: you will be very happy.*

Holly would be satisfied with that.

Not that Camilla Constantina would ever say *just kidding.* Or kid, for that matter.

"That is it," was her grandmother's response, every time, her gleaming black eyes giving nothing away. "The stones have spoken."

A month ago, her hand trembling, her heart hoping, Holly had set a plate of *sa cordula* in front of John Reardon, the man she loved. As she'd been living in California, thousands of miles away from her grandmother in an attic apartment with no oven, she'd paid the Italian butcher's eighty-six-year-old great-aunt to prepare the dish. Holly and John had been a couple for almost two years. She was practically a stepmother to his four-year-old daughter Lizzie. And more than anything, Holly wanted to become part of their family.

Why had her grandmother saddled her with this fortune? Who could possibly like *sa cordula?* Holly had tasted it three times before, and it was so . . . slimily awful that even Holly's grandfather, who, per legend, ate even more reviled "delicacies," had hated it. But the love of Camilla's life wasn't supposed to like it. Her Great Love was to have blond hair and blue eyes, and when in 1957 twenty-two-year-old single Camilla had turned down another eligible, dark-eyed, dark-haired man in her small village near Milan, everyone worried she was crazy like her spinster aunt Marcella, who mut-

12

tered in a back room. But some months later, the dashing Armando Constantina, with his butter-colored hair and Adriatic blue eyes, had come to town and swept her off her feet all the way to America, and Camilla's reputation as a fortune-teller had been restored.

Holly's father, Bud Maguire, had taken one bite of *sa cordula* during Thanksgiving dinner in 1982 and forever refused to taste anything his mother-in-law cooked unless he recognized it and knew what it was. Bud liked plain old spaghetti doused with jarred Ragu and a piece of garlic bread, which was just fine with Holly's mother, Luciana Maguire, who went by Lucy and had no interest in her heritage or cooking. Or fortune-telling. Especially because Camilla Constantina's supposed source of knowledge was a trio of small, smooth stones she'd chosen from the banks of the Po River as a three-year-old. "I'd sooner believe in a crystal ball from the clearance aisle in Walmart," Holly's mother had often said with her usual disdain.

It had taken Camilla Constantina until Holly was sixteen to tell her granddaughter her fortune. As an adolescent, Holly had asked her grandmother over and over to sit her down with the stones and tell Holly what she was desperate to know — would Mike Overstill ever ask her out? Would she do okay on the American history test worth 85 percent of her final grade? Would her mother ever stop being such a killjoy? Camilla would just take both her hands and tell her all would be well. But finally, on Holly's sixteenth birthday, when Mike Overstill had not shown up at six thirty to escort her to the junior prom (he had called twenty minutes later to say, "Sorry, um, I forgot I asked someone else"), her grandmother, who was visiting, reached for her white satin pouch (out of eyesight of Holly's mother, of course) and said *si,* it was time. Camilla took the three smooth stones from the pouch and closed her hands around them. As Holly held her breath in anticipation, her grandmother held Holly's hand with her free one and closed her eyes for a good half minute.

And the long-awaited revelation was that the great love of Holly's life would like lamb intestines tossed with peas. In butter sauce.

This, from a woman who'd rightly foretold the fates of hundreds of year-rounders and summer tourists on Blue Crab Island and the nearby mainland towns, who'd drive over the bridge to pay twenty-five dollars to sit in the breakfast nook of Camilla Constantina's famed kitchen and have their fortunes told.

Holly had said she was sure there was something else. Perhaps her grandmother could close her eyes a bit longer? Or just do it all over again? Camilla would only say that sometimes the fortune could not be understood readily, that it held hidden meaning. To the day Camilla Constantina had died, just two weeks ago, the fortune had not changed. Nor had the meaning become clear. Holly had been taking it literally from the first time she'd fallen in love. At nineteen. Then again at twenty-four. And yet again two years ago, at twenty-eight, when she fell in love with John Reardon.

Because she couldn't, wouldn't serve lamb intestines to a guy she was crazy about, she'd wait until she knew she was losing him, knew from the way he stopped holding her gaze, started being impatient, started being unavailable. And unkind.

And so to console herself that this man was *not* her Great Love, she would serve him the *sa cordula* as an appetizer — a small portion so as not to tip the scales in her favor (who *would* like a big portion of sheep guts?). And each time, bittersweet success. The love she was losing was not her Great Love. He was just a guy who didn't like *sa cordula* — and didn't love her. It made it easier when he broke up with her.

This time, though, *this* love, was different. Despite John's pulling away. Despite his impatience. Despite the way he stopped calling her at midnight to tell her he loved her and wish her sweet dreams. She loved John Reardon. She wanted to marry John Reardon, this man she'd fallen for on a solo vacation to San Francisco, where she'd gone to get over a lesser love. This man she'd stayed for, uprooting herself from Boston, hoping to finally find her . . . destiny, what she was meant to do with her life. And she thought she'd found it in this mini family of two. She wanted to spend the rest of her life baking cookies with Lizzie every other weekend during the child's visitation with her father; she wanted to shampoo those golden curls, push her on swings, and watch her grow. Everyone, namely her mother, had told her she was crazy for dating a newly divorced man with a kid. But Holly adored Lizzie, loved almost-stepmotherhood. And she loved John enough to wait. Though the past few months, he'd stopped referring to "some day" altogether.

And the past few weeks, he was more distant than ever. They always got together on Wednesday nights, so there Holly was, changing Lizzie into her favorite Curious George pajamas after her bath while John avoided Holly. He was on his cell phone (first with his brother, then with his boss), texting a client, emailing a file, looking for Lizze's favorite Hello Kitty cup. He was everywhere but next to Holly.

She sat on the brown leather sofa in the living room, Lizzie cross-legged next to her as Holly combed her long, damp, honey-colored curls and sang the ABC song. Lizzie knew all her letters except for *LMNOP*, which she combined into "ellopy." Usually when Holly gave Lizzie her bath before dinner and brushed out her beautiful hair and sang silly nursery rhymes that made Lizzie giggle or they got to the "ellopy," John would stand there with *that* expression, the one that always assured Holly he loved her, that he was deeply touched at how close she and his daughter were. That one day, some day, maybe soon, he would ask her to marry him. And that this wish she walked around with, slept with every night and woke up with every morning would come true.

This wasn't a fairy tale, though, and Holly knew in her heart that John wasn't going to propose. Not in the near future and probably not ever. She knew this with 95 percent certainty, even though she wasn't psychic like her grandmother.

But how was she supposed to give up on John? Give up on what she wanted so badly? To marry this man, be this child's step-mother, and start a new life here in this little pale blue house on a San Francisco hill? Yes, things were strained between her and John, though she wasn't sure why. But that didn't mean things could not be unstrained. A long-term relationship went through lulls. This was a lull, perhaps.

There was only one way to know.

And so, when Lizzie was occupied with her coloring book and a new pack of Cray-olas, Holly went heavy-hearted into the kitchen to make the dinner she'd promised Lizzie, cheeseburgers in the shape of Mickey Mouse's head (the only food she cooked really well) and to heat up the Great Love test. With the cheeseburgers in front of them all, a side of linguini for Lizzie in butter sauce with peas (which looked a bit like the *sa cordula*) and two small plates of *sa cordula* before her and John, Holly sat down beside this pair she loved so much — and waited.

If John liked the *sa cordula,* she could relax, accept what he said, that he was just "tired, distracted by work." Etcetera, etcet-era. He *was* her Great Love. If he didn't like it, then what? No, she wouldn't let herself go there. Her breath caught somewhere in her body as John placed his napkin on his lap and picked up his fork, eyeing the *sa cordula*. In one moment, everything between them would change because of hope or lack thereof, and yet John looked exactly the same as he always did, sitting there at the dinner table in front of the bay window, so handsome, his thick sandy-blond hair hand-swept back from his face, the slight crinkles at the edges of his hazel eyes, the chiseled jawline with its slight darkening of five o'clock shadow.

Holly sucked in a quiet breath and took the quickest bite, keeping her expression neutral — despite the gritty, slimy texture of the *sa cordula*. The intestines of a lamb did not taste "just like chicken." Did not taste like anything but what it looked like. Savory butter sauce or not. And as if the peas could help.

John forked a bite and stared at it for a moment. "What is this again?" he asked.

"An old-world Italian dish my *nonna* sometimes makes," Holly said, trying not to stare at his fork.

Lizzie twirled her fork in her linguini the way Holly had taught her. "I wish I had a *nonna*."

"You do, pumpkin," Holly said, treasuring the idea of Camilla Constantina showing Lizzie how to roll out pasta with a tiny rolling pin. "You have two. Your mom's mother and your dad's mother."

"But if you and Daddy get married, then I'll have a *nonna* Holly too."

Out of the mouths of babes. Holly smiled. John stiffened. Lizzie twirled her linguini.

And then, as if in slow motion, John slid the fork of lamb intestines, topped with one pea, into his mouth. He paled a bit, his entire face contorting. He spit it out into his napkin. "I'm sorry, Holly, but this is the most disgusting thing I ever ate. No offense to your grandmother."

Or me, she thought, her heart breaking.

Maybe her grandmother was wrong.

But forty minutes later, after Holly had helped Lizzie brush her teeth, pulled the comforter up over her chest, read half of "Goldilocks and the Three Bears" and then kissed the sleeping girl's green-apple-scented head, John had come right out and said it. That he was sorry, it-wasn't-her-it-was-him, that despite not meaning to, he'd fallen in love with his administrative assistant, and she had a young son, so they really understood each other. And no, he didn't think it was a good idea if Holly continued to see Lizzie, even once a month for a trip to the playground or for ice cream. "She's four, Holl. She'll forget about you in a couple of weeks. Let's not complicate anything, okay?"

Holly wanted to complicate things. She wanted to complicate this whole breakup. And so she pleaded her case, reminded him of their two years together, of Lizzie's attachment to her, of the plans they'd made for the future. Which, Holly had had to concede, had dwindled to maybe going to the San Francisco Zoo the weekend after next. And when he just stood there, not saying anything and taking a sideways glance at the clock, she realized he was waiting for her to leave so he could call his new girlfriend and tell her he'd finally done it, he'd dumped Holly.

As if in slow motion, Holly went into the bathroom, afraid to look at him, afraid to look at anything, lest she start screaming like a lunatic. She closed the door and slid down against the back of it, covering her face with her hands as she cried. She sucked in a deep breath, then forced herself up to splash water on her face. She looked in the mirror over the sink, at the dark brown eyes, the dark brown hair, and the fair skin, so like her grandmother's, and told herself,

He's not your great love. He's not meant to be. It was little consolation.

And what if he had liked the *sa cordula?* Then what? How could she fight for a great love with someone who'd said he didn't love her as easily as he'd said the *sa cordula* was disgusting?

After a gentle yet impatient, "Holly, you can't stay in there all night," she came out of the bathroom. He handed her a shopping bag of her possessions he'd clearly packed earlier that day in anticipation of dumping her — a few articles of clothing and her toothbrush, and again said he was sorry, that he never wanted to hurt her. And then she stood in the doorway of Lizzie's room, watching the girl's slight body rise and fall with each sleeping breath.

"Good-bye, sweet girl," she whispered. "I'll bet if I'd given you a taste of the *sa cordula,* you would have asked for another."

TWO

One month and three thousand miles later, as Holly stood at the stove in her grandmother's kitchen — *her* kitchen now, she had to keep reminding herself — the breakup, the final good-night kiss she'd blown to sleeping Lizzie — was the One Sad Memory that went into the bowl of risotto on the counter.

In the month she'd been living in her grandmother's house, going through Camilla Constantina's easiest recipes, she still wasn't used to wishing into a pot of simmering marinara sauce or recalling a moment that made her cry while pounding a thick breast of chicken. She wasn't used to pounding a chicken breast, period. She wasn't used to anything — being alone in this country kitchen with its Tuscan-yellow bead-board walls and gleaming white-tiled center island, the copper pots and black cast-iron frying pans hanging from the rack above her head. The six-burner stove. And especially the recipe book. The very thing that had saved her, given her something to do, something to focus on.

She would not be bested by a bowl of risotto. If one could call the sticky mess in the bowl risotto. It tasted nothing like her grandmother's famed risotto alla Milanese. And now, Holly, who wouldn't even call herself a passable cook, unless you counted omelets, Micky Mouse–shaped cheeseburgers, spaghetti (if she didn't overcook it), and the homemade chicken nuggets she'd made often for picky-eater Lizzie, was attempting risotto al salto when she couldn't make a Bisquick pancake without half of it being burned and half being undercooked.

She glanced at the loose-leaf binder of Camilla's Cucinotta hand-scrawled recipes, which lay open to page twenty-three: *Risotto al salto.*

Risotto al salto
Leftover risotto alla Milanese
1 pat butter
1 sad memory
1 fervent wish

All of Camilla Constantina's recipes called for wishes and memories, either sad or happy or unqualified. They were as essential to Camilla as were the minced garlic or the tablespoon of olive oil. Her grandmother had told Holly that when she first started cooking as a young girl at her mother's hip, she began the tradition of adding the wishes and memories, which had delighted her elders. "She is saying her prayers into the osso buco," her mother and grandmother and aunts would say, patting little Camilla on the head. And since little Camilla would invariably wish for her father to return safely from war — and he did — the tradition was born. Much later Camilla would wish her own husband would recuperate from his heart attack and it would not be, yet she'd explain as best she could to Holly that the magic was in the wishing, not so much the getting. And that memories, particularly the sad ones, had healing properties, just like the basil or oregano she regularly used in her dishes.

During the past month, the memory of saying that final good-bye to John, of watching Lizzie sleep for the last time, of missing both of them with a fierceness that stopped her breath, had made it into quite possibly one hundred overcooked pastas, countless too sweet or too salty sauces, and three rubbery veal scallopinis alla something. She'd been trying not to think about John and Lizzie and the breakup that had brought her to her grandmother's house on a rainy September evening. Or what had happened since — on the chilly October morning she woke to find her grandmother lying lifeless in her bed, a tiny painting of the three Po River stones watching over her from the iron headboard. But Holly's new life — and the white binder containing her recipes — *insisted* upon memories.

No, she didn't want to think about John, who would likely be putting Lizzie to bed right then (it was his weekend, a schedule she'd have in her head forever), or Lizzie, who was probably asking him to read *Green Eggs and Ham* for the third time. Because if Holly let herself remember too much, she'd remember herself in that scenario, of hoping every weekend for a proposal, an engagement ring, that never came. And the pain of what she'd lost would knock her to her knees, as it had many times since she'd come running to her grandmother's house. The place she always ran to. And now the house was here, but the source of the comfort was gone.

What was left was this kitchen and the recipe book, her grandmother in the form of walls and ceiling and stove and hundreds

of utensils — and recipes. Very *original* recipes.

She pulled a broad-based black frying pan
from the wall of pots and pans adjacent to
the stove (the other day she'd had to type
broad-based frying pan into Google for a
picture, since her grandmother had so many
pans), set it on a burner, and sliced a pat of
butter into the center. Risotto al salto was
simply (ha — supposedly simply) a thin
pancake made from leftover risotto. She
reached for the binder and checked the
recipe for how high to set the burner and
for how long to let the pancake fry in its
swirl of butter. She had to get this right.
Camilla's Cucinotta was hers now, hers to
keep going for her grandmother, who'd left
her the house and the business — the
popular Italian cooking class and the tiny
takeout pasta shop. There was no time for
sobbing against the refrigerator for what
she'd lost. There were pastas and sauces to
make for tomorrow. There were recipes to
get right so that Holly could teach her
students how to make them like her grandmother did.

There was learning to cook.

Though Holly had spent a month every
summer of her childhood with her grandmother on Blue Crab Island, helped cook

beside her, rolled out fresh pasta so thin it was almost see-through, knew which pastas took which sauces, Holly was not a cook. She might have been, had she not almost killed her grandmother with her culinary experiment at the age of seven. She'd made her grandmother a sandwich piled high with ridiculous ingredients like a slice of cheese, a spoonful of ice cream, two slices of hard salami, a mashed scoop of banana, and, unknowingly, rat poison. Her grandmother had been in the hospital for almost two weeks, and despite her assurances that Holly was only seven, that it was an accident any child could make, and that the sandwich had been delicious otherwise, Holly had developed a fear of the kitchen, of what lurked inside cabinets and inside food, like the weevils her mother had always cautioned her about. She'd lost the love of cooking. During subsequent summers, Holly still helped in the kitchen, still loved sitting at the table, peeling potatoes, watching her grandmother hum along to the Italian opera that always played on a CD player. But she'd stopped trusting herself as a cook that day and she'd never gotten the trust back. Now, though, she had to trust herself. Her grandmother's bank account, one combined for personal and business, totaled $5,213, when property tax was due in December. When heating oil was $2.57 a gallon. When a half pound of veal was over six bucks. Her grandmother had always said she was doing fine financially. But clearly she'd been scraping by. If Holly couldn't keep the cooking course going, keep the little pasta business going, Camilla's Cucinotta would disappear with her grandmother.

Holly reached for a spatula from the row of canisters holding every imaginable utensil, still unsure if she should use plastic or wood or metal. What made her think she could do this? She was thirty years old — *thirty* — and had never been able to succeed at something like a career except when it came to kid-focused work, like manning the aquarium tank at the children's museum during the marine educator's maternity leave (Holly had memorized every sea creature, from anemones to starfish, and thrilled four-year-olds) and she was a decent waitress, which was how she'd earned her living in San Francisco, but at a la-di-dah coffee shop that sold eight-dollar bowls of basic coffee and fifteen-dollar sandwiches a gourmet chef created. Her ability to make spaghetti with jarred marinara and a side of garlic bread, a passable lasagna and veal parmigiana (for the nondiscerning, such as herself) did not qualify her to teach her grandmother's famed Italian cooking class. Her grandmother hadn't even considered lasagna and veal parmigiana Italian food. "Those are American dishes," she'd scoff.

"How am I going to keep Camilla's Cucinotta going when I can barely make a decent tomato sauce?" she asked her grandmother's ancient gray cat, Antonio, who was grooming himself in his red cat bed by the side door. The class started in one week. One week. One week left to learn the recipes for the eight-week fall course and sound like she knew what she was talking about. She stared at the risotto, nothing more than a clump of rice, and told herself she could do it. "You follow the recipe," her grandmother used to say. "That's all there is to cooking."

There was a world of difference between Holly Maguire and Julia Child. Julie Powell, even.

A glance at the recipe, handwritten in her grandmother's beautiful scrolling script, in red ink, told her she'd forgotten one of the essential ingredients. The fervent wish. She'd been so focused on studying the steps for spreading the risotto in the pan, and then she'd interrupted herself to do a Google search of *gilded* to see exactly what was meant by *gilded edges of the risotto pancake,* and then she'd gotten lost in the One Sad Memory and forgot all about the last essential ingredient. When she'd made the risotto alla Milanese earlier that day (both too salty and too tasteless at the same time), the recipe had called for a wish, just a plain old wish, not a most fervent one, and a memory, neither happy nor sad. Just a plain old memory.

And so after adding the dry white wine into the beef marrow broth (she had not liked the sound of that the first three times she'd attempted the risotto but had gotten used to it) and then letting the rice absorb it, she'd closed her eyes and let a wish come to her, and the one that formed fully inside her was that her grandmother would come back. Would once again be standing at the island in the middle of the bungalow's kitchen, stirring, chopping, talking.

"Nonna, my most fervent wish is that you're watching over me, guiding my hand so I don't mess this up," Holly said as she spread the sticky risotto into the pan. She couldn't mess this up. Not her grandmother's kitchen, this magical place.

She studied the recipe for how long before she was supposed to flip the pancake. Not that the risotto al salto would be any good; it would be as good as the risotto it was

31

made from, which Holly would grade a solid C. But it was better than her first five attempts. Risotto and the risotto al salto were on her grandmother's list for week two of the cooking class that would start next week, but Holly would switch it to a later week. Her students knew that Camilla Constantina herself would not be teaching Camilla's Cucinotta Italian Cooking class this term (except for one student, who Holly couldn't reach). They knew there would be changes to the proposed menu of recipes in her grandmother's little brochure, which Holly saw all over town.

At the funeral, Holly's mother had been stunned to hear that Holly was taking over the course. "For God's sake, Holl, just sell the house and be done with it." But Holly couldn't — wouldn't — do that. She would not sell the house or business she'd inherited. She would not sell out her grandmother. The grandmother who'd been so kind to her while Holly was growing up, never fitting in anywhere except in her grandmother's kitchen, where Holly could barely peel a potato without slicing the skin off her finger. Camilla's Cucinotta had been her grandmother's life. It had been her grandmother. And despite being a so-so cook, Holly was determined to continue what her grandmother had started as a young widow with a young child in 1962. For the past two weeks, since her grandmother had died, she'd spent her days surrounded by flour and eggs and garlic and onions and veal, following the recipes for the pastas and sauces so exactly that they'd come out okay for the past several days. Progress. Not with that extra delicious quality of her grandmother's, but enough to satisfy your basic penne in vodka sauce lunch eater in Maine.

And Holly had four students enrolled — the same number of students Camilla had had in her first cooking class in 1962. The other twelve had requested their money back at the news of Camilla's death, but Holly could understand that. After all, Holly wasn't the seventy-five-year-old Milanese Love Goddess Camilla, whose *maccheroni* in secret sauce had supposed aphrodisiac properties, whose exotic black-eyed gaze upon you, her Italian stones in your hand, could determine just the man for you, the *life* for you. Whose very essence had earned her the title Love Goddess and her business The Love Goddess' Cooking School.

Holly as the love goddess. That was laughable. Cryable too.

Holly had students. Enough for a class.

Enough to purposefully buy fresh ingredients at the supermarket and farmer's markets in Portland. Some neighbors and past students had assured her (she couldn't tell if they were just being kind) at Camilla's funeral and later at the bungalow that her grandmother's magic was in her blood, that if she wanted, she could do it. Holly desperately wanted to believe this, but all her practice tiramisus and pumpkin ravioli with their ingredients of wishes and memories hadn't changed a thing for *her:* John hadn't come back with that diamond ring, saying he'd made the biggest mistake of his life, that he wanted a future with her, that his daughter missed her. In fact, she hadn't heard from him at all. Her crying voice mail about her grandmother's death got her only a text message the next morning:

Sorry about your gm's passing.

Perhaps she hadn't needed *sa cordula* to tell her this man was not her great love.

Holly was about to turn on the gas burner when a banging interrupted the stillness in the kitchen. For a moment she thought the wind had dislodged the screen door again. It was early October, and the wind rolled off Casco Bay a quarter mile into the center of town, where the cottage stood at the end of the road, nestled between a stand of evergreens that separated the house a bit from the rest of the houses and businesses that lined the main street.

The banging continued and Holly glanced up through the large archway that led into the entryway, surprised to see someone at the door, knuckles against the glass. It was a girl, around eleven, maybe twelve, holding something in each of her hands with the hopeful, confident expression of a child about to attempt to sell a magazine sub-scription or Girl Scout cookies, which Holly would happily buy. A sleeve of Thin Mints and a glass of Chianti while watching an old movie later sounded great. Holly glanced at the wall clock. It was just after eight p.m. *Risotto al salto, you will just have to wait.*

Holly walked over to the door, slid the silver bolt, and was immediately struck by the girl's coloring. Her long, shiny hair was the color of chestnuts, which Holly had used to make Italian chestnut cake yesterday morning, and her eyes the beautiful dark blue of blueberries. The girl reminded Holly of one of her favorite (to look at) custom-ers, a man who'd been in several times since Holly had come to the island, the always-in-a-rush, two containers of penne and two containers of vodka sauce. Mid-thirties. Tall, lanky, yet muscular. He had those same blueberry-colored eyes. But his hair was darker.

"There isn't really vodka in the sauce, is there?" he'd asked the first time he'd come in, a woman, wearing a very pink and frilly suit with black patent leather heels, beside him.

"Silly," the woman had said, smiling and resting her pink-manicured hand on his arm. "It burns out in the cooking." She'd turned to Holly and added, "Men," with a delighted headshake. And Holly had smiled and filled the orders, surprised that this man, this stranger she'd never seen before on the island, had registered on her radar at all.

"May I help you?" Holly asked the girl.

"This is all I have." She held up the twenty-dollar bill. In her other hand was a brochure for Camilla's Cucinotta's Italian cooking course. "I know it's not enough. But I can wash dishes or sweep up. Whenever I try to cook or my dad does, half of everything ends up on the floor, so I know you'll probably need a sweeper for your students. And I could fetch stuff, like from the pantry or the markets or anything. Every report card I've ever gotten says I'm a good listener."

Holly smiled. Her own report cards had always said the opposite. "Are you saying you want to take the class but you don't have enough money?"

The girl bit her lip and looked away, and Holly realized she was trying very hard not to cry. "My dad's going to marry that totally fake pink bobblehead if I don't learn how to cook." Tears pooled in those blueberry-colored eyes.

So. Her father *was* the two containers of penne and two containers of vodka sauce guy.

"Why don't you come in and sit down for a moment," Holly said, gesturing to the tasting bench just to the right of the doorway. The bungalow's Tuscan-inspired foyer constituted Camilla's Cucinotta's takeout shop. One hundred rectangular square feet, it held a chalkboard menu of the day's pasta offerings, and one wall was a built-in refrigerated shelf from which customers could choose their pastas and their sauces. A large, open archway separated the entry from the kitchen; Camilla had discovered that folks liked to see her cooking, that it helped business. "Does your dad know where you are?" Holly asked, glancing again at the clock on the wall.

"My curfew's not till eight fifteen and I live just down Cove Road," she said, glancing out the window and pointing her thumb across the street to where Cove Road led to the bay. "When I turn twelve next month, I get to stay out till eight thirty. Not that there's anything to do on this lame-o island, anyway. When we moved here a few months ago from Portland, I asked my dad if we could go looking for blue crabs, and did you know there are *no* blue crabs in Maine? The whole island is totally made up. Like the bobblehead."

Holly couldn't help the smile. And she knew all about the history of Blue Crab Island, from her grandmother, who thought the old story was hilarious.

"Well, since you have fifteen minutes, how about a cup of hot chocolate?" Holly asked. "My name is Holly Maguire, and I recently inherited this house and the cooking school and the pasta shop from my grandmother. She's the Camilla of Camilla's Cucinotta." She pointed at the cameo-esque photo of her grandmother on the brochure.

"What does *cucinotta* mean?" the girl asked. "Oh, and my name is Mia. Geller. And I love hot chocolate. But I hate those gross, hard little marshmallows."

Holly laughed. "I hate those too. And *cucinotta* means kitchen in Italian. Little kitchen, really. And it's very nice to meet you, Mia." Mia smiled and tucked the brochure in her pocket, and Holly went into the kitchen and within minutes had made two steaming cups of hot chocolate. She sat in the antique rocker across from the bench, the one her grandmother always sat in to discuss the pastas of the day with her customers. Holly wanted to keep the girl in view of the big window, just in case Mia's father came looking for her.

Mia sipped the hot chocolate. "Wow, this isn't from a packet, is it?"

So. Add that to Holly's small list of achievements in the kitchen. "My grandmother would turn over."

"You know who'd totally use an instant mix with those gross hard minimarshmallows? Jodie, the bobblehead. And get this, her name is really spelled Jodi with just an *i,* but she added the *e* because it's supposedly 'more interesting,' which I don't think it is at all — it's *fake.* Why doesn't my dad see it? Oh, wait, I know why. Because she wears these tiny pink skirts and tight pink shirts. Has she ever heard of feminism?" Mia took a sip of her hot chocolate and leaned her head back against the windowsill, her

39

chestnut-colored hair falling behind her narrow shoulders. "When I ask my dad if he's going to marry her, he always says he doesn't know, *maybe,* that we can't live on his burned cooking and grungy housekeeping skills and that it would be great for me to have a mother figure who understands almost-twelve-year-old girls. Like Jodie the Fake understands anything but which lipsticks have SPF and match her shoes."

Holly was loving this girl more and more by the minute. She took a sip of her hot chocolate. "*Can* she cook?"

"She made a great lasagna the other day," Mia said, her shoulders slumping. "It was so good I had seconds. I would have had another piece, but I noticed my dad smiling at Jodie just because I actually was shoveling her lasagna into my mouth. God, I'm such a traitor to myself. So I *have* to learn how to cook, especially Italian, my dad's favorite, so that he won't need to marry her. Plus, I *know* that my mom is gonna come back. Maybe even for my birthday. She's married to some rich guy and lives in L.A. and France like half the year, but I know she's going to come back — for good — when she gets her fancy life or whatever out of her system. It's already been two years, and that's a long time."

Over a plate of the chestnut cake, which Mia took one bite of and then ignored, Holly learned that Mia's father, whose name was Liam Geller, was an architect who specialized in the very unfancy building of dairy and cattle farms with their outbuildings and barns and chicken coops. Apparently, the chicken coop in the backyard of the Gellers' antique farmhouse in Portland, which had been Liam's concession to city living, even though they weren't downtown, was one of the final straws that sent the wife running two years ago. From her backpack, Mia took out a wallet-sized photo of her mother and father in happier days, Mia as a toddler on her dad's shoulders.

And there he was. Younger. With a more hopeful look in those dark blue eyes. He was so attractive. There was something in his serious demeanor combined with an absentmindedness that had managed to actually charm Holly out of her misery for the past few weeks. Liam Geller had been in to Camilla's Cucinotta five or six times over the past month — only once with the girlfriend — and the very sexy sight of him, always in a hurry, barely noticing anything around him, like that during the past two weeks, the penne was a little too toothsome

41

and the sauce either too sweet or not enough — or the woman wearing the yellow and blue Camilla's Cucinotta apron — had motivated Holly to put on a little makeup herself, a little spritz of something sexy from her grandmother's perfume collection.

"Very attractive man, *si?*" her grandmother had said with her Mona Lisa smile the day Holly had come downstairs one morning wearing a sweep of mascara and a touch of lipstick, her long dark hair in a low ponytail instead of the slapped together atop her head as it had been for the prior two weeks. Holly had smiled for what seemed the first time since arriving. It wasn't so much the man, but what he represented. Hope. Optimism. That flirtatious, sweet feeling of a crush.

Twice, the call for wishes in her grandmother's recipes had turned unexpectedly erotic at the thought of him. He was her secret nameless crush, and because she felt gutted out from the inside, she was grateful for his lack of small talk, his lack of interest in her as even the person selling him his penne. She didn't want to like him beyond her harmless crush.

Even more so now that she knew he had a girlfriend — and a daughter. Another man *and* another child to love and lose? Holly wouldn't even go there.

"So can I be your helper?" Mia asked in a rush of words, the blueberry eyes pleading. She gnawed her lip for a moment. "I'll do anything you need. I'll even risk stinking of garlic. Even though that will totally turn off Daniel. Well, in American history, because that's the only class where he sits next to me. Not that he ever talks to me anyway. He doesn't even know I'm on this earth."

"Daniel?" Holly repeated, thinking about the girl's request. She *could* use a helper. But a preteen girl wasn't what she'd had in mind.

"He's this boy at school. He's so cute I can't even bear to look at him sometimes. You know?"

"I know," Holly said, her heart opening. "I know exactly. And I'll tell you what. I *could* use a helper, an apprentice. You can take the course for free that way."

Mia's face lit up and she pocketed the twenty-dollar bill. "Oh, my God, thank you!"

"If every Monday night from six to seven-thirty is too late or interferes with your schoolwork, you can come after school as often as you'd like and do practice runs of the weekly recipes and even help make the daily pastas and sauces if you want. I need all the help I can get."

Mia threw her arms around Holly and squeezed. "That's so perfect. Like you're my own cooking tutor! The bobblehead is so gonna be history!"

Holly tried not to laugh. She liked Mia's exuberance. She could use some of it. "You'll need to let me know your dad said it was all right, though."

"Are you kidding? He'll be thrilled. I'll actually be 'taking an interest in something, getting a hobby, something that is just mine.' Ha. How funny is it that my hobby is actually getting rid of his beauty pageant loser girlfriend?"

Holly couldn't help laughing. The girl had verve. Camilla Constantina would not only approve of what Mia was trying to do, she would come up with her own special wish-mix of ingredients to add to the penne in vodka sauce.

THREE

When Mia left, Holly returned her attention to the risotto al salto. Though she'd already made her wish, she said, "Please don't burn to a crisp," into the garlic-scented air, then turned on the burner, low-medium. She stood at the stove, staring at the risotto pancake, which began to slightly crackle, and then leaned over to the counter to reread the instructions. *Melt butter in skillet.* Check. *Spread risotto on bottom of pan, forming a pancake.* Check. *On low-medium heat, cook until gilded a golden brown, then cover pan with a lip-less lid. Flip pan and lid — risotto should now be on the lid. Return pan to the burner. Slide the risotto from the lid back into the pan and cook other side until gilded.*

All was well until she flipped the pan. This was her fourth attempt at risotto al salto, and the pancake stuck to the top of the lid and couldn't be pried off.

"If the dish does not turn out as you expected, you simply try again," her grandmother had always advised her students. And Holly.

This was what Holly did like about cooking. The do-over aspect. There were no do-overs in love, in relationships, unless the It's Not You, It's Me was willing. But risotto, overcooked pasta, underseasoned sauce — there were not only second chances but hundreds.

After washing the dishes and pots and pans and utensils, she cleaned up the center island, counters, and stove and swept the floor until it was spotless, then made sure Antonio's water bowl was full, shut the kitchen lights, and headed up the narrow, steep stairs to the second floor, which held two bedrooms and a huge bathroom with a claw-footed tub. She took a fifteen-minute soak in her grandmother's soothing lavender bath salts, which did wonders for her tired muscles, then changed into her comfiest pajamas and pulled her wet hair into a ponytail.

It was only nine thirty, but she was exhausted and wanted to fling herself under the covers, forget about pancakes made out of arborio rice, and perhaps let her mind wander over the hotness of a six-feet-plus guy with blueberry-colored eyes and a slight cleft in his chin. But instead of going to her bed, she was drawn to her grandmother's room.

The bedroom was both spare and cozy at the same time, dominated by the queen-sized iron bed, its black headboard adorned by the tiny oil painting of the three Po River stones. The bed was covered by a white down comforter with four plump pillows. A huge mahogany wardrobe with intricate carvings stood in one corner; in another was a wrought iron vanity with a huge round mirror and a chair covered in white velvet. There was a dresser by the window, topped by a glass tray of old-fashioned perfume bottles, the kind with sticks, and surrounded by photos of Holly and her parents. She loved this room. Holly moved over to the vanity and picked up the photograph her grandmother had slid inside the beveled edge, of Holly and her grandmother the day before she died, a photograph her grandmother had taken by holding the camera at arm's length. Holly treasured it.

She turned off the lights and switched on the lamp on the bedside table, then got under the covers and picked up the white-satin pouch of stones next to the lamp. She slid the stones onto her palm, closed her eyes, and waited, hoping the stones would tell her something, reveal something. Such as: *You will be all right. You will wake up one day and not feel a gnawing emptiness in your heart and stomach. And you will not let your grandmother down. She left you Camilla's Cucinotta because she believed you could carry on her legacy your way.*

Did she even have a way? That was the question. She'd graduated from Boston University with a degree in English literature and no idea what to do with her life. And so she'd tried a bit of everything. She'd been everything from a private investigator's assistant, which involved lots of simple background checks via Google, to a dog walker. She'd sold ads in the back of a newspaper. She'd volunteered at a hospital, reading to children awaiting surgical procedures. She'd temped everywhere from a literary agency, sending out form letters that said *This isn't quite right for us,* to a real estate agency. And nothing gripped her. Not even the three months she'd thrilled children with the facts of sea life at the children's museum. She liked being a waitress except when someone, usually a flirting guy, would ask, "So, what are you — a waitress slash what?" And Holly would have to say, "Just a waitress."

"What do you love doing?" John had asked, exasperated. He was an investment banker and had had his heart set on money from his first finance course in college.

Holly had shrugged. She knew she loved Blue Crab Island and her grandmother, yet instead of moving to Maine after college graduation, she'd stayed in Boston for a guy with whom she'd fallen deeply in love. And then another. Until she'd followed John Reardon to California, three thousand miles away. She'd let her relationships take center stage of her heart, mind, and soul. Maybe because she'd never found her niche.

So what did she love doing? She loved watching cats, even old, lazy ones like Antonio. She loved walking across bridges. She loved sitting in the little alcove in her grandmother's kitchen, sipping tea and watching Camilla Constantina, a Sophia Loren lookalike who wore dresses every day for every occasion, roll out her fresh pastas, stuff the gnocchi, breathe in the aroma of her sauces with a satisfied expression.

"So maybe you should go to culinary school," John had suggested. "I'm sure you picked up the basics by osmosis. You could go to that famous French cooking school, Le Cordon Bleu."

That had been one of the first hints that

John Reardon wouldn't be devastated if an ocean separated them.

I'm not a cook, she thought then and now, the memory of her grandmother clutching her stomach in pain because of seven-year-old Holly forcing its way into her mind. She wished she could get back the way she'd felt that day in the kitchen, when she hadn't realized she was sprinkling rat poison on her grandmother's lunch. The wonder and intrigue and possibilities and fun of choosing ingredients. She wanted . . . what? To feel the way she did in her grandmother's kitchen that day. Completely absorbed in what she was doing. In love with what she was doing. Confident, despite her inability to roll the pasta thin enough without ripping it, something her grandmother never did. And like she belonged, despite everything. She'd never felt that way anywhere else but in Camilla's Cucinotta. And now that it was hers, she was scared. Despite not having a clue how to cook, how to teach people how to cook, she felt inexplicably safe in this house, in the kitchen.

Holly gripped the stones tighter in her palm. *Tell me I can do this. Just tell me that.* But the stones said nothing. She didn't expect them to, of course, but she wouldn't mind a sign. A crackle of lightning, perhaps.

She sighed and put the stones back in the pouch and onto the bedside table. She'd slept in the other bedroom since she'd come a month ago and for the past two weeks since Camilla had passed. The room she'd slept in every summer of her childhood. It was the smaller of the two bedrooms upstairs, but Holly still wasn't ready to move into her grandmother's beautiful master bedroom with the ornate bed she had shipped from Milan when she'd first moved to Blue Crab Island. For the past two weeks Holly had kept the door to both rooms open so that Camilla's spirit would flow through into her bedroom. And because Holly loved looking inside, loved sitting on the bed with its pristine white covers, loved looking at the painting of the Po River stones, at the large painting of the Po River that had soothed her grandmother to sleep every night.

Holly glanced at the photos on the dresser, of her parents, and one of her mother as a little girl and another as a teenager, and she tried to imagine her mother disliking this magical house, biding her time until she could leave at eighteen. Her mother's childhood room, which had become Holly's room, held nothing of Italy or her heritage; it was full of white Maine cottage furniture and glass bowls of seashells. Holly's mother found Camilla and her sexy dresses, fortune-telling, and busybody matchmaking an embarrassment and left the "creepy" island the minute she could to settle in a suburb of Boston, where she lived with Holly's father, who had no appreciation of his exotic mother-in-law or Blue Crab Island. Luciana Maguire couldn't understand why Holly wanted to spend as much time as possible on the island when she herself had wanted to escape, but Holly's mother never claimed to understand her. And so Holly spent every school vacation and summer with her grandmother and loved the island and the lore surrounding Camilla. She'd grown up with comforting assurances of what was to come (a constant "You will be fine," which Holly believed, whereas her own mother, a self-professed realist who didn't believe in "that nonsense," was just a big old cynic).

Growing up, when Holly used to spend an entire month every summer on Blue Crab Island, the locals would ask Holly if she'd inherited her grandmother's gift of "knowing." She hadn't. She could not, as Camilla Constantina could, assess someone and know that her true love wasn't the man beside her but the next man she'd meet, perhaps at the supermarket. Or that she really shouldn't wear her new suede boots the next day because it was going to rain by late morning, despite what the forecast said.

Holly had inherited the Maguire trait of not knowing.

She recalled her grandmother telling her last year at Thanksgiving that she wasn't so sure John was the one, that he didn't seem to be serious about Holly in that place deep inside him. John and Lizzie had been invited for Thanksgiving, but John went to his parents instead with Lizzie and Holly hadn't been invited. Yet the next day he'd told Holly he loved her, and as she sometimes did, though it made her feel bad, she thought perhaps her grandmother didn't *really* know, that it was just old-world wisdom and worry.

But of course she'd known.

The night John had broken up with her, she'd picked up the phone to call her grandmother to find Camilla had left her a message. "Thinking of you, as always." She'd somehow known. She'd called her grandmother and explained that she'd served the *sa cordula* to John and that he'd hated it and spat it out, but that it was little consolation that John wasn't her great love because he was. And her grandmother told her to change her flight to Maine for the next day, even though they'd recently made plans for Holly to visit in two weeks. And when Holly had called her boss in the morning to call in sick (well, brokenhearted), she'd asked if she could switch her vacation, and her boss had told her he'd planned to have a talk with her when she came in that day, that she was too slow and they had to let her go, sorry. She would soon have been out of a place to live too, since her roommate's boyfriend, who was always over lately, had now officially moved in. Since the roommate had the apartment first, Holly had been told a couple of weeks prior that she'd need to move out, sorry. She'd thought she'd be invited to move in with John. But he'd been sorry too.

Everyone was sorry and Holly had had nowhere to be.

Her grandmother had known she was dying, which was why she'd asked Holly to come in September. To be comforted by her granddaughter before she died. And to be there.

Camilla Constantina wasn't truly psychic; 30 percent of the time, in Camilla's own estimation, she was wrong, but usually involving things that were asked of her — "Will I get married?" (Pamela Frumm, who managed Blue Crab Island Books, was forty-two and still hadn't found her guy after her grandmother had told her for ten years that "Yes, of course you will." But sometimes Holly would wonder if her grandmother was just being kind. Why say no? What would that have done to Pamela Frumm, who could often be seen in high heels and lipstick and awaiting her Match .com date, who *could* be the one?) And her grandmother had been sure that her great-aunt Giada's cancer would take her around Christmastime, and two years later, she was still waking up at five every morning to roll out pasta for her son's restaurant in Milan.

But 70 percent of the time, Camilla was right. Whether about the Red Sox or some-one's true love or a tornado. Holly had often wondered if it was more difficult to know than not to know.

She got out of bed, walked over to the dresser, and opened the top drawer, where she knew she'd find her grandmother's diaries, a stack of four black-and-white composition notebooks that she wrote in English. She took them out and put them on the dresser, stopping to open one of the bottles of perfume and drawing out the stick, rubbing just a bit on her wrist, the smell of her grandmother's favorite perfume as soothing as her hugs.

Holly had found the diaries the day of her grandmother's funeral, when she'd come upstairs to get away from her mother, tsk-tsking Holly for refusing to sell the house, and her father, stuffing his face with plate after plate of buffalo wings, a kitchen full of food that her grandmother would never have touched, delivered by neighbors she'd done so much for. Holly hadn't felt right reading her grandmother's diaries, wasn't sure she should or even wanted to, but now that Camilla's life was hers, Holly hoped to find a secret or two hidden in the pages, something to make this new life feel more like hers — and something that would help her understand her own mother, from whom Holly was pulling further and further away. Her mother had lost her own mother, and though Holly had seen her crying at the funeral, her tears seemed less about her grief than about something else — the unbridgeable gulf between them, Holly thought. Luciana Maguire rarely talked about growing up on Blue Crab Island, except to say she'd been miserable there from her first memory.

Holly had a feeling that if her grandmother hadn't wanted her to read the diaries, they would not be front and center in the top drawer of her dresser when she clearly knew she was dying. She took the top notebook, with her grandmother's beautiful handwriting, declaring: *This notebook belongs to Camilla Constantina.* She lay back in bed and opened the first notebook.

August 1962
Dear Diary,

A few days ago I tacked the ad (LEARN TO COOK ITALIAN FOOD) in the large space between Annette Peterman's call for a babysitter (the poor infant is colicky and no one responded to the ad, according to the proprietor, despite Annette's willingness to pay three dollars an hour) and a black and white signed glossy photograph of President Kennedy. The bulletin board in the general store is also Blue Crab Island's suggestion box and complaint bureau. *Please lower your car radios when driving along Blue Crab Boulevard* was one complaint. *Someone is not picking up after their dog on Shelter Road* was another. The poster of Kennedy is reassuring. Armando loved him, the first Catholic president of our new country. "You see," he said, "we belong."

But now he's gone. A full year has passed since Armando died from a heart attack while pulling weeds from the garden. The grief counselor in Portland suggested I start a diary to help me get out my feelings, especially because I have so few people to talk to now. I was not interested in writing about my grief, but oddly enough, today, the very day I begin what feels like my third life (the first being Italy, the second with Armando in America, and the third as a widow with a child to raise), I bought this notebook from the general store here on Blue Crab Island. It's amazing that just one month ago I woke with the notion to go to Blue Crab Island, where Armando and I rode bicycles along the bay one fine summer day. The feeling was so strong and I knew I was meant to go, meant to take Luciana, who is now five, to the Island, where there are no blue crabs, and there was the bungalow, this two-story apricot-colored gingerbread cottage at the far end of the main road, nestled against evergreens. I knew instantly it was meant to be our house. It's small, just two bedrooms, and a bit run-down, but the kitchen is the biggest room in the house, and there's a small backyard where I can grow herbs and vegetables.

The moment I drove over the long bridge that connects Portland to Blue Crab Island,

I felt my knowing come back. This past year without Armando, I woke up each morning with nothing more in my head, my heart, my bones, than what even my dear Luciana could plainly see: that I was grief-stricken. But we have been five years in America, in Portland, and I will be fine. That I know even without the help of my comfort stones. It was time to take Luciana out of that house of loss and into a house of beginning. Now, just one month later, the rooms are painted the cool shades of the Mediterranean, the kitchen is stocked and ready. And I am ready to give this newfangled idea a try, teaching a class in Italian cooking. I have a decent amount of money tucked away, but I want to try to earn my own living, to show Luciana that a woman can be enterprising.

Today I had my first class. Four students. Four surprising students. They are the fancy women of Blue Crab Island: Lenora Windemere, whose great-great-grandfather bought Blue Crab Island in the late 1800s, and who owns the general store, and her friends. When I tacked up that ad, I didn't know who, if anyone, would take my class; I consulted the stones and was overcome with peace, which meant offering the course was the right thing to do, but I had no idea in what way.

My students arrived together earlier today, a glorious spring day, these women who'd stopped by the day I bought the run-down bungalow at the edge of Blue Crab Boulevard (as if a paved road on the town's main street were a boulevard). "What country are you from?" they wanted to know. "What happened to your husband? Does your daughter speak English? Do you always wear dresses to clean?"

I've always felt their stares as I walked from the bungalow, Luciana in hand, to the general store for provisions. The store does not have everything, but over the past five years, I know which butchers and markets in Portland have vegetables and fish and meats that rival the markets back home. They don't like me, these women, because I am Italian and speak English with a heavy accent. Because I do wear pretty dresses every day, even to clean. Because one of their husbands, I have no idea who, said right in the middle of the coffee shop, which serves terrible coffee that I will never get used to, "Do you know who you look like? Sophia Loren."

I suppose I do look somewhat like Sophia Loren, except that my hair and eyes are almost black. I have the hairstyle, the figure, the accent. Another reason I am not liked by the women of Blue Crab Island.

So I was surprised when promptly at noon on a Thursday, these four prominent women turned up at the door with their ten-dollar bills. They walked in one at a time, in order of their rank, I understood instantly. First was Lenora Windemere, with her shellacked blond beehive, cream-colored mohair sweater, and tight peach pedal pushers. Annette Peterman was next, also blond, also in pedal pushers, who would have been very attractive were it not for the dark circles and fatigue etched on her face. From the colicky baby, I assume. Jacqueline Thibodeux, PTA president, councilman's wife, with her auburn curls and fine features, looked like a porcelain doll. And Nancy Waggoner, who rarely spoke and only agreed with whatever the other three said.

"Welcome to Camilla's Cucinotta!" I said with my practiced big smile. "I am prepared to teach you the secrets of Italian cooking." I reached for the aprons I bought for the class and held them out.

"No rush, is there?" Lenora said, not taking an apron, so of course the other three put their hands back down. "What is that perfume you're wearing? I don't recognize it, and I'm always trying new fragrances. Is it from Italy?"

"Actually, I made it myself, from mixing oils," I told her. "I can make some for you for the next class."

She stared at me. "How nice. It's interesting how you extend your eyeliner on your top lashes but don't use any at all on your lower lashes. Why is that?"

My eyeliner?

"Why don't you wear pants?" they wanted to know. "Do you buy your bras around here? What brand of shampoo do you use? Do you use the regular type of hair curlers? Or is that a permanent?"

What I quickly learned was that they wanted to learn my secrets without actually giving me the compliment. They wanted to study me up close, see how I wore my makeup and styled my hair and outfits so that it all enhanced rather than empowered. They are not interested in learning to cook; they already know how or think they do, anyway.

"Okay, ladies, we'd better get started on the lesson," I said to them. "Osso buco takes quite a while to prepare —"

"Ossco buco?" Annette interrupted. "That

sounds kind of, what's the word? Exotic. We're interested in learning how to make Italian dishes the way they do in restaurants. You know, veal parmigiana. Lobster fra diavolo."

Veal parmigiana? Veal with cheese on top?

I'd planned a typical three-course menu: a small plate of pasta to start, tagliatelle with a simple tomato sauce, the osso buco. And so I ignored Annette and began the lesson for a classic Italian dinner, the small plate of pasta, the osso buco, a salad, and fresh fruit for dessert.

"I'm really interested in learning how to make veal parmigiana," Annette said. "Lasagna too, but mainly veal parm. It's my husband's favorite meal, and I'm planning a huge party for his fortieth next weekend. Everyone's invited, and —"

At least she'd thought to stop herself. Everyone *wasn't* invited.

"Well, then," I said. "I'll teach you how to make a delicious veal parmigiana." Veal I had, of course. And there was always Parmigiano-Reggiano in my refrigerator.

And so the women finally put on their aprons and gathered around the center island, learning how to season the veal, how to make the sauce, when to lay on the cheese.

But as Annette Peterman placed the cheese over the veal in the pan, I knew, quite suddenly, that her husband would not attend that party. There was only his absence that I felt. He was going to die. I had no idea in what manner or exactly when. I only knew he would not be at that party.

And so I sighed, my heart going out to Annette with the colicky baby, who talked about her husband nonstop. Bob says. Bob and I. I don't like her — or the other three. But they were grudgingly here to learn my secrets and that made them vulnerable enough. And now I would know more about them, things that would make me care, make me worry. I knew what it was like for your husband to suddenly not be there.

And so I allowed these women I don't like to teach me the American way of Italian food.

And I learned something. Quite a few things.

The entry finished, Holly wanted to keep reading, to find out what happened next, if Annette's husband did die, if the women came back the following week, but she was so tired and her eyes were drifting shut. She took the three stones from the pouch on the bedside table and held them to her chest, shutting the lamp and glancing out at the crescent moon in the dark sky, her last thought of John and Lizzie making a surprise visit, John magically charmed by the idea of moving to Maine and taking up photography, Lizzie walking through the woods, picking blueberries. She pulled the comforter up to her chin, wondering what it was like to *know*.

FOUR

Holly stretched in her grandmother's bed
— *her* bed, she reminded herself — the
bright morning sun slanting through the
white gauzy curtains. The stones had fallen
on the braided round rug next to the bed,
and Holly hoped that didn't mean she'd
broken something inside them. Not that
they were of use to her. If there were magic
in those stones, they worked only for Camilla Constantina.

She replaced the stones in their pretty
white pouch, then got up and took a long
shower, enjoying the scent of her grandmother's seventies-popular shampoos, like
Wella Balsam and Flex with its sticker price
of $1.99. She dressed in jeans, a warm
cream-colored sweater, and her trusty
brown Frye Harness boots, then headed out
to the Farmers Market in Portland with her
shopping list — recipes that she needed to
master for the first two classes. She had

some money saved up of her own, not much, and combined with the four months to keep the house and business going, she needed to be careful with what she spent.

As she drove over the half-mile span of beautiful bridge that connected the island to Portland's harbor, she felt the same peace she always did at the glittering blue water, the boats docked along the shores where Holly could see cottages and mansions nestled among the evergreens. She parked in a harbor lot along Commercial Street, the seagulls swooping amid the boats and busy street.

Holly weaved her way to her favorite farmer's market in an open area between two low buildings. The market was crowded with vendors and shoppers. She was becoming something of a regular here, and she liked that one of the vegetable vendors, who had an enormous tattoo of a snake on his bicep, knew her by sight enough to wave. She passed trucks unloading what looked like cabbage and moved past the huge baskets of colorful peppers and hovered by the bushels of onions, trying to remember what her grandmother had said about onions. Big was good? Small? Sweet? Yellow? There was so much to know, so much to hold in your head. She'd been here at least five times the past two weeks and she couldn't remember what type of onion to buy. And basil — was she supposed to choose leaves that had flowered or not?

"What's that, Daddy?" a little voice said.

Holly glanced over to see a girl about Lizzie's age sitting on her father's shoulders, a half-peeled banana in her hand. She pointed to a basket of eggplants.

"Those are eggplants," he told her.

Well, at least Holly knew more than a toddler about vegetables, she consoled herself.

"They look like Grandpa Harry's feet," the girl said.

Holly laughed and the man and girl smiled at her before moving along. She closed her eyes at the fresh pierce to her heart. Had Lizzie forgotten her already? Had John? She imagined Lizzie atop John's shoulders, chewing at cotton candy, the administrative assistant walking beside them where Holly should have been.

Holly stood amid the baskets and bushels, of vegetables and fruits, every color and size imaginable, of organic eggs and artisan breads, and what looked like jar after jar of jams, and it was all so overwhelming that Holly had to close her eyes for a moment and remember this was about buying some tomatoes, sage, basil, and onions. Just ask

68

for help, she reminded herself. Ask the tattooed vendor which onions were best for Italian cooking. Her grandmother had once told her that one of life's best lessons was not being afraid to look foolish — to just ask the question.

She waited until a woman plucking several small, round purple-ish somethings and long green leafy somethings had paid before announcing she couldn't select a simple onion without help.

"The plain old everyday yellow onion," the man told her, tossing one up in the air and catching it as he multitasked with another customer. "Does its job by being itself. Good motto for life, eh?"

Holly smiled. Certainly was. She'd always been trying to be herself, but she couldn't seem to pin down what that was. Female was all she was certain about. And unlucky in love, when it came right to it.

An hour later, everything on her list in bags in the trunk of her grandmother's trusty little Toyota, Holly drove back across the Blue Crab Island Bridge, the WELCOME TO BLUE CRAB ISLAND sign a comfort, as always. This was home now. She followed Bridge Road, waiting for the curve that never failed to send goose bumps, good ones, up along her arms as the thick of evergreens stopped to reveal the open blue waters of Casco Bay. Holly drove on to the center of town, down the mile-long main street (the entire island was only two miles long and two miles wide) with its charming downtown: a small library funded by the wealthy Windemere family, the tiny town hall, the bakery, which had been expanded to include a small café, a general store, a bistro called Avery W's (Lenora Windemere's none too nice granddaughter), a yoga studio/knitting shop, a used bookstore, and a seafood restaurant. A very expensive hotel, the Blue Crab Cove Inn, jutted out in the bay a mile away from the center of town.

Next to the yoga/knitting shop (two things Holly could not do), and right in the middle of Blue Crab Boulevard, Holly noticed a banner in the window of Avery W's. COOKING CLASSES — STARTING OCTOBER 22. SIGN UP NOW! EACH WEEK A DIFFERENT REGION, FROM JULIA CHILD'S BELOVED FRENCH CUISINE TO GIADA DE LAURENTIIS'S ITALIAN TO YOUR FAVORITE CHINESE! TAUGHT BY AVERY WINDEMERE — WHO HAS A CERTIFICATE IN COOKING FROM USM!

Holly frowned. There had never been any competition for cooking classes on Blue Crab Island. And of course, her sudden rival

70

was Avery Windemere, who, along with her friends, particularly the vicious Georgiana Perry, had been mean to Holly every summer, starting when she was seven, old enough to be dropped off on her own, her parents returning for her a month later. Holly could remember the way Avery had treated her as though it were last summer.

"Could her pants be any stupider?" Avery would say, giggling, a few other girls surrounding Holly as she'd sat on the front porch, peeling carrots or snapping peas. "Aren't you like *eight?* No one wears little lobsters on their clothes." Laughter. "And, omigod, is she really wearing a red and green and white striped scarf?"

They're the colors of the Italian flag, she wanted to scream at them, but Holly had learned at school that it was better to ignore bullies than to react.

And when Holly would continue with her peeling, Avery would add, "Your grandmother is a witch; my mother and grandmother say so. The only reason they're nice to her is because they're afraid she'll cast a spell on them and make them funny-looking like you."

And when they tired of bullying her and continued on their bikes past the house into the woods, where they probably stepped on

71

chipmunks and slugs for fun, Holly would run inside and tell her grandmother how mean they were and ask her to assure Holly that their lives would turn out terribly. Her grandmother would hug her and assure her that everyone got theirs, that there was such a thing as karma that took care of meanies.

The bullying had stopped when Holly was a teenager, around sixteen. Avery and her friends had basically ignored her as they walked around town in their bikini tops and shorts, holding the hands of cute boys. Ever since, when Holly would visit her grandmother — and for the past month — Avery simply pretended that she didn't know Holly. Fine by her.

A certificate in cooking. Ha. Not that Holly had even taken a single cooking course. But she'd learned at her grandmother's hip. That was worth a degree and then some.

Still, if Holly lost her remaining four students to Avery, she'd never be able to prove herself, never be able to start something of a grassroots, word of mouth campaign that Holly had inherited her grandmother's cooking skills. If just a little. No one would continue buying the pastas and sauces. No one would take the courses. And Camilla's Cucinotta would become a memory.

Holly would not let that happen. Not to her grandmother's legacy.

She drove on down Blue Crab Boulevard and parked her car in the driveway, then headed up the winding cobblestone walkway to the porch, her arms laden with shopping bags of ingredients. A replica of an Italian statue stood by the door, holding a stone sign that read:

CAMILLA'S CUCINOTTA: ITALIAN COOKING CLASSES

Fresh take-home pastas & sauces daily
Benvenuti! (welcome!)

Holly loved walking into Camilla's Cucinotta, loved the Tuscan-inspired entryway, with its golden-yellow walls and painted blue wooden floor, the beautiful round rug. The blackboard listed the two pastas of the day (Camilla had always done three, but Holly couldn't keep up) and the sauces. Today there was penne, and gnocchi, and the sauces were vodka, Bolognese, and Camilla's famous garlic and oil. A carpenter had built in the refrigerated shelf with French style doors, from which customers could come in, choose what they wanted,

73

ring the little bell, and chat with Camilla while they paid. The antique cash register on the counter worked. Often when customers stopped in for pastas, they would ask if Holly told fortunes, but she had to tell them she did not.

She glanced at the row of brochures on the counter. Just before her grandmother had passed away, Holly had helped her plan the menus for the fall class. Camilla had offered the same class for the past three seasons and wanted to do something a little different, go back to basics, almost like she had when she first started teaching. When Camilla had arrived on Blue Crab Island in 1962, a widow with a young daughter, and offered Italian cooking classes to the residents from her bungalow's kitchen, there were no written recipes, only memory and instinct. But Camilla had forced herself to write down the ingredients, the amounts, the steps in a way that her neighbors could understand (apparently they hadn't been able to understand her shorthand those first few times).

When Holly had first arrived last month, Camilla spoke a lot about wanting to offer a course that would lure those attracted to Avery Windermere's American bistro, which had opened this past spring and was an instant hit with the summer tourists, not that Blue Crab Island attracted summer visitors the way Peaks Island did. Camilla's classes had always been so popular among the locals that she'd never had rivals, except for catering that didn't involve Italian dishes. But Avery had moved back to the island with her husband and opened the bistro. And was now offering cooking classes. And an Italian segment.

The night before her grandmother died, Holly had cooked alongside her, making gnocchi stuffed with potato and cheese. She'd added the garlic to the pan while Camilla excused herself to answer the jangle of bells and sold eight containers of pasta and seven quarts of her sauces.

"I must move with the times, yes?" Camilla had asked, moving slowly back into the kitchen. She was seventy-five and appeared in good health, but she grew tired easily and often needed to sit down at the kitchen table for a rest. "They come and buy my old-style pastas and sauces, but perhaps the cooking class needs a little something, like on the Food Network?"

"You should have your own show on the Food Network, Nonna," Holly had said. "Your food is what people really want and crave. Classic. The real thing."

Camilla smiled. "I hope you're right." She glanced in the pan and patted Holly's hand with her tiny, age-spotted one. "What are we up to?"

Holly glanced at the binder, open to the recipe. "A happy memory."

"Ah, I love the happy ones," she said. "Since we're cooking together, I will share mine."

Holly expected her grandmother to recall either of her two favorites: the day four-year-old Holly had dislodged a sheet of fresh pasta, which had draped over her and had to be combed out of her long hair for two hours under the shower. Or the time Holly had pretended to cook for a previous boyfriend's very traditional parents, then fessed up during dessert that her grandmother had made everything. The boyfriend had been embarrassed and dumped her a week later, since "It's not like I could marry you now." Holly had called her grandmother, barely able to get the breakup out because she was laughing so hard. "Definitely not your great love," Camilla had agreed.

"A happy memory I will always keep with me is the night you arrived here two weeks ago," Camilla had said as she'd stirred the sauce. "You were brokenhearted, *si,* but you were home, Holly."

Home. She'd never thought of Blue Crab Island as home because she spent such little time there, except for the month every summer growing up and a few school vacations. And then her romances and trying to find where she belonged and what she should do with her life had kept her moving around, first in various Boston neighborhoods and then west to Seattle and Portland, and then east to Philadelphia and then back to Boston and then to San Francisco, where she'd lived for the past almost two years. Until lately, she'd never noticed how good she felt when she drove over the bridge from Portland.

I will not let you down, Nonna. I will be ready on Monday when my students arrive. I will not let Avery Windemere drive Camilla's Cucinotta out of business.

And so, with her Camilla's Cucinotta apron tied tight around her, which always made her feel a bit armored, she set to work on one of the day's special pastas, which she was also retesting for the third week of class: ravioli al granchio, with fresh crabmeat, one of Camilla's homages to her adopted home state.

Holly's first three attempts were awful. The first time she hadn't sealed the edges

77

of the ravioli squares tight enough, and the crabmeat came out in the boiling water. The second time, she'd forgotten a step entirely, to let the dough for the pasta sit for a half hour to allow the gluten to rest, and the dough was ruined. And the third time, she'd gotten everything right, but the results were meh. Still, at least once a day, someone stopped in to ask if she'd be offering it soon.

She liked making her own pasta, creating the well inside the heap of flour and cracking in the eggs and the kneading and twisting until it was elastic. As she rolled out the pasta on the big wooden board on the center island, remembering to roll it thin, but not so thin that it ripped, she glanced at the white binder, open on the counter to ravioli al granchio. The final ingredient was One Sad Memory.

She sighed, setting aside the stretchy, shiny sheet of dough to rest. She refused to think about John Reardon. Or Lizzie. She took a Diet Coke break and stared out at the evergreens through the big window over the sink, her mind too full of the next steps for the ravioli to let a sad memory enter. She went back to the dough and cut out the squares using an espresso cup, as her grandmother had always done. As Holly put a thimble-sized drop of the crab-meat mixture onto each square and then carefully covered it with another square, pressing down on the edges to form a seal, the sad memory came with such force that it brought tears to her eyes.

Two weeks in her grandmother's loving, magical care almost had Holly feeling better, almost had her waking up without that dull ache, when she'd remember that John and Lizzie were at that very minute just going on without her, that she wasn't part of their lives. Every morning that ache was less pronounced because of her grandmother's TLC, because she'd come downstairs to the smell of strong Milanese coffee, to which she had to add half a cup of milk, and the subtle scent of dough, to find Camilla in the kitchen in her shirtwaist dress and Clarks shoes, opera playing softly, Antonio batting at his mouse toy, and she'd have a purpose that required following directions, adding flour, collecting two cans of tomatoes, taking Camilla's list to the supermarket or farmer's market.

But *that* morning, two weeks ago, Holly awoke in the white bedroom to the sound of silence. She'd gone downstairs and realized Camilla wasn't awake, making gnocchi or tourte Milanese and discussing the three essential steps in classic Italian cooking with someone on the porch where she had her morning tea, Antonio at her ankles. The soothing kitchen, with its wide-planked pumpkin floors, white-tiled counters, and the Tuscan blue of the painted wood cabinets and the pale yellow walls that were not the colors of Nonna's Milan but nonetheless made Nonna happy, were as they'd been last night, when Holly had come downstairs for a cup of tea, unable, again, to sleep, unsure where she would go, what she would do with her life now. Perhaps she would stay here forever, she'd thought, breathing in the utter peace of the kitchen, the comfort of knowing her grandmother was upstairs, sleeping, a balm to her heart.

Some mornings, depending on when Holly woke up, her heart so rended that she'd sleep until ten or eleven, her grandmother would be out, walking the path of the bay with Antonio, who waddled beside her like a dog and had not run off in sixteen years. But it was too early for her grandmother's walks, and so she knocked gently on her grandmother's door and went in. "Nonna, are you feeling all right?"

Silence.

And when Holly went in, there Camilla lay, the three Po River stones loose beside her on the bed. She had passed away in her sleep. The loss had both shaken Holly and slapped her across the face with the need to get up and take care of her grandmother's business, to keep her lore and legacy alive. The past weeks, studying the recipes her grandmother had planned for the fall class, trying to remember her grandmother's words as she'd cooked beside her, had saved Holly from staying in bed with the blankets pulled over her head.

The night before she'd died, her grandmother had sat with her on the rocking chairs on the porch, holding Holly's hand as they sipped Nonna's special wine. At her usual sad, wistful expression, her grandmother said, "He's a fool, Holly, so you're lucky he's not your great love. Trust me."

Holly had nodded. "Is *anyone* going to like *sa cordula?*"

"*Si,* your great love," she'd said, unwinding the pins in her braided bun and letting the silver braid fall to her narrow shoulder.

Holly wasn't so sure she believed in great loves anymore. How could you think you'd found it, only to be mistaken a year or two or three, or in some cases twenty-five years later?

Forget about great love and focus on great cooking, she ordered herself now, the final ingredient hovering over the ravioli. When

81

she was little, she used to think the sad memories in the food would make those who ate the food feel sad, but her grandmother had assured her time and again that only the heart's call went into the food and not the memory or wish itself. It had taken Holly a while to understand what that meant.

The sad memory was taken care of. So now, with the sauce recipe calling for a wish, she couldn't help it. Her heart spoke first into the pan of seasoned chopped tomatoes, sautéing in garlic-infused olive oil.

Come back to me.

The image of John, Lizzie on his shoulders, his hands raised up to keep her steady, came to mind. "Come back to me. Tell me you were wrong. That it wasn't love with your administrative assistant. That you know that now. Beg my forgiveness."

But he's not your great love, she reminded herself.

According to a dish no one would like. And her grandmother wasn't always right with her fortunes. Seventy percent of the time. But Holly believed in her grandmother's abilities. One hundred percent of the time.

He wasn't her great love. She knew that; she'd known that for months. And her life was *this* now, she thought, glancing down into the crackling sauce and realizing she'd forgotten to remove the garlic before she'd put in the tomatoes.

The bells jangled over the front door. Holly jumped; for the briefest moment she thought it would be John and Lizzie magically transported via her wish. But it was very likely a customer stopping in to check on the pastas for lunchtime. Or another student wanting her money back for the cooking class. While Holly had been at the farmer's market, one of her four students had left a message on the Cucinotta's answering machine. *Sorry, can't take class, after all. Please mail refund to . . .* Which thankfully *still* left four enrollees, since Mia was as much a student as her assistant.

Holly turned down the burner on the sauce, wiped her hands on a kitchen towel, and headed to the front door. It was Liam Geller standing there. His dark wavy hair was still damp in places and he was dressed nicely, in dark gray pants and white button-down shirt, no tie. A gray messenger bag was slung over his torso, a long tube extending out of the top edge. Blueprints, Holly figured.

At the sight of her, he smiled through the glass, and she slid open the bolt.

"I'm sorry to bother you so early," he said, "but I saw you cooking through the window so I figured it would be all right."

Holly smiled. "No problem."

"I'm on my way to work and I wanted to double-check with you — my daughter Mia was here last night, and she said you invited her to be your apprentice?"

His eyes were beautiful. Such a vivid dark blue, like Maine's blueberries or the darkest stripes of the Carribbean Sea. And so like his daughter's.

"Yes. I told her I'd love to have her as my apprentice if it's all right with you. The class is every Monday night for eight weeks, six o'clock to seven thirty."

"It's more than all right. It's great. She could really use a little hobby right now, something besides school and friends and she doesn't seem to have found her extra-curricular interests yet."

Actually she has, Holly thought. *Getting rid of your girlfriend. Poor guy.*

"She'll be a great help," he said, glancing at his watch. "Well, I'd better get going." He glanced at the hand-painted wooden sign, CAMILLA'S CUCINOTTA, hanging on the wall above the cash register. "Camilla, is it?"

Holly stared at him. He'd been served by

Camilla at least five or so times during the two weeks that Holly had been here with her grandmother. How could he not know who Camilla Constantina was? "Camilla was my grandmother. Beautiful, elderly Italian woman with pitch black eyes and silver bun?"

Recognition dawned in those gorgeous eyes. "Oh, yes, she waited on me a few times. Tell her I said the sauce she'd suggested for the macaroni was great; I was going to get the usual, but she talked me into it."

Are you that self-absorbed? Holly wanted to scream at him. "She passed away two weeks ago." How could he not know? This was a small island, and he'd moved here months ago, Mia had said. He was in his own world, distracted, unnoticing. Holly could envision him going through the motions, marrying a bobblehead who was superficially kind to his daughter, his daughter who was in emotional pain.

It was interesting how crushes could end just like that.

The bell jangled again. Two attractive women in their late twenties or early thirties, whose expressions reminded Holly of her mother, came in. They were dressed similarly, in slim-fitting jackets and low-slung, dark-washed jeans tucked into riding boots. They both ogled Liam.

"Liam, isn't it?" the redhead said. "We met at our daughters' school the other day. You're new to Blue Crab Island, right?"

"Few months," he said.

They stared at him, watching his face, his muscles. They both moved a bit closer to him.

"Divorced?" the blonde asked, tapping his ring finger. God, they were intrusive. And obnoxious.

He nodded with a Hugh Grant smile.

"May I help someone?" Holly asked.

"Please, go ahead," he told them, and they smiled seductively and came closer to the counter Holly stood behind.

The one with the auburn hair said, "I bought this pound of penne yesterday and it was overcooked. And the Bolognese sauce was . . . I don't even know, missing something. Like not enough meat or garlic, maybe. I'd like my money back."

"Al dente is one thing, but rubber is something else," her friend added.

Holly felt her cheeks burn. This was the third time in the past two weeks that someone had complained about the pastas or the sauce and asked for her money back.

"Really?" Liam said to the woman. "I

86

bought the penne yesterday and thought it was great." Those blueberry-colored eyes were sincere. "And the Bolognese? I finished the entire quart. I'd better stop coming in here so often or I'm going to have to add a mile to my running routine."

Damn. He was absentminded and attracted to pink bobbleheads and so distracted he didn't notice the penne was overcooked and the sauce too bland, but he was *nice*. Holly felt her crush creeping back inside her heart.

FIVE

For the past few days, Holly had spent all day and night in the kitchen, channeling her grandmother by listening to Italian opera and talking to Antonio as though he cared. "Okay, Antonio, now we stuff the ravioli with the spinach and three cheeses." She had sold half of the pastas and sauces she'd made and had only three requests for money back or another try. Her marinara sauce was still missing something (it was ironic that the simplest thing to make was among the most difficult) and her pasta always seemed either overdone or underdone, but she was getting better. Her gnocchi with crabmeat had been much, much better, so much so that she might include it for week three, after all. And now that today, tonight — the first class — had finally arrived, she wasn't as nervous as she thought she'd be.

Oh, who was she kidding? She was seriously nervous.

She'd spent the afternoon scrubbing the kitchen clean and rechecking that she had all the necessary ingredients for the class. She'd opened and reopened the refrigerator ten times to check that the veal scallops were there. That the white binder was leaning against a heavy ceramic bowl full of cinnamon scented pinecones. And then at five forty-five, she went outside and moved the blackboard easel a bit closer to the road. This end of Blue Crab Boulevard didn't attract many shoppers, since it was mostly woods and paths leading to the water, but occasionally someone would be headed out for a jog along the bay and would walk the length of the boulevard and start down at this end. So far today no one had asked about the class, not even the three people who'd stopped in to buy pasta and sauce.

"The fall cooking course begins tonight," she'd said brightly to those who came in, shoving brochures at them. But all she got were nice smiles and "how nice," and "have a nice day."

She had four students. That made a class. It was how her grandmother had started and look where it had taken her.

Ha. Holly would be lucky if she got through the first night without everyone demanding their money back. She took a deep breath and moved the sign even closer to the road, angling it so that it could not be missed.

CAMILLA'S CUCINOTTA ITALIAN COOKING CLASS

Starts tonight at 6:00
Spots still available!

Each class would be devoted to an entrée and an appetizer, and if there was time, a dessert. Holly had changed the class a bit; she'd had to. She wasn't ready to make osso buco, so shifted it to week six. Risotto alla Milanese — class seven, at least. This new course syllabus didn't claim to be her grandmother's, the famed Camilla Constantina's. It only claimed to be Holly's, who would learn as her students did.

She went back inside and glanced around the gleaming kitchen. She lowered the opera, took another deep breath, and straightened the four aprons hanging on the wall.

The bell jangled and a woman appeared at the archway. An unhappy woman, Holly thought, surprised at how she stopped in the archway and stared at the floor for a

90

moment as if taking a necessary breath. She wore only shades of charcoal gray — casual cotton pants and a long-sleeved T-shirt and even gray canvas skimmers. Her fine brown hair, barely long enough for its ponytail, looked unbrushed, as if the woman had just woken up from a nap, realized she had to hurry, and slapped her hair into an elastic band. No makeup, no artifice whatsoever on her delicate, pretty features. The only thing that sparkled was her diamond ring, resting above a gold wedding band. She toyed with the gold chain around her neck, which disappeared into the V of her T-shirt.

Holly mentally ran through the students. Juliet Frears, Tamara Bean, Simon March, and her apprentice, Mia Geller, the only one she actually knew by sight. The woman seemed familiar, though her name wasn't. As the woman stood there, she wrapped her fingers around the pendant, then rested it above her T-shirt. A gold locket encircled with tiny rubies. Holly gasped. She *knew* that locket.

"Juliet?" Holly said softly, fearing any loud or sudden movements would send the woman out the door. She was sure it was Juliet Andersen — the one friend she'd made on the island as a little summer girl. But Juliet had moved away when they were twelve and hadn't kept in touch much past the first year.

For the briefest moment the woman's face almost lit up. "Holly?"

"Yes, it's me!" Holly walked over. Her instinct was to wrap her in a hug, but Juliet's body language said to give her space.

"I had no idea you'd be visiting your grandmother. Lucky for me. God, it's been what? Fifteen years?"

Juliet looked entirely different from what Holly remembered. She'd always had long hair, down to the bra strap (they'd both gotten their first bras together during that final summer they'd spent on Blue Crab Island). And her green-hazel eyes used to sparkle with ideas and enthusiasm. She was going to be a marine biologist and figure out why there were no blue crabs on Blue Crab Island. She was going to be a neurosurgeon and fix the synapses that made kids' great-uncles have agoraphobia, like her great-uncle Nathaniel. And she was going to be a teacher and focus half the school day on anti-mean assemblies, showing girls like Avery Windemere what happened when they grew up being mean to others and what constituted mean.

This woman, with her gray-yellow pallor to match her clothes, the nothing in her eyes, the resignation in the expression and slump, was hurting. Bad.

Holly was unsure if she should initiate conversation or let her be. "Frears is your married name, then?" she asked.

Juliet nodded and glanced away. She touched her wedding ring for a moment, then glanced at the white binder Holly had set on the large island in the center of the kitchen. "The summer my father died, your grandmother taught me how to make spaghetti and meatballs. She told me that every time I missed him like mad, I could make his favorite meal and add a happy memory of him as a special ingredient and I'd feel him close to me, and for a few fleeting seconds that would bring comfort. And then I'd have a delicious home-cooked meal to eat while remembering all the wonderful things about him."

Tears came to Holly's eyes. "I remember that, Juliet. I remember when you and your mom drove away in her blue car, and I was so sad, and my grandmother told me that when I missed you and wanted to feel you with me, I should make chocolate milk. Whole milk and one heaping tablespoon of sweetened cocoa. It worked. And now I remember her telling me that day you left that one day you'd be back. I miss her so much."

Juliet stiffened. "Miss her? Oh, no, Holly. Don't tell me."

"Three weeks now. I came here a month ago, crying over a breakup, and she passed away in her sleep. I'm glad I was here, though. I'm glad I spent those days with her before she died."

Juliet sucked in a breath and stared out the window.

"I'll understand if you want to drop out of the class, Juliet. I did call and leave two messages on your answering machine, to let you know my grandmother wouldn't be teaching the class, but I didn't connect your married name to you, of course. You clearly need my grandmother. I can see that. Please don't feel that you need to stay just because I'm teaching the course."

"Thanks for understanding," Juliet said, and turned around and walked out.

But I didn't mean it, Holly wanted to call after her. She wanted to run after her, tell her to come back, that Camilla's recipes were still magic, even if Camilla weren't there. *The magic is in the wishing, is in the remembering. . . .*

Go after her, Holly told herself. *She needs someone to go after her.*

Holly ran outside, the October air chilly against her thin black sweater. "Juliet!" she called, glancing around. There was a man walking down the road, coming toward the house. And a car with its signal on, turning into Holly's driveway. But no sign of Juliet.

Holly glanced around, and there she was, sitting on the swing her grandmother had made for Holly's mother when they'd first moved to Blue Crab Island. Juliet faced away from the house, toward the wooded edge of pines. She managed to appear both stiff and slumped at the same time.

"Juliet, please come back in," Holly said. "Whatever it was you needed from my grandmother, it's in the kitchen. It's in her recipes."

Juliet said nothing, and then a wail escaped her, so sad that Holly covered her hand with her mouth. What should she say? Do? She moved to the side of the swing, so as not to get in Juliet's face.

"The air here is just like I remember," Juliet said, staring ahead. "I couldn't breathe in Chicago, Holly. I couldn't *breathe.* There was just no air. I wonder if it was always like that and I just never noticed. It had to have been, though."

"What do you mean?"

Juliet stared at the ground and said noth-

95

ing, and Holly had no choice but to let it go for the moment since the other students began arriving. A man walked up the cobblestone path. A woman got out of a car that she'd parked in the driveway and was heading up the three porch steps.

Holly held out her hand, unsure if Juliet would take it or if she'd run off, get into her car, and disappear.

She slipped her hand into Holly's. "Okay," she said.

Okay, Holly seconded silently.

The small group stood in the entryway. "Hi, everyone," Holly said. "I'm Holly Maguire, granddaughter of Camilla Constantina, who began this cooking class in 1962. I don't claim to be as good a cook as my grandmother, but I grew up cooking at her hip every summer, watching her every move, listening and absorbing. And I'm the keeper of her famed recipes, Camilla's Cucinotta recipes."

She'd practiced that monologue last night. It was amazing how you could sound confident, like you knew what you were talking about, like you *believed,* when you felt like you might fall over any second.

The other woman, who by reasons of deduction must be one Tamara Bean, was

96

in her early thirties, Holly guessed, with long, wildly curly brown hair, narrow brown eyes the color of peppermint bark, and a long nose that made her look both regal and Eastern European. Tamara raised an eyebrow and glanced around. "Is it just us three — two women and *one* guy?" she asked. "My mother gave this class to me as gift certificate to meet men. She'd heard this course attracts men."

That would explain the fitted sweater, pencil skirt, and high-heeled, knee-high black leather boots. *You can't leave,* Holly sent telepathically. *No one is allowed to leave!* "There's one more student, my apprentice, but —"

"Oh, thank God," Tamara said, pulling her hair into a low ponytail like Juliet's. She set her tote bag on the tasting bench and took off her boots, exchanging them for a pair of black ballet flats. "I'm willing to try, you know? The cutesy outfit, showing up. But I am so sick of my mother throwing men at me. My sister is getting married — my *youngest* sister. The middle one is already married and pregnant, of course. I'm so sick of meeting men." She turned to the man standing across from her. "No offense, of course."

He smiled. "None taken."

"You're Tamara Bean, right?" Holly said, glancing at her roster.

Tamara nodded. "At least here I can actually learn to cook, something I enjoy doing. I'm thirty-two — so what? All my relatives do is throw men at me and make me feel like a loser for not being in a relationship. And they're full of reasons for why my relationships don't work out."

"It's never the reasons anyone thinks," the man said, then seemed to realize he'd spoken out loud. Simon March was tall and lanky and quite attractive, with sandy-streaked blond hair and dark blue eyes. "I mean, it's never the things you can do something about, really. It's always about who you are, intrinsically. Simon March, by the way."

"Well, that's depressing, Simon March," Tamara said.

Juliet stared at her gray-clad feet.

"Not really," Simon said, "If you think about it."

Was this good? Student conversation? Tangents? The meaning of life? It had to be good. It was certainly better than awkward silence. If they kept it up, perhaps they wouldn't notice that Holly often had to look up ingredients or certain pans and utensils on Google. She would have them do the same, though, if they didn't know the difference between a cast iron pan and a ravioli pot.

"Welcome, Simon, Tamara, and Juliet," Holly said with a nod at each of them. "Mia, my young apprentice, should be along soon." Holly glanced at her watch. It was five minutes after six. Time to get cooking.

You can do this, she told herself. *It's not like anyone here is a home cook or a chef who'll make everyone realize you're totally unqualified.*

"Okay," Holly said. "Let's move into the kitchen and get started. Let's all stand around the island, the perfect size for five. If your feet get tired, feel free to grab a stool and bring it over."

"Sorry I'm late!" a girl's voice called as Mia came rushing in, out of breath, in jeans and, Holly counted, at least three layers of slim-fitting T-shirts. Her hair was in a loose braid that had come partially undone from her run over. "My dad insisted I finish my book report on *Island of the Blue Dolphins.* Isn't it crazy there's a book called that when we live on Blue Crab Island?"

"You're right on time, Mia," Holly said with a smile. "Everyone, this is Mia Geller. Mia is almost twelve years old and will be my helper for the class. First, let's all put on our Camilla's Cucinotta aprons." Her grandmother had twelve made up, in all different sizes. They were a pale yellow with a white enameled pot with *Camilla's Cucinotta* written across it in blue.

Juliet seemed about to say something but gnawed her lip and glanced around, her gaze settling on a photograph of Camilla and Holly on the counter next to a huge bowl of green apples. "I'm so sorry about your grandmother, Holly."

"Me too," Tamara said. "I didn't know her personally, but my sister speaks about her in hushed tones. Camilla Constantina had quite a reputation as a cook and a fortune-teller."

"Maybe Holly inherited her grandmother's abilities," Mia said, tying the apron behind her back. "What am I thinking, Holly?"

"That it's time to start class?" Holly said, trying to sound authoritative but warm. Her grandmother use to tell her how sometimes the students would get to talking to the point that some recipes never got made. She moved behind the island, her four students gathering around, eyeing the empty surface. There was nothing to indicate any cooking would be going on. "If you're wondering why you don't see the ingredients for to-

100

night's menu crowding the work area, it's because my grandmother believed that part of learning how to cook involves learning about the ingredients and where they're kept, as well as what types of bowls, pots and pans and utensils you'll need. So, as we need our ingredients, we'll fetch them and anything else."

So far, so good, Holly thought. She'd sat in on a couple of her grandmother's cooking courses as a teenager and was surprised at how much she remembered of her grandmother's lectures. About how collecting the ingredients for the recipes was part of the cooking process. How the gentle sautéing of onions and garlic in olive oil was the base of almost every Italian dish, how the final ingredient of each dish — whether a fervent wish or a sad memory — was as essential as the first.

"Tonight, for our first class, we're starting with a simple, classic Italian meal, a perfect meal for fall's chill. Chicken alla Milanese with a side of gnocchi and a salad. We'll start with the chicken cutlets, since the gnocchi takes no time at all, as we'll be using gnocchi I made from scratch yesterday. My grandmother often made her own pasta, but she also used boxed pastas whenever she was short on time or wanted a quick dinner. I've made you all copies of tonight's recipes from the Camilla's Cucinotta recipe binder. Mia, will you hand out the recipes?"

Mia took the stapled sheets and handed three to each person. The chicken Milanese, the gnocchi in a cheese sauce, the salad.

Simon flipped through the pages. "Looks quite achievable. Ah, and there it is, the famous last ingredients. For the chicken, a wish. For the gnocchi, a happy memory. And the salad, a sad memory."

Holly noticed Juliet stiffen. "You can add the final ingredients silently or aloud. Whichever feels right to you."

"So for the wish," Mia said, "we just wish for something like when we're blowing out birthday candles?"

Holly smiled and nodded. "Exactly like that. Anything you want."

"How many wishes go into the chicken?" Mia asked. "Just one? Or do we all put wishes in?"

"We all do," Holly said. "The recipe calls for one wish from the person making it. As we're all making it, we all put our wishes in. But we're getting ahead of ourselves. First, Mia, will you get the packages of chicken breast from the refrigerator?"

Mia retrieved the two packages and set them on the island counter.

"My grandmother always told me that you can buy meat fresh from a butcher or look for fresh from the supermarket, the best you can afford," Holly said, opening the packages of chicken and setting them on the large wooden cutting board. "Tamara, can you find out from the recipe how long the chicken will take to cook?"

Everyone glanced at their copy of the recipe, and Tamara said. "Six to eight minutes, depending on thickness."

"All right then, that's pretty fast," Holly said. "So we might as well start the water boiling for the gnocchi, since that will take several minutes in itself. Simon, we'll need a large pot to boil fifty pieces of gnocchi, big enough so that the gnocchi isn't too crowded, as when they're done they float."

"Like fish," Mia said. "That's how you know your goldfish is dead. Floats."

Simon laughed and reached for the largest pasta pot on the shelf of pots running the length of wall above the stove. "I never could keep a goldfish very long."

Holly asked him to fill the pot half with water and to set it on a middle burner to boil. That done, she asked Mia to read the first two steps for the chicken.

Mia scanned the sheet for where to begin. "Pound the chicken breasts between two sheets of plastic. Season with salt and pepper, then dredge in flour, then beaten egg, then polenta. What's polenta?"

"Polenta is a cornmeal, an alternative to bread crumbs. My grandmother loved the flavor it added."

Holly directed Juliet to get three large, flat plates from the cabinet marked *Plates* (her grandmother had long ago labeled everything to make it easier for her students to feel at home in her kitchen) and to fill one plate with flour, one with the polenta and cheese, and one with egg beaten with a splash of water. Once the plates were arranged, Holly handed each student a small can of tomatoes and asked them to each pound on a chicken breast until it was a quarter of an inch thick.

"Take that!" Mia said, slamming down the can on the poor plastic-wrap-covered breast. She laughed. "Cooking is more fun than I thought."

Even Juliet smiled at that.

"Now everyone take your piece of chicken and move through each plate," Holly said, "coating it in the flour, then in the egg, then in the polenta cheese, and then you can lay them on a cooking tray. Tamara, can you find a large cooking sheet in the cabinet marked *Cooking Trays*?"

As her students moved from plate to plate, Holly watched them, unable to hold back her burst of glee. She was teaching. Really teaching. The students were following her steps and clearly enjoying themselves. Juliet seemed absorbed in her task as she dredged the chicken in the flour and then the egg, carefully laying it on the polenta cheese.

"When do we add our wishes?" Tamara asked as they moved on to the next step of selecting a frying pan, pouring in oil, and turning the burner on to medium-high. "I know what I want."

"What?" Mia asked.

"For my family to lay off and stop making me feel like a loser for not being married when my younger sisters are."

Simon nodded, his blue eyes on Tamara. "I think we all want our families to lay off." He seemed about to say something else, but he clamped his mouth shut and handed Holly a stick of butter.

"You can each add your wishes any time you begin cooking," Holly said, adding a pat of butter once the oil was hot. "What you don't want is for the food to be done before you've added the final ingredient."

As Mia collected the plates from the island and put them in the sink, she said, "I wish that my dad won't marry that stupid, fake bobblehead. That's my wish. Please come true. Please come true. Please come true," she added, hands in prayer toward the ceiling.

"Who's the bobblehead?" Tamara asked, dipping the end of a cutlet into the pan to see if it sizzled, per the instructions. It did, and everyone crowded around the stove, carefully laying down their cutlets in the pan.

"My dad's girlfriend. She's a pretty good cook, I hate to say. How such a fake bobblehead makes such good lasagna is beyond me. I have to learn how to cook even better than she does so that my dad won't think he has to marry that makeup face so we won't starve. My dad keeps saying we can't live on his burned steaks. I'm so afraid he's going to marry her. If I can just learn to cook and get Daniel to ask me to the dance, then he won't marry her."

"What does Daniel have to do with it?" Simon asked, keeping an eye on the chicken. Now that it was almost done, he briefly consulted the recipe, then dropped the gnocchi into the boiling water.

"My dad's also always saying that he doesn't know enough about the needs of twelve-year-old girls and dresses and dances and all that stuff," Mia said. "Like I care about any of that? So if Daniel does ask me to the dance, which I so hope he does, then my dad will really see — I can cook, I'm doing girly things on my own, and we're just fine on our own."

Simon nodded at Mia. "Very clever girl. If this Daniel doesn't ask you to the dance, he's a fool."

She studied him for a moment. "Can I ask you something? What makes a boy like a girl?"

Simon gave the gnocchi a stir. "When I was twelve, I fell madly in love for the first time with a girl named Christy. She had bright red hair and freckles and she was so skinny that she could squeeze through the slight opening in the locked fence between our houses. She talked about all sorts of interesting stuff, like her family, that she was waiting to see a shooting star, that she liked to spend her Saturdays clam digging with her father."

Mia frowned. "Nothing I have to say is all that interesting."

"You'd be surprised," Simon said, taking the cutlets from one pan with a large spatula and setting them to rest on covered paper-towel-lined plates. "I just knew that I liked girls who spoke their minds, said how they felt, were full of ideas. Like . . . my wife.

And I guess I'd better make my wish, since the gnocchi is almost done. I wish she'd — I wish she'd change her mind."

Tamara drained the gnocchi, everyone watching the steam rise up to the ceiling. "About . . . ?" Tamara prompted as she returned the gnocchi to the pan.

"Wanting a divorce," he said, eyes on the floor. "Having an affair." He glanced at Mia and sucked in a breath, as though he realized he was saying too much in front a kid.

"Won't you be mad at her, though?" Mia asked. "For cheating on you? My friend Emily hasn't talked to her ex-boyfriend for three days. Even though they're in four classes together. And she says she's never going to talk to him again. He kissed someone else during lunch period — in front of everyone. That's how he broke up with Emily."

Simon nodded. "Mad, yes. But I think I'm full of forgiveness at this point."

Everyone was quiet for a moment. And then Mia turned to Holly and said, "What's your wish?"

"We don't need to say our wishes aloud," Holly said, adding the remaining cheese and butter to the gnocchi as Tamara gently stirred it. "You can say them aloud, of course, but you can also wish them silently into the recipe."

"It won't work anyway," Juliet said.

Everyone turned at the new voice. Juliet stood at the stove, a small bowl of dried sage in her hands. She measured out the amount and added it to the pot. "I can wish and wish and wish but what I want will never come true."

"Some things can't," Holly said. "For the past three weeks I've wished my grand-mother would come down the stairs, put on her apron, turn on the Verdi she loves so much, and begin humming as she starts making the pasta. But it'll never happen."

"So why wish it?" Mia asked. "That's kind of like a wasted wish, since you only get one per recipe."

"The heart wants what it wants," Holly said, repeating her grandmother's words. She could see that Juliet had tears in her eyes, so she added, "Mia, could you and Tamara grab the ingredients for the salad?"

Mia glanced at Juliet and took the binder over to Tamara and together they began col-lecting the romaine and spinach.

Everyone (except Juliet, who remained silent) put their memories, happy and sad, into the gnocchi and the cheese sauce while giving it a stir. Holly's happy memory was that her grandmother had taken a photo of the two of them the night before she died. Camilla had printed it out and stuck it inside the beveled edge of her vanity mirror, and when Holly had noticed it the next day, she was so happy to have it. Her sad memory was the loss itself. Juliet remained silent and had twice left the room, but she had returned. Simon's sad memory was the day he moved out of his house, his daughter crying in her room and refusing to come and say good-bye. And his happy memory was seeing her face every other Saturday, even if she'd only agree to visit for the day and not the entire weekend. Mia's sad memory involved meeting her mother's "loser husband who smelled and had no shoulders." Her happy memory involved catching Daniel checking her out in American history that afternoon. Tamara's happy memory had been the day she'd broken up with her last boyfriend, a control freak named Laird. Her sad memory was the way her sisters had made her feel for breaking up with a good-looking doctor just because he was "a little controlling" — and then explained the "controlling" included coaching her on what to say at lunch with his parents, who were Yale graduates.

"What a jerk he was," Tamara added as

she washed the lettuce and spinach. "Holly, did you know that your grandmother is responsible for my sister's wedding? Francesca came in to have her fortune told, and Camilla told her she would meet the man she would marry the next week by the pier. And she did. Isn't that amazing?"

"Did my grandmother ever tell your fortune?" Holly asked Tamara.

"I made an appointment, but I canceled it three times. I'm not sure I want to know. I mean, what if my sister didn't want to spend an entire week painting by the pier? She felt she had to because her destiny was awaiting her. I'm a little afraid of that."

"I can understand that," Juliet said, and again, the sound of her voice was so unexpected that everyone stopped and turned to look at her.

"Your grandmother must have told your fortune," Mia said to Holly.

Holly rolled her eyes. "I almost wished she hadn't. Supposedly, I'll know my true love if he likes this disgusting Italian dish called *sa cordula.* Sautéed lamb intestines and peas." She mock-shivered.

Simon laughed. "Who would like that?"

"No one so far," Holly said.

He collected the ingredients for the salad dressing, a simple garlic and oil. "Fate and fortunes are a funny thing. Tamara, do you think it was fate or did your sister engineer that meeting *because* she knew it was her fortune?"

Tamara shrugged and gave Simon the huge bowl of salad, ready for his dressing. "I have no idea. We've gone over that question so many times. I just know it's so romantic."

"You know what would be totally weird?" Mia said. "If Holly found a guy who actually liked lamb guts and even though he was really ugly and mean, she still felt like she had to marry him just because he was supposedly her great love."

"That would be weird," Holly said. "Which is why it's a good thing no one on earth could possibly like the dish."

"I'm not sure I believe in fate," Simon said, drizzling the salad with the oil and garlic. "When I first saw my wife, I wasn't attracted to her at all. I thought she was too pretty, if that makes any sense. Almost plastic-pretty, you know? But as I got to know her — we used to be coworker scientists at the same laboratory — I fell madly in love."

"That could still be fate," Mia said.

"True, but now I'm living in a small two-bedroom apartment in some hideous condo complex, and Cass, that's my daughter, hates the room I tried to set up for her and now she doesn't want to come over. I don't want to force her to stay over and make things worse, but I'm her dad — I want a close relationship with her."

"How old is she?" Tamara asked, ladling the gnocchi into a serving bowl.

"Eight," Simon answered. "The last time she came over, a month ago, I tried to make her favorite meal, spaghetti and meatballs, but it came out awful — chewy spaghetti and hard as rock meatballs and the sauce was bitter, and the entire day was a mess. I guess that's why I signed up for this class — I thought I'd learn to cook her favorite meal and maybe that would help. She loves spaghetti. She'd eat spaghetti for breakfast, lunch, and dinner if her mother would let her. With butter, with tomato sauce, with meatballs. And I don't want to open up a can of Chef Boyardee again. She's only eight, but I feel like she knows that it's canned garbage. I care what she thinks."

"We'll definitely put spaghetti and meatballs on the menu for next week's class," Holly said as she placed each cutlet on a plate. "You'll learn how to make killer meatballs and spaghetti that she'll want to come over every day for."

He gave a brief smile, but then stared at the floor. "Three months ago, my life was one thing and now it's —" He glanced around as if embarrassed at much he'd revealed, then stared down at his hand — the left one, Holly realized. "Every time I look at this ring on my finger, for a moment I forget that it's not exactly symbolic of anything, you know?" All eyes went to the silver ring on his left hand. "And now, because my wife left me for some sleazeball rich ambulance chaser, I see my eight-year-old daughter every other weekend and alternating Wednesdays." He shook his head.

"I'm glad you love your daughter so much and care what she thinks," Mia said. "That gives me hope."

Simon smiled at Mia and brought the huge wooden bowl of salad over to the kitchen table. "Good."

Holly glanced at Juliet, who'd been so quiet. She was staring out the window at nothing in particular, just the gathering dark.

"You're a good dad," Mia said. "What if *my* dad doesn't care what I think?" She picked at the ends of her apron tie. "I mean, shouldn't what family thinks count?"

Tamara stared at her. "Well, of course your dad should care what you think, honey.

Who your father marries will have a big effect on you. I'm sure he realizes that."

"I'm not so sure of that at *all*," Mia said, setting the bowl of gnocchi on the kitchen table. "God, this stuff smells amazing. I'm *starving*."

"Then let's sit down to eat," Holly said, placing a plate of the chicken at each place setting.

The five of them were about to take their seats when the front door bells jangled and a familiar woman rushed in, her heels clicking against the wood floor. She wore a tiny pink suit, a little froth of a sheer scarf around her neck, knotted at the side, and high-heeled black patent-leather peep-toe pumps.

The Bobblehead.

"I'm not too late, am I?" she asked, her smile bright white. "I'd love to sign up for the class. The board outside said there's room?"

Holly shot a glance at Mia, who was staring at the woman with contempt and disbelief.

Mia's eyes narrowed. "You already know how to cook Italian. Why do you need to take this class?"

"Hi, sweetie!" she directed at Mia, blowing her the equivalent of an air kiss. "Yes,

I'm a great cook and Italian is one of my specialties, but wouldn't it be lovely for us to do something together!" She dashed a smile around the room. "Oh," she said, her gaze landing on Juliet. "Gray is not your color, hon. I'm a certified colorologist and an Internal Beauty Cosmetics saleswoman. I'd say you're a summer. No, a *spring.* Springs can't wear gray — and certainly not that shade."

Mia was shooting Holly a very satisfied *I told you so* smile.

Juliet stared at Jodie for a moment, then her gaze moved out the window.

"Oh, pah," Jodie singsonged. There I go again. Always the businesswoman. I would love to take this cooking class, even though it looks like I missed the cooking part tonight. Which one of you is Camilla?"

"I'm the teacher," Holly said. "Holly."

"Oh." Jodie looked confused. Mia shook her head. "Holly. Well, anyway. Is there a spot available?"

Holly could feel Mia's eyes boring into hers. *No. Tell her no.*

"I'm sure there isn't," Jodie rushed to add, with a tight smile. "But I at least wanted to stop in and check."

Ah. She didn't mean it. That would make

it much easier for Holly to lose her course fee.

"I'm so sorry," Holly said, "but since this is my first time teaching my grandmother's course, I've capped the number of students at four."

Holly could see the woman's relief. The idea to take the course had clearly been Liam's.

"Oh, darn," Jodie said. "Mia, I was so hoping we could enjoy an activity together. Well, then, bye, all. Oh, and I'll just leave some Internal Beauty Cosmetics pamphlets and my card on the table if any of you want to discuss fall colors. Now that summer's gone, we all start looking a little washed out."

As the door bells jangled behind her, Juliet suddenly started laughing. "I'm sorry," she said, catching her breath. "But that was funny."

"You should hear her try to tell a joke," Mia said. "Opposite effect."

There were snickers, and then when they sat down to test their first meal, there was a chorus of "not bad" and "this is pretty good" and a long discussion about next week's menu, which everyone agreed to change to spaghetti and meatballs so that Simon could learn to make the kind that would keep a kid coming back for more.

Class one: A-plus.

As Holly finished cleaning up the kitchen (Mia had missed a lot), she headed out to the porch swing with a cup of tea and her grandmother's diary. She couldn't see the bay from here, but the sounds of water lapping and the warm rush of breeze almost lulled her to sleep. She could probably fall asleep out here and be perfectly safe, except for a raccoon poking up to steal the slice of leftover tiramisu from yesterday.

"Nonna," she said to the dark sky. "Tonight was a success. I did it. No one stormed out and called me a fraud. No one demanded their money back." She was dying to find out what had happened with the four women who had taken her grandmother's class. Had they come back? Did Annette's husband die? Holly opened the diary and read.

August 1962
Dear Diary,

They came back the following week with their ten-dollar bills, the four women full of excitement. They had each made their husbands the dishes the way I taught them, and there were changes. Big changes. Annette's husband came home from work the day after she'd made him the veal parmigiana and said she deserved a nap after being home all day with the colicky baby. This, after telling her baby care was the mother's responsibility. Nancy's husband brought her a bouquet of lilies, her favorite flower, when he could just have easily chosen the cheaper carnations. Lenora Windemere's husband booked a dinner cruise around Casco Bay. And Jacqueline's husband made love to her for the first time in over seven months.

After a week of my recipes, they come home with different expectations than a scotch and a newspaper. They come home kinder. Peering into the mysterious pots on the stove. Sniffing the air and smiling. And at night, they were amorous. Jacqueline confessed to me in a whisper over the barrel of apples in the general store that her husband wanted her in a way he hadn't in two years. Was there a secret ingredient she could use on his steak or baked potato, his other favorite meal? Was it the basil?

What could I say? I had to honestly report that I truly didn't know. There was nothing magical about my ingredients. The recipes simply called for wishes and

119

memories and they had come true.

Or, more likely, the women were changing. Hoping for more. Expecting more. I tried to explain this, but Lenora said her husband insisted that "Eye-talian" cooking was full of aphrodisiacs, like oysters were, reportedly. I reminded them they didn't use oysters in the recipes they copied down.

During the second class, as they prepared eggplant parmigiana and linguini in clam sauce, the wishes and memories went into the pots and pans. As Lenora pounded the eggplant, she wished for another baby. I can't fully describe the funny feeling I got as she added the "Please, Lord, let this come true." I just know it was a funny feeling, not quite bad, yet not good either. I'm not sure what this means. Twins, perhaps?

As she shook salt into the big pot of boiling water, Annette wished that the birthday bash she was throwing for her husband would be a huge hit and that her snooty sister-in-law would come. I find it hard to imagine the person Annette could possibly find snooty, since she and her friends are as snooty as they come.

Nancy sliced cheese and wished her sister would move back to Maine from Florida.

And Jacqueline slid the linguini into the pot, wishing her husband would sleep in their bed again tonight.

Within a few weeks, everything had come true. Lenora learned she was six weeks pregnant. Nancy's sister came for a visit and announced her husband was being transferred to the Boston office, which was as good to Nancy as if they were moving to Maine. Jacqueline's husband bought her a black silk teddy.

And Annette's snooty sister-in-law did RSVP yes to Annette's husband's fortieth birthday party. But two days before the party, he died of a massive heart attack while jogging. His fortieth birthday was turned into a memorial service.

I don't know Annette well, of course, and she's mostly unbearable and materialistic and obsessed with having what her friends and neighbors have. But now what she wants most of all is to join her husband in heaven — which is what she told me when I stopped by her house the night of the memorial, once everyone was gone. I could hear the baby crying, and when Annette didn't answer the door, I gave the doorknob a jiggle and it opened. I found Annette sobbing on the kitchen floor, her back against the refrigerator door, containers of food on the table and counters. I let her know I was there and was going to take care of the baby, and that's when she said she wished she were dead too, then added, "I wish I were with him. I just want to be with him."

I let it go at that and hurried upstairs to the baby, who I hoped had been tended to by family and friends that had come over after the funeral. The baby was wet and hungry, so I changed him and warmed a bottle and put him back down, but when he started crying again and Annette slammed her hands over her ears, I said to her, "Honey, I'm going to take the baby home with me and give you some time. You come get him when you're ready." She nodded and burst into tears, so I helped her upstairs to her room, where she lay down on her bed and sobbed.

I knew all about that.

I put the food away in the refrigerator, went through the nursery, and packed a bag for the baby, wrote a note to remind Annette that I was taking the baby home with me to care for until she was ready to come get him, and then left.

Luciana was thrilled to have a baby in the house and helped me diaper him, even after he sprayed right on her neck. Three days later, Annette came for her baby. Something was completely gone from her eyes, that spark of jealousy and competitiveness.

"Thank you for helping me," Annette said, taking the baby from the bassinet I'd bought at a secondhand shop.

"Whenever you need some time to yourself, you just bring him here," I told her.

I let her know I'd cancel class out of respect, but Annette shook her head and said it would be a help to be among her friends. The following week the four of them were back. Annette was still as standoffish as ever with me, as though I hadn't done her a kindness it seemed her friends hadn't. And when it came time for her to make a wish into the gnocchi, she wished she'd find another husband who was as good a provider as Bob had been.

Lenora smiled at Annette; it was clear Lenora had told Annette it was time to take control of her life. I would have thought Annette had a tiny heart, but when the recipe called for a happy memory, she told of her husband reading her terminally ill father the sports scores during the Super Bowl, and how she knew that despite how he seemed on the outside, he could sometimes be a caring man. It turned out that

Bob, as went the American expression, was a bit of a shit.

And so that was that for Annette's grieving period. She now wished for a new husband who would not mind a colicky baby. Lenora spent her wishes on not miscarrying, which had happened the previous year. Nancy wished her in-laws would decide to move in with her husband's sister in New Hampshire instead of them, and Jacqueline wished that her husband was not carrying on an affair with his secretary, which would account for the previous year's dry spell.

They came back week after week, becoming decent cooks of Italian-American food. And through it all, I can't say I was ever really included in their little group, despite being privy to their most personal hopes, dreams and fears.

Holly closed the diary and wrapped her arms around herself, unsettled by all she'd read. The women who'd taken her grandmother's class sounded so selfish and cold, despite tragedy, infidelity, unhappiness. Or, perhaps, because of those things. Holly shivered as the wind swirled through her sweater. She thought of Juliet, grieving someone or something, alone here in Maine, where she had no family but at least one friend.

She collected her mug and the composition book, headed inside, and picked up the phone to call Juliet, then realized she only had the number where no one called back, in Chicago. Juliet was grieving a loss. Her husband? She sounded exactly like her grandmother had described Annette — before the perky interest in finding a new husband, anyway. Why hadn't Holly pressed Juliet on where she was staying? Now she wouldn't be able to find her and could only hope she'd show up next Monday for the class.

Watch over her, Nonna, will you? Holly said, her gaze on Antonio, who sat on his perch, staring out at the inky night sky and the twinkling stars.

Six

The next morning, as Holly checked the Bolognese sauce simmering on the stove and kept an eye on the timer for the tagliatelle, one of her favorite pastas, she realized no one had come in during the three weeks since she'd been making all the takeout foods, with wide eyes and a sly smile and asking, "What was in that sauce?" She had no idea what accounted for the amorous quality of Camilla's food, but then again, Camilla herself was the magical ingredient.

The Bolognese sauce had called for a wish, just a plain old wish, nothing fancy, and Holly's thoughts turned back to Juliet with her grieving eyes and gray clothes. "I wish Juliet peace," was what went into the sauce along with finely chopped pancetta.

Someone rang the doorbell twenty times in a row. Holly figured it was Mia (who else would?) and there she was, her expression frantic, shivering in the morning chill in just a thin light blue hoodie and jeans.

"Mia, honey, what's —"

Mia burst into tears, and Holly ushered her in, closing the door with her foot. She led her into the kitchen and sat her down in the breakfast nook, quickly making her hot chocolate, which did seem to have magical properties, at least as far as Mia was concerned.

"He's going to propose to that moron," Mia wailed, flinging her head down on her arms. She lifted up her head and covered her face with her hands. "I can't believe it. How could it be? He knows how I feel about her." Tears streamed down Mia's face, and Holly hurried over and sat down beside her.

"How do you know?" Holly asked, reaching out to tuck Mia's hair behind her ears and out of her face.

"Five minutes ago I was going into the kitchen to get some cereal, and I passed his bedroom, and he was standing by the window, with his back to me, holding an engagement ring. He was just staring at it, like he was rehearsing his proposal." She burst into tears again and flung her head back down.

Holly stroked Mia's hair and got up to pour the hot chocolate into a mug, which she brought back to the table.

Mia lifted her head again. "You can help me!" She picked up the mug, wrapping her hands around it. "You could come over tonight and back me up. Like, I'll say, 'Dad, you can't marry that fake moron who doesn't even like me,' and when he says, 'Honey, *of course* she likes you,' you can say, 'No, really she doesn't, she made that clear when she was totally relieved there was no room for her in the class.' And then he'll say, 'Come on, that's crazy, she came in to take that course and there was no room.' And then he'll go into a half-hour discussion on what it means to *project,* which is his new word. And then you can tell him to lose the psychobabble *and* the bobblehead, that I'm *right.*" Tears filled Mia's eyes and Holly knew she'd have to tread carefully.

"Honey, it's not my place to interfere in your dad's life. I don't even know him, really."

"His life? It's *my* life. And you know *me.* I'm your apprentice. Please, Holly?"

"Mia —"

She looked at Holly with those teary, blueberry-colored eyes. "All he ever says is that he'd never do anything bad for me. But he's blinded by Jodie without an *e*'s big boobs and miniscule skirts and high heels.

128

There's no way she loves him. And she hates me."

"I'm sure she doesn't hate you, Mia."

She stood up, her lips tight. "You sound just like him."

Holly's shoulders slumped. She was out of her element here.

"Just come for dinner tonight, Holly. You don't have to say anything if it doesn't feel right or whatever. But should you suddenly feel like saying something, you can."

"And I'm there because . . . ?"

Mia bit her lip, then her eyes lit up. "Because I'm your apprentice, and since you saw how little I know about the kitchen and its inner workings, you wanted to give me a lesson in my home. Like to familiarize me with how ovens work and what potato peelers are."

Holly raised an eyebrow.

"Please, Holly. You don't have to say anything if you're not comfortable. But if my dad should say something that strikes you as completely weird, even though you don't know him very well, you could say something like, 'Wow, it must be really hard to propose to a woman your daughter hates.' And that will just get the conversation started. And he won't be able to say, 'When you're an adult you'll understand,' because he'll be talking to an adult. You."

"Mia, this is not my pla—"

"Please, Holly. Just come over to teach me how a kitchen works, what to do if a pilot light goes out or whatever. Why I shouldn't use a fork to stir scrambled eggs in a nonstick pan. That kind of stuff. I really need to learn."

Holly sighed. "Oh, fine. You do need some pointers. But I can't promise you I'll say anything at all about your father's love life. That's *not* my business."

Mia beamed. "Like sixish?"

"Like sixish." With that, Mia raced out. Holly watched her dash across the road and down the path toward the bay.

Talk about sticky.

Holly had sold three tagliatellis and three quarts of Bolognese sauce and had only one returned pumpkin ravioli (too toothsome). Progress. Despite how well the class had gone, she'd been expecting the phone to ring all day with at least one of her students dropping out and demanding his or her money back, but the phone remained blessedly silent while the front door chimes happily rang. Also progress.

When the bell jangled again, Holly covered the minestrone soup she was attempting for the third time (too flavorless, despite all the herbs, and too thin), and headed into the foyer, prepared, she realized, to chat about today's pasta special and what was still fresh and available from the past few days. She smiled at the strikingly pretty woman with long, red hair and dark blue eyes and the most translucent skin Holly had ever seen. The woman had been in a few times when her grandmother was alive, and Holly had noticed her at the funeral.

"Hi," she said. "I'm Francesca Bean. Tamara's sister."

Tamara's sister? Holly studied her face, and yes, there was the same aquiline nose and the elfin chin, but otherwise they looked nothing alike. "Oh, yes, the bride to be," Holly said. "Congratulations!"

"Thanks. In fact, my wedding is why I'm here. I'm getting married in six months, March twenty-first, the first day of spring, at the Blue Crab Cove Inn. And I'm in the process of arranging for a caterer. I was wondering if Camilla's Cucinotta would like to prepare a tasting menu for my fiancé and me and our testers, aka our mothers who are footing the bill and insist on agreeing to the band, food, and photographer."

Holly's mouth dropped open and she quickly shut it, reminding herself that appearing stunned that anyone, let alone someone planning a wedding lavish enough to be held at the Blue Crab Cove, which was one of the ritziest bed-and-breakfasts in southern Maine and accounted for most of the summer tourists, was not how to score this job.

"I'm honored, Francesca," Holly said. "But since I saw you at my grandmother's funeral, I know you're aware she's passed on. I'm doing all the cooking for Camilla's Cucinotta."

"I know. My sister told me all about you and the class last night. She said she had a blast and loved everything you all made."

Thank you, Tamara.

"Your grandmother is the reason I'm marrying the guy of my dreams," Francesca said. "I would have hired her to cater the wedding whether my mother or future mother-in-law approved or not, but now that she has passed, they raised a huge fuss at our wedding-agenda breakfast this morning when I said I'd like to give you a chance to cater. They insisted you prepare a tasting menu for their approval or they won't pay, and to be honest, both my fiancé and I are in grad school and totally broke, so I kinda need to bow before them when it won't kill me."

"I totally understand," Holly said. "And I'm really touched that you're giving me this opportunity. I can't tell you what that means to me."

"Well, I can't tell you what your grandmother meant to me. To me and Jack."

Holly smiled. "Your sister said my grandmother's fortune brought you two together?"

Francesca's face lit up. "Can you believe that one twenty-five-dollar fortune changed both our lives? I was deciding between two doctoral programs, one here at Bowdoin and one in California, and my mother was driving me nuts to choose Bowdoin, which made me want to choose California, and I had no idea what to do, so I went to Camilla."

As Holly made a pot of Earl Grey tea and led Francesca over to the breakfast nook, Francesca told Holly the story of how she'd sat in this very chair and listened to Camilla tell her to take her paints and her easel — and Francesca hadn't even mentioned to Camilla that she painted — every day for one week by the pier, and that she would meet the man she would marry by that pier, paintbrush in hand. And that would help her choose her program, in Maine or California.

"And she was right," Francesca said, sipping her tea. "The fourth day, I was backing up to check my painting from a distance and a very cute guy came up to look at the painting and he said it was a beautiful depiction of the Blue Crab Island bridge, and if the painting was for sale when I was done, he'd buy it in a heartbeat. While we were talking, I totally forgot about your grandmother's prediction. I was so caught up in talking to him, about Blue Crab Island, about Maine, and he said something like, 'Maine is a part of who you are, and it really shows in your work,' and I realized I did want to do my program here in Maine, that I was only thinking of leaving to escape my overbearing mother. But cute Jack helped with that because I suddenly had a date every night of the week."

Holly smiled. "That's a great story."

"I don't know if your grandmother was right or if fate just works that way or what would have happened if I'd gone to California. I just know I met the man of my dreams and I'm marrying him in March. I'll bet you've gotten some great advice from your grandmother."

Holly smiled. She had gotten great advice her entire life from Camilla. But she hadn't always listened.

"So you see why I have to give Camilla's Cucinotta a chance, even if Camilla herself won't be doing the cooking? This is her place. I can feel her in here, I think." She glanced over at Antonio lying in a spool of sunlight in his cat bed. "That cat was here when she told me to spend my lunch hours at the pier for one week. And that cat will be here when you create the tasting menu."

"Are you saying you think Antonio has special powers?" Holly asked with a grin.

Francesca laughed. "No. Just that he belonged to the Love Goddess. And now he belongs to you. All this belongs to you. I assume you wouldn't be here, making the pastas of the day and teaching the cooking class, if you weren't serious about cooking."

"I'm very serious about it," Holly said. And she realized how true it was.

Over another cup of tea, Francesca told her about her and Jack's first date, and the engagement party, which Camilla had gone to, giving them a beautiful box with their names carved on it, and then she got into the details about the how and when of the tasting. The mothers wanted the matter settled within two weeks, so Francesca named a date and time to meet in the drawing room at the Blue Crab Cove, because according to Jack's mother, it was as impor-

135

tant to ensure the food went with the décor and ambiance as it was for it to be delicious.

"About the menu," Holly said. "What did you have in mind?"

"Since Jack comes from an Italian family, we all like the idea of celebrating the mix of our heritages. Maine meets Italy. Camilla's lobster ravioli, which she made for our engagement party, was amazing. Three courses. Oh, and each course should have a vegetarian option. You don't need to worry about dessert, of course. The cake is being made in Portland, by my mother's favorite bakery."

"And you'd like a sampling of a few different items per course for the tasting?"

"Three of each would be perfect."

Three of each. Nine dishes to make and perfect within two weeks. If she secured this job, she would be hired for other catering jobs. For the Blue Crab Cove. For parties, corporate and academic and private.

"Francesca, I'm just curious. Who is my competition?"

"You have two competitors. One is Portland Cooks and the other is Avery Windemere. Do you know her? She grew up on Blue Crab Island. She's now offering cooking classes too. My parents are good friends with the Windemeres, so I have to offer her a trial run too, even though" — she leaned in — "she's not my favorite person. Plus, Lenora Windemere is a good friend of my grandmother's, and especially because there was some kind of bad blood between Lenora and your grandmother, I feel like I have to give Lenora's granddaughter a chance."

"Bad blood?" Nothing in the diary hinted at bad blood — yet, anyway. Though, as Camilla had written, despite the confessions and secrets she was privy to, she had not quite been welcomed into the group of four as a friend. "Like what?"

Francesca shook her head. "I don't know. My grandmother isn't much of a gossip, so she's never said. And the one time I thought to ask my mother, who does love gossip, she said she didn't know either, just that it had something to do with Lenora Windemere's youngest son, who died young."

Died young? The baby she'd finally conceived?

"Apparently, Lenora tried to get your grandmother kicked off the island for a long time when they were in their twenties or thirties, but then Lenora just took to ignoring Camilla and stopped talking about her altogether. She tried to get her friends to stop going to Camilla for fortunes and classes, but they snuck over to see her anyway and soon enough Lenora accepted it."

"I wonder what happened," Holly said, her grandmother's words in her diary coming back to her. *When she dropped the gnocchi into the water and added, Please Lord, let me get pregnant, I got a funny feeling. . . .*

Francesca shrugged. "Whatever it was, it was something bad. When my grandmother mentioned to Lenora in passing a couple of months ago that I planned to hire Camilla to cater the wedding, she said that would be a big mistake, that Camilla might poison the food to spite her for being a family friend. Of course, everyone told her that was nonsense, and my grandmother reminded her it was because of Camilla that I was getting married and staying in Maine in the first place. My family loves Jack and his family. So Camilla has serious points with some of the Beans, if not the Windemeres. But I'll tell you, my mother thinks the Windemeres walk on water, and she'd like to hire Avery to score suck-up points, so do the best cooking of you life for the tasting."

But no pressure! "I'll spend the next week creating a tasting menu to assure you and your family that they should choose Camilla's Cucinotta to cater your wedding,"

Holly said.

"I'm sure you will. I just have a good feeling. And you've got Tamara all jazzed about something other than dating. Though now she's talking about how she can cook for her dates."

Tamara, enthused about dating? Interesting. Maybe she talked about dating so much with her family to get them off her back, to assure them she was "working on it." She had a feeling Tamara had long lived in Francesca's shadow. Or maybe Tamara did want to meet someone, did want to get married like her sisters — and didn't want to admit it, especially under all that pressure, perceived or otherwise.

"I owe Tamara too, since she found my gown for me. I must have looked at a hundred dresses and none of them was the one. And then Tamara said she saw the perfect Francesca dress in a small boutique in Portland's Old Port, and she was right."

"Did you have to get mother and future mother-in-law approval?" Holly asked, unable to imagine someone nixing a dress she loved and having to put it back.

Francesca laughed. "No way." She whipped out her cell phone from her purse and flashed through five photos of herself in a beautiful, delicate wisp of a dress that suited her fragility.

"It's stunning," Holly said. "Tamara must know you well."

Francesca looked thoughtful for a moment. "Better than I thought."

Holly had tried on a wedding gown once, just six months ago, right before John had started changing, becoming more distant. She'd passed a bridal boutique and had gone in and couldn't help the big fat fibs that had come out of her mouth, that yes, she was a bride to be, thinking of a summer wedding, and could she try a few? She flipped through stunning gowns on the rack until she found the one she'd wear if John ever did propose, and when she tried it on, it was so fairy-tale perfect that she'd burst into tears. The proprietor had her tissue box handy, of course, and had said that was often how you *knew.* Holly supposed that was true. She'd cried when she'd realized John was pulling away from her in a way that was different from those times he'd needed a minor break. She'd *known.*

She wondered if Jodie without an *e* was visiting bridal shops and trying on dress after dress and then dumping them on the floor with a disdainful, "That particular white doesn't suit my coloring at all." Which was mean of Holly, since she didn't even know the woman. But Mia had been right about Jodie's attitude when she'd come in about the class; she'd been disingenuous about wanting to do something with Mia and all about scoring points with Mia's father by being able to tell him she tried. And those cracks about Juliet's colors? Just plain obnoxious.

As she walked Francesca to the door, Holly was torn between wanting to find out what the "bad blood" was between her grandmother and Lenora Windemere and preparing for a very big job interview. She decided the Camilla–Lenora feud would just have to wait. She headed back into the kitchen and stood in the center of the room and felt as though the air was filled with tiny invisible bubbles of possibility. "I have a chance to do something," she said to Antonio. "Something meaningful. Something that would make my grandmother proud. Something that would make me proud." She bent down to scoop up Antonio and scratched him under his white chin, the only spot of white on his gray coat. "Antonio, I want that catering job. If you are at all magic like my grandmother was, twitch your whiskers to help, okay?"

Antonio only twitched to get down. He didn't love Holly and clearly missed his owner of sixteen years. She set him down in his little bed, then grabbed the recipe book and held it tight against her chest. Almost two weeks to prepare the menu, based on Camilla's menus and recipes. Almost two weeks to perfect it. The money that a major job like this would bring in would pay that property tax, months of groceries, and allow Holly to offer a winter class and keep Camilla's Cucinotta going.

She would secure that wedding. She had to. Even if she had to wish into every pot and pan for the next two weeks.

SEVEN

At a little before six, Holly scooped up the bag full of ingredients she'd collected from the refrigerator and pantry and headed across the street and down the oak-strewn unpaved path to Cove Road. She'd often biked down this road as a kid, the pretty cottages with their picket fences and porches so appealing. The Gellers' cottage was the last one on the left, Mia had said, the bay opening up right behind it. It was getting dark now and Holly couldn't see the water, but she could hear the seagulls and feel the bay breeze in her face, in her hair.

The house was fairy-tale wonderful, made of stone with a red wood door, the name GELLER in multicolored letters on the lobster-shaped mailbox. Two bikes were leaned against a stone carport, helmets dangling from the handlebars. Two beagles scampered up to greet her, their barks alerting Mia she was here. The red door opened and Mia beamed and raced out. "I'm so glad you came, Holly. I was so nervous you were going to bail on me."

If only I could, she thought. "I brought an easy-to-make meal. I thought we'd make chicken Milanese again so you can wow your dad with how much you learned and how easy and fast it is to make, and we can do a basic linguini primavera as a side. Plus a delicious loaf of Italian bread for bruschetta — that just means toasting the bread and topping it with fresh chopped tomatoes and olive oil."

"Prima who?"

Holly smiled. "It means spring — and in this case, spring vegetables. And trust me, scrumptious."

One eyebrow shot up in the air. "If you say so. Everything we made last night was incredible."

"It was, wasn't it?" Holly said. Not Camilla incredible. Not four-star restaurant incredible, but incredible because they'd made it themselves. "So is your father here?"

"He's not home from work yet. Come on in."

Holly followed Mia up the three stone steps into a foyer with a wrought-iron coat rack, on which she hung her jacket. Through an archway they entered the large living

144

room with its huge stone fireplace; brown leather sofa and love seat, both covered with colorful throw pillows; and oriental rug. There was an upright wood piano against one wall and a gallery of photographs of Mia in varying ages behind the love seat.

"Very nice," Holly said, looking all around. And much cozier and "a family lives here" than another single father's home had been, she thought, recalling how stark John Reardon's house was.

"Give the bobblehead a day as official stepmonster and everything will be pink and made out of plastic, trust me." Mia led Holly down a short hallway into the kitchen, a good size, with old-fashioned appliances — a white stove and refrigerator and no dishwasher, as far as Holly could see. There was a beautiful wood table set below a bay window with three chairs.

"There used to be just *two* chairs at the table until Dad and Fakie got serious and she started coming over for dinner all the time. I hate looking at that third chair every day."

Holly didn't feel it was her place to respond to that in Liam Geller's own house, so she set down the bag of ingredients on the counter and busied herself by putting away the perishables, unable to help noticing the to-do list scrawled in black ink and stuck to the refrigerator with a Downeast Energy magnet: *Put $10 for field trip in M's backpack. Pick up dry cleaning. Oil change. Say thanks to the cooking teacher. Kibble.*

Only *Say thanks to the cooking teacher* and *Put $10 in M's backpack* for field trip had big check marks through them.

Holly smiled.

"My dad is totally anal," Mia said. "I just learned that word in our psychology segment."

Holly slid over a large wooden bowl and began placing her vegetables in it. "Everyone keeps to-do lists. You will too."

"I keep mine up here," Mia said, pointing to head. "Number one: Lose the soon-*not*-to-be stepmonster. Number two: Get Daniel to notice I exist on this earth. Number three: Find perfect dress to wear for the Fall Ball."

"Are you going to ask Daniel to the dance?"

"No way. I'd be totally mortified if he said no. Especially if anyone found out I asked him. And my one new friend already knows I like him. One person knowing is enough."

"That's great that you have a new friend," Holly said. Friends were everything, especially when you were turning twelve. Holly

146

remembered how much Juliet had meant to her, how much Juliet had helped her feel not only okay, but good about herself at that awkward age.

"Her name is Madeline Windemere," Mia said. "Isn't that the most gorgeous name? She's thinking of letting me in her M Club, but so far, the other Ms have been kinda snotty about it. Like Morgan Leeson and Megan Grist. Madeline's one of the most popular girls at school, so if she lets me in, I'm in."

Huh. That didn't sound good. Life on a tiny island. The Windemeres were every-where.

"I met Madeline at a welcome party her mother threw for us when we moved here at the end of August," Mia said. "Madeline said I had killer hair and a totally possible amazing body and that because my name started with *M,* I could be in her club, but only if the other Ms voted me in at the end of the month."

Ugh. Holly remembered this crap from middle school. She supposed it would go on forever. And either Mia would be wel-comed into the glittering girls' society and find true friends there, which was possible, Holly knew, from watching the cliques Avery had as a tween and teen and in her own school in Massachusetts, or she'd be cast out and find her own group, her own people. Being "voted in" to a group of friends didn't sound like the basis of a beautiful friendship.

She imagined Jodie coaching Mia into the M Club. Maybe Jodie *did* have to go. "Mia, I just want you to remember one thing. *You* get to choose too. If you decide you don't want to be an M, you get to decide that too."

Mia looked at her like she had four heads, but before she could say anything, the sound of a car pulling up had her jumping down off the counter. "My plan is to ease into the topic. Not hit him all at once with the fact that I saw him with the ring. He hates confrontations. You have to work up to a conversation with my dad."

Holly had a desperate urge to run out the door and back up the path to Blue Crab Boulevard. What was she doing here, in the middle of this family drama that had nothing to do with her? How had she gotten here?

Mia took Holly's hand and pulled her into the living room, where Liam, looking his usual rumpled, handsome self, was being welcome-mauled by the two beagles jumping at each of his knees. At the sight of Holly, he straightened.

"Dad, look who's here to give me a home lesson in the basics of Kitchen 101 and Italian cooking? Isn't that awesome? Holly is so amazing. We're going to make dinner! It would be so cool if you could learn too, Dad. Holly is the best cook and can teach us to make all our favorites. I'm getting to do my own trial run of what we made last night — chicken Milanese."

Holly's eyebrow shot up. She hadn't cleared this with her father? Holly didn't love being manipulated, especially by a preteen. She'd have to make things clear with Mia later. And she was hardly the "best cook." Lesson number one for Mia: one exaggeration could topple your entire plan.

"That's great," he said, taking his messenger bag from where it was slung around his torso and hanging it around the coat rack. "But honey, I wished you'd let me know. I have plans for dinner tonight. Important plans that I can't break."

Mia's lips tightened and she looked like she was trying to stop herself from crying. "You mean with *Jodie?*"

He glanced uneasily at Holly. "Yes, with Jodie."

"What's so important?" Mia asked through gritted teeth. "Why is *tonight* so important?"

Holly wanted to disappear. Liam glanced at her with an embarrassed *I'm sorry about this* expression, and then stared at his daughter. "Mia, we have a guest, so —"

"Yeah, we have a guest so let's not talk about the fact that my father is going to propose tonight to a totally fake beauty pageant loser who hates me." With that, Mia ran out the front door.

Liam rushed to the door, but Mia was out of sight. "Mia!" he called out.

Silence.

He came back in, leaning his head against the wall and sighing.

Holly put on her jacket. "Which direction do you think she went?"

"There are four places she likes to go when she's upset. She could be at any of them." He put his jacket back on and they went out, the dogs following them. "Stay in the yard," he told them, and began walking around back, where Holly could see a stretch of inky water and a rowboat moored at a short wooden dock. "I often find her in the rowboat," he said as he headed around the house.

Was she supposed to follow? Go home?

She followed. "This must be tough on you, your daughter reacting this way to the news that you're going to propose to your girlfriend."

She realized she'd just done exactly what Mia wanted — a little late, though.

"News? I don't know where she got the idea that I'm going to prop—" He stopped dead in his tracks and ran a hand through his dark hair. "Oh, man. She must have seen me holding her mother's ring this morning and thought I'd bought one for Jodie."

"Her mother's ring?" Holly asked, not sure she should even be in this conversation.

"I was looking for a parking pass and couldn't find it anywhere and thought I'd thrown it in the top drawer of my desk in my bedroom, where I throw everything I never use, and sitting right in there was my ex-wife's diamond ring. She left it, and her wedding ring, on my pillow the morning she moved out, and I flung it in the drawer. I saw it in there this morning — for the first time since, and it just floored me, you know? A few years ago I had a very different life. I guess the ring reminded me."

Lord, this was awkward. She barely knew this man and now she was privy to the breakup of his marriage *and* his escalating daughter drama.

"So you're not proposing to your girlfriend?"

"No," he said. She waited for him to add a *yet* or an *I don't know* or a *we'll see what the future brings,* but the *no* was all he seemed willing to say on that subject.

He took a deep breath and let it out slowly, kicking at rocks along the path up to Blue Crab Boulevard. "Things have been a little tense in the house lately. Mia thinks her mother is going to come 'home' for her birthday. Literally and figuratively. God, I hate these huge setups of disappointment. Her mother likes making these grand gestures that make it seem like she went through heaven and earth for someone. But she'll come and she'll go after the birthday cake. If she comes at all."

"To be honest, Mia seems more wrapped up in the idea of you marrying Jodie than about her mother coming or not. It's all she talks about."

"Well, she'll calm down when I explain about the ring." As they stepped onto Blue Crab Boulevard, he said, "She likes that huge tree with the low climbing branches behind the library. She might be there."

And so they went there next. The small library was on its own lot in the center of the mile-long main street. "Ever been married?" he asked, glancing at her as they walked up the brick walkway to the library and followed it around back.

"Me? No."

"You're lucky, then," he said. "Still not cynical."

"Oh, I'm plenty cynical."

He smiled. "When I was standing there this morning, just staring at the ring, all I could think about was the night my wife left, saying that I talked her into a life she never wanted. Including motherhood. Do you believe in that? Do you think you can talk someone into a life? Doesn't the other person have to want it to say yes to it?"

Oddly enough, Luciana Maguire came to mind. When Holly asked her mother why she never wanted to visit Camilla, why she never wanted to stay for a few days when she'd drop off Holly, her mother would sometimes say, "I don't want to live in your grandmother's life. I had to growing up, but I don't now." When pressed for whys, her mother would say she didn't want to talk about it. Luciana would sometimes mutter that kids didn't have much choice, then add that was why she didn't keep Holly from visiting as much as she wanted to — so as not to force or project her own negative feelings about Camilla or the island onto Holly. Her mother was complicated. Holly didn't think she'd ever understand her.

But as much as Mia would want Holly to shift the focus to forcing a *kid* into a certain life, with a certain stepmother, say, Liam wasn't talking kids right then. This was about adults. Relationships. Love. And lack thereof.

"On some level, yes," she said. "I would think. But if the other person is persuasive and you don't know what you really want and the life being offered sounds appealing, maybe on paper, I guess you could say yes and not be sure."

It had been her idea to move to California after three months of a long-distance relationship that Holly had been so sure of. And John had finally said, "Sure, why not, but of course we can't live together because I have Lizzie every other weekend," and so she'd moved into the attic apartment with a roommate who was rarely there until she was suddenly always there with the boyfriend who ended up squeezing Holly out. Maybe she'd talked John into a life and he'd halfheartedly said yes. She had no idea how any of that worked.

"What about right now?" Liam asked, as though he'd read her mind. "Do you feel like you got talked into the life you're living right now?"

"Literally right now, yes," she said, smiling. "Your daughter engineered this whole thing, hoping I could back her up somehow. I'm sorry I got involved. I mean, in your personal business."

"Don't be. She clearly trusts you and she doesn't have a lot of female role models. She hates all but one of her teachers, and the one friend she's made seems a little snotty. I thought Jodie might be a good influence on her, but as you heard Mia say, she hates Jodie."

Holly offered a small smile, unsure what to say.

"You took over your grandmother's business," he said suddenly as they walked along the cobblestone path behind the library. "Did you want to?"

"I think deep down, yes. I was kind of between lives at the moment and suddenly one presented itself. A meaningful one. I spent summers here with my grandmother when I was growing up. She meant the world to me."

He glanced at her. "Then it sounds like you're where you belong."

They checked the big tree and the few ornate benches in the backyard, but Mia was nowhere to be seen.

"Where next?" Holly asked.

"Down toward the far end of the island

155

there's a little gazebo at the start of the nature conservancy. She likes to take her iPod and books there to read sometimes. It's a bit of a walk but she might have run there."

As they crossed Blue Crab Boulevard, Holly could just make out the Blue Crab Cove Inn way off in the distance, along the rocky edge of the island. They headed toward the woods, about a quarter mile away. "So why did you think Jodie would be a good influence on Mia?" Holly asked, hoping she wasn't overstepping despite how much he'd told her already.

"Jodie is very positive, always smiling, always optimistic, and she's so feminine, so . . . opposite of me. She makes me forget everything because she's so different from me. We talk about things I've never talked about before, like why I bought this shirt, why these colors appealed to me."

"And that appeals to you from an architectural perspective?" she asked.

"No, it appeals to me from an 'I need to be distracted' perspective. Mia is kind of intense, as you may have noticed. Add that to my work, which is very demanding, and just trying to be everything Mia needs in one person, and I need a big distraction sometimes. Jodie's a great distraction." He stopped walking again. "Oh, damn. I forgot to call her to tell her I'd be late or had to cancel."

Mia was not at the gazebo. He excused himself to make his call, and Holly stood inside the pretty structure while he walked ahead a bit and pulled out his cell phone. In a minute he was back, and they headed toward town. The only other place Liam thought she might be was her new friend Madeline's house, but he didn't have high hopes, as Mia had mentioned she was a little nervous about doing something wrong to mess up the friendship, and showing up unannounced after a fight with your divorced dad over his new girlfriend had a sordid sound he didn't think the highfalutin Windemeres would appreciate.

Holly stopped in her tracks. "I wonder if she went to my house. Not inside, of course, since it's locked, but the side garden has this beautiful swing that my grandmother had built between two apple trees."

He pressed a hand to his forehead. "I should have thought of your place first, and we practically walked right past it an hour ago. "The cooking class is all she's talked about since you agreed to let her be your apprentice. It's special to her, and I'll bet she is there. If she's not, I'll call the Windemeres and see if she did go over to their house."

But Mia *was* at Holly's, so close to where they'd first started out looking for her, sitting on the swing, facing away toward the evergreens, slowly swinging back and forth.

"Mia," Liam said and she got off the swing and stood there, heels dug in as though she refused to budge, tears streaming down her face. He walked over to her, and Holly stayed where she was to give them some privacy. But she heard him say, "I'm not proposing to Jodie. When you saw me with a diamond ring this morning, it was the ring your mother left behind. I found it in my desk drawer and I was just looking at it, thinking about some stuff."

Mia glanced up. "So you're not going to marry Jodie? Ever?"

He sighed. "I have no plans to ask Jodie to marry me."

"Ever?" she prompted.

"Mia, I can't talk about ever or never. I can only tell you that I have no plans to ask anyone to marry me."

The relief on Mia's face was something to see. She rushed over and hugged her father so tight he had to step backward.

"Let's go home," he said, and with his arm slung around his daughter, the pair walked over to Holly.

"Can Holly still come over and give me that cooking lesson?" Mia asked. "You have to try the amazing chicken Milanese. That's where Holly's grandmother came here from — Milan, I mean. And she's making linguini primasomething. I'm totally starving."

He glanced at Holly, then turned to his daughter. "That all sounds delicious, Mia, but I think we've all had enough of a lesson tonight. Rain check?" he said to Holly.

Holly smiled. "Absolutely. See you soon, Mia," she added, then headed up the steps to her house.

"Holly," Liam called out as she turned her key in the door, and Holly turned around. "Thank you."

She smiled and stood there like an idiot for a second, unable to take her eyes off his face. She wanted to go with them, she realized. Back to that stone cottage by the bay with the beagles and fireplace and makings for her success story as a teacher.

But he had a girlfriend. And an ex-wife who Mia was sure was swooping into town for her birthday. And a daughter, who Holly already was starting to care too much about.

She turned to go inside and the moment she closed the door, she felt their absence, as though she hadn't spent only an hour in their company.

"That's trouble, Antonio," she said to the cat.

He stared at her and then trotted off. Some welcome home committee he was.

Liam had waited until she was safely inside and a light turned on, Holly saw as she peeked out the window. He and Mia stood on the sidewalk in front of the house, and when Holly glanced out, he held up a hand and then put his arm back around his daughter and they started across the street.

She liked that, liked that someone cared again that she was home safe. Until she saw him standing there, saw his hand go up, the briefest of smiles, she didn't realize how much she missed someone caring. Before John had stopped, she loved the way he'd call a few times a day to check in, to check up. And when she'd come to Maine and woken up those first two weeks to the smell of her grandmother's strong Milanese coffee, the smell of onions and garlic of her *soffrito* just beginning for her sauces, she felt so *safe*.

Holly let out a deep breath and closed her eyes. She wouldn't have minded going back to their house, making that meal, talking about cooking or school or anything. Maybe it was the intensity, the unexpected intensity, that accounted for the fact that she missed Liam and Mia all of a sudden.

She stood in the quiet kitchen for a moment, unsure what to do with herself. She called a girlfriend she'd made in California and updated her about the class and her broken heart, which was healing day by day. Talking to someone from her former life helped ease something in her chest. Afterward, she called Laurel, one of her oldest friends from Boston, but her toddler daughter was throwing a major tantrum in the background, and Laurel had to hang up after thirty seconds. For a moment Holly thought about calling John, just to hear his voice, just to say hi, but she knew he'd either not pick up or leave her feeling even worse. She started to press her mother's number into her phone, but the few times they'd spoken during the past three weeks had left Holly feeling unsettled. Luciana wouldn't be happy to hear that the first class had gone well, that Holly was serious about keeping the course going. About making a life for herself here. She put down the phone and stared out at the night sky.

She thought of Juliet, alone somewhere, a hotel, maybe, in her gray clothes, staring out at the night the same way. She was a long way from home, a long way from somewhere she couldn't breathe. Holly headed to her laptop and googled Portland hotels and called five of the most popular, but there was no Juliet Frears or Juliet Andersen registered as a guest. She could be anywhere.

Like right here, Holly realized. On Blue Crab Island. The place that held so many good memories for her, when her father was alive, when her family was last together. Holly shook her head at herself for not having thought of it last night. She looked up the number for the Blue Crab Cove and asked if there was a Juliet Frears registered.

"Yes, ma'am," said the clerk. "Would you like to be connected to her room?"

Now it was Holly's turn to be relieved. "Yes, please."

The phone rang and rang and rang, but voice mail picked up. "Juliet? It's Holly Maguire. I hope you don't mind that I tracked you down to the Blue Crab Cove. I had a feeling you might be staying here on the island. I'd love to see you, before the next class, I mean. Lunch or dinner or even just coffee. Whatever you're up for. Anyway, I just wanted to let you know I'm thinking about you and I hope you're all right. Talk to you soon."

She clicked her cell phone shut and headed upstairs to take a long, hot bath, and by the time she got out, fingers wrinkled and smelling like her grandmother's lavender body salts, she was too tired to even think about menus for lavish weddings, let alone working on a recipe. She was even too tired to open her grandmother's diary, though she was dying to know if Camilla had written of the bad blood between her and Avery Windemere's grandmother.

For the second week in a row, Holly lay down in her grandmother's bed, the Po River stones over her head, and fell fast asleep.

EIGHT

Liam starred in her dream, of course. A brief dream, no nakedness, but he was there, with her in the gazebo, standing very close to her. She lay in bed and thought of his face, a very handsome face, just slightly craggy with that cleft in his chin. Her crush had turned to *like,* unfortunately. Which meant it was time to get up and focus on what was important: the job interview of her life. She took a shower in which she only briefly thought of Liam, and this time there was a little nakedness, but by the time she was dressed in her comfiest jeans and the red cashmere sweater had grandmother had brought her back from a trip to Italy a few years ago, Liam was shoved out of her mind.

She shook some kibble in Antonio's bowl and he came waddling over, then headed to the front door and batted at something lying there. It was an envelope that someone must have slipped under the door. Decorated with strawberries — scented, she realized as she picked it up — the envelope was addressed to Holly. She ripped it open and pulled out more scented stationery in looping red ink.

Dear Holly,
  I'm really, really, really sorry about last night.
                              — Mia Mae Geller

Holly smiled and sniffed the strawberries again before tucking the letter in her back pocket. She well remembered being a confused almost twelve-year-old, and dealing with a dating father and an absent mother hadn't been among her problems. That had to be tough stuff.

She brewed a pot of coffee, using her grandmother's almost-gone stash of imported Italian beans, which she had to make weak since the taste was so strong, but at least the beans lasted longer that way. She liked how the kitchen smelled the way it always had when Holly had visited — like strong Milanese coffee, like Maine, like onions and garlic and the sweetness of simmering tomatoes.

A wedding. A lavish wedding at a fancy inn on the coast of Maine on the first day of spring. That was what she had to keep in mind as she thought about the tasting menu, what would suit the basics and what would suit the little she knew of Francesca Bean and a romantic named Jack. The menu would need to be romantic. And elegant, like Francesca.

Mulling it all over, Holly made herself a quick breakfast of toasted Italian bread and the strawberry jam from her grandmother's collection, then took the recipe book out in the backyard with a mug of coffee and stretched out on a chaise. Antonio had darted out the moment she opened the door and was chasing a white butterfly, a last holdout from summer. Holly had grabbed her heavy cardigan from the peg by the side door but had no need to even tie it tight around her; the mid-October Maine morning was still warm enough for her to be outside with a jacket, the sun shining bright. She took a guilty glance at her grandmother's garden off to the side; a few lone tomatoes were turning green, and herbs that Holly couldn't name were withering. She could learn to cook, but she couldn't take up gardening too. At least not yet. For now, the herbs and vegetables would come from the supermarket or the farmer's market, and one day she'd take out a book on creating your own edible garden.

Three courses. Each with a vegetarian option, unless it was vegetarian, of course. A starter. A light dish. An entrée. *If I were going to a wedding,* she thought, *a wedding with Italian food, what would I hope was on the menu?*

An incredible pasta. Perhaps some kind of interesting lasagna. A scallopini in a to-die-for sauce. It was a start, and for the next hour, which included two more trips inside for a refill on the coffee, Holly went through the recipe book and brochures, creating lists of possibilities. Her grandmother had often talked about how Americans were drawn to food that would make them seem more sophisticated for liking it yet reminded them of their own best memories. Give them an Italian dish that evoked a special trip or Thanksgiving dinners at home, and they'd be hooked. Holly had never understood how that could be accomplished with an unpronounceable Italian dish with ingredients no one had ever heard of, but her grandmother would serve said something, and it was the equivalent of comfort food, Holly's favorite, yet it would be infused with the dark spices that reminded Holly of her first trip to Italy with her grandmother, when she fell madly in love with a sixteen-year-old boy named

Marcello.

I want to try a recipe, she thought, popping up and heading inside. This was new, she realized. Three weeks ago, when her grandmother had passed away, Holly had been motivated to try the recipes, of course, the tie to her grandmother more soothing than anything could possibly be. Yet fear had been the extra ingredient she'd unknowingly, unconsciously added to every recipe along with the wishes and memories. And right then, she didn't feel scared. She felt . . . kind of excited.

She lay her notes, covered in scribbles and Post-its, on the counter. White bean pâté on crostini; ravioli stuffed with grilled eggplant, spinach, and cheese; antipasto platter, Tuscan roast beef tenderloin roasted with pancetta, herbs, and red wine; risotta alla Milanese; gnocchi filled with herbs and mushrooms and served with asparagus; cotoletta Milanese, her grandmother's favorite dish, with roasted pine-nut and fontina cheese sauce.

Holly was dying to try the white bean pâté on crostini for lunch, but since she needed to soak the cannelloni beans overnight, she flipped through the recipe binder for the three-cheese spinach ravioli, and perhaps she'd also try crab ravioli or gnocchi in an herb sauce as starters. She eyed the pasta machine, which was not her friend, and decided not to think about it until it was time. She chose one of the large wooden boards and set it in the middle of the center island, then brought over the canister of flour and salt, measuring the amount onto the surface and making a well for the eggs. She drizzled in the olive oil, then kneaded the dough and sprinkled it with a little extra flour to keep it from sticking.

Holly smiled at the thought of how she hadn't known where to work the dough for pasta when she'd first started alone in the kitchen. Despite watching her grandmother cook for so many years, cooking right beside her, she'd missed so much. But she'd absorbed much as well. And what she knew, without realizing it, often took her by surprise. Such as kneading the dough until it was elastic and then letting the gluten relax for a good ten minutes. She'd seen her grandmother do that at least a hundred times.

While the dough rested, she turned back to the recipe book and got the cheeses she needed from the refrigerator, the buffalo mozzarella, ricotta and parmesan, the baby spinach and the basil leaves. On her way to the herb baskets for garlic she switched on her iPod from its dock on the windowsill and "Beautiful Day" by U2 filled the room.

A half hour later, she'd pulled the rectangular pieces of dough through the pasta machine, making sure they were thin but not too thin. As she cut out her squares and stuffed each ravioli with the spinach and cheese, she checked the recipe for the final ingredient. A wish.

"My wish is that job. I want that job."

She felt eyes on her, and there was Antonio, staring at her. She could swear he was smirking at her. She headed over and scooped him up, despite his wriggling against her, and scratched behind his ears. "I'm going to get that job, Antonio cat." She danced him around to U2 for a few moments, then let him down. He waddled back to his bed and stared at her. Holly laughed. She felt in control for the first time since coming to Maine. And it felt good.

She would save the butter sage sauce for the last minute, since it only took five minutes to make. Eight raviolis stuffed and sealed so that the edges wouldn't open during the four-minute boiling, she dropped the ravioli in the pot and was about to set the timer when she heard the bells jangle. She raced over, wiping her hands on her apron, unable to place the four women who stood in the entry, one of them holding a container of ravioli and a pint of her vodka sauce.

The woman looked so familiar. She'd seen those cold green eyes before but couldn't place her. "My mother bought this ravioli and sauce here yesterday," she said, practically spitting the words, "and we heated it up exactly as the direction label said, but the ravioli was inedible. And the sauce, way too bland. I hope you have a return policy."

Holly felt her cheeks burn. Were the women all together, or were they separate customers who'd likely leave now?

"Of course," Holly said. "And I apologize." She opened the old-fashioned register, in which she kept very little cash, and returned the woman's eleven dollars and tax. "I'd love for you to take this penne and vodka sauce," Holly said, confident about both, "with compliments and apologies."

"Um, I don't think so," the woman said in the snottiest voice Holly had ever heard, and Holly suddenly placed her.

"You're Georgina Perry," Holly said, staring at her.

"Georgina Perry *Handelmann*."

Whoopdie-doo, Holly wanted to say.

"Oh, wait a minute. You're the previous owner's granddaughter, right? Hailey, right?

"Holly."

"That's right, *Holly*." She upped her chin at the blonde behind her, who tapped into her iPhone. "Carly has a dog named Holly. Her husband gave it to her on Christmas. Isn't that adorable?"

Georgina Perry had been Avery Windemere's little sidekick when Holly was a girl, with a mean mouth and buck teeth she'd clearly had fixed.

And Holly was Avery's competition.

She knew the penne and the vodka sauce were perfectly fine. Three weeks ago she would have burst into tears over a returned pasta, knowing she was barely passable as a cook. Now it was personal taste — or a friend of Avery's — that would merit a return.

"Have a nice day," Georgina said with a smile, then the rattlesnakes left.

They're still in middle school, Holly thought, hoping Mia's friend hadn't inherited her mother's or mother's friends' ways. Yeah, right.

At the sound of a short hiss, Holly remembered the ravioli.

No. No. No. All that work! She raced to the stove to see her ravioli bubbling over the edge of the pot. Several had fallen onto the stove.

Well, there was another wish that might not come true.

Holly was so dejected by the hours of work wasted that she changed into her comfortable walking boots and headed out for the two-mile walk to Blue Crab Cove, hoping the beautiful inn would reinspire her to work on the recipes later. Plus, Juliet hadn't called back and perhaps she'd run into her, if she weren't holed away in her room. Holly had only been inside the Blue Crab Cove once, to have a birthday lunch with her grandmother, and she'd gotten a peek into one of the rooms, which was so lush and romantic Holly could imagine living there.

The inn jutting out on the craggy cliff seemed much closer from a distance, but the road to it wound around the bay in such a way that it was a mile from the main road. As she neared the inn, the fairy tale–like gray Queen Anne with its turrets and decks came into full view and almost stole her breath. She, Holly Maguire, former dog-walker, temp, and sea anemone lecturer, could very well be catering a fancy wedding in this amazing place.

The grounds, the surrounding bay, the majestic Queen Anne were so beautiful that Holly stopped to take it all in, then headed in to the posh lobby with its oriental rugs and huge Renaissance oil paintings. She walked down the hall to where she could see inside a banquet room with its imposing chandeliers and floor-to-ceiling windows draped in velvet.

She was making a mental note to soak the cannelloni beans for the white bean pâté when she saw Juliet through the wall of windows, down by the cliff's edge, just past a stand of trees lit by its yellow-orange leaves. She was standing there, in jeans and a long gray sweater, looking out, and then she sat down and began digging at the pebbly sand-dirt with her bare hands and put something in the ground, then covered it with earth.

And then she dropped down to her knees, as if she were crying, and Holly wanted to run out there, but she knew she shouldn't.

Oh, Juliet, what happened? she wondered. Perhaps she would hang around the lobby until Juliet came back inside. Holly settled herself into one of the overstuffed chairs by the fireplace with her brochures and menus and the notes she'd taken to fine-tune her ideas for the tasting menu. If Juliet came in and spotted her and wanted to talk, so be it.

Holly spread out her work, plugged in her

netbook, and ordered a pot of Earl Grey and a plate of cookies when Juliet did come through the side door, her gaze stopping on Holly. She came over, her hands on each end of her sweater's sash. "Sorry I haven't called back. I appreciated your call. I'm just not . . ."

"That's okay, Juliet." Holly reached up and squeezed her hand briefly. She waited for Juliet to say more, and when she didn't, Holly rushed to add, "I'm trying out for a catering job for a wedding here, so I figured I'd soak up the ambience while I worked on the tasting menu."

"That's wonderful, Holly. I know you'll do great. I was so impressed with the class. You're a natural teacher. And the way you set up the class, so that we all do everything together and learn about pans and technique as much as simply following a recipe, that was so helpful."

Holly beamed, the compliment making her very happy. "I think I might have found my place, Juliet. Do you remember how we used to talk about that, how we felt like we didn't belong anywhere? I feel like I'm meant to be here, meant to be doing this."

Juliet smiled, but the smile faltered and she sat down on the edge of the chair beside Holly's as though she might have fallen otherwise. "I'm sorry if I cast a gray pall over everything. Until that pink woman mentioned how gloomy I look, I didn't even think about what impression I give. I don't really care how I look, but I don't want to turn your class into a downer."

"Don't give it another thought," Holly said.

Juliet stared at her feet for a moment. "I'll see you Monday night for the class. I did really enjoy the first one. I liked hearing all those wishes and memories. I've been so . . . insular lately that I almost forgot other people *have* wishes and memories. My husband thinks that's selfish, that *I'm* selfish for closing myself off and running away out there, but we're such different people. . . ." she trailed off and moved to the windows, gazing out at the blue-gray water.

Holly was relieved to hear Juliet's husband was alive and well.

"Well," Juliet said. "I'll see you Monday, then." And with the briefest of smiles she was down the hall and gone.

Back at the house, after cooking for hours, an exhausted Holly glanced around the spotless kitchen, which she'd just finished cleaning. There was no sign of the huge mess she'd made, including knocking a bottle of expensive olive oil off the counter with the pot of soaking cannelloni beans that she'd moved to the stove. She'd had a good night. Her fifth attempt at risotto alla Milanese had come out pretty darn good. She would absolutely include the risotto on the tasting menu.

Holly turned off the lights, headed upstairs to her grandmother's room, and began moving some of her clothes to the closets, wondering what she should do with Camilla's beautiful collection of dresses. She hated the idea of giving them away, but she wouldn't wear them herself, so perhaps she could donate them. When she was too tired to lift even a stack of her sweaters, Holly settled in under the fluffy white comforter with her grandmother's diary.

September 1962
Dear Diary,

Since Lenora *did* become pregnant and Jacqueline's unbearable in-laws *did* choose to live with their other son in Massachusetts, word spread that if you wished for something in my home, it would come true. Lenora suggested I charge money for wishes, but that seemed a little greedy for something that took no effort on my part. And so their friends came to make wishes, which turned into conversations and questions about their lives, about their future, about their marriages and children and jobs, and suddenly I was bringing down the three Po River stones and using them more for comfort for myself than for any answers. The women seemed to like that, that what I "knew" seemed to come from the magic Italian stones. Finally, I did take Lenora's suggestion to charge money and settled on five dollars. Every day I have at least one customer for a fortune, so I created a private nook in the kitchen by the side window with its view of sky and trees.

Despite this, despite all the phone calls and knocks on my door, despite how much I know about these women on the island, I haven't made any real friends, even though I've tried, both with the locals and the mothers at Luciana's school in Portland. I remain on my own. It is just as well. I am now the keeper of secrets here on the island, and since I know so much about so many, perhaps that is why everyone keeps their distance.

Today the class worked on making tagliatelle Bolognese. Of course they want nothing to do with learning how to make fresh pasta; they say they have no time. But they have plenty of time. As Annette added the meats to the pot, the veal and the pork and the pancetta, she said, "Do you believe my mother is already trying to fix me up with her doctor? My husband has been dead for one month."

The others were mincing vegetables, the carrots and garlic and onion and celery. I waited to see if something would come, a vision of Annette and a man canoodling in a doctor's office, but there was nothing.

"I wish you knew everything," Lenora said, adding the crushed tomatoes to the pot. "I wish you could tell us everything that's going to happen."

"I'm not sure any of us would really want to know," I said. "Had I known my Armando was going to suddenly die, like your husband, Annette, then what? I would have suffered an additional two weeks, two months? Been unable to focus on the time I had with him because I'd be already grieving when he was alive."

Annette glanced up at me. "That's very wise, Camilla."

"I wonder if my baby will be a boy or a girl," Lenora said suddenly, dipping a spoon into the pot for a taste. "Oh, my, this is good."

Lenora mistook my silence as a polite

reminder for her to pay up, and she rummaged in her purse for a five-dollar bill, which she slapped on the counter.

But I wasn't thinking about fortune-telling disguised as questions a close friend would ask another, for support, assurance. I was thinking that Lenora's baby would be a boy — and that there would be trouble. The funny feeling I originally had was now just something of a gray cloud.

"What?" Lenora asked, the spoon poised midair. "Oh, God, don't tell me it's twins!"

"A boy and a girl!" Annette exclaimed.

"Identical twin boys," Jacqueline added. "Lenora already has the girl she always dreamed of."

Lenora ignored them. "I want to hear what Camilla has to say."

No, you really don't, I thought, pretending great interest in peeling an extra clove of garlic.

"Boy, right?" Lenora asked. "I heard if you're carrying low, it's a boy. And girls are supposed to steal your beauty, but I've never looked better."

As her friends agreed with that last bit, I turned away for a moment. I knew the baby was a boy, but I didn't want to tell Lenora that, didn't want to make this baby so definite in her mind, something she could name and shop for, buying out the blue onesies at the new department store in Portland.

"I do have the feeling the baby is a boy," I told her. "But —" And I added this in front of everyone so that they would pressure her or gossip to her doctor — "but there is some feeling of a difficult birth."

She stared at me. "Amanda's was an easy birth, so I don't know why this one wouldn't go as smoothly. Right?" There was hard emphasis on the *right*.

"You delivered at home with Amanda, using a midwife?"

Lenora glanced at her friends. "Yes, and everything was fine. It's what I'm going to do for this baby too."

"No, Lenora," I said. "This baby should be born in a hospital."

Her sharp blue eyes bored into mine. "Why? What are you saying?"

I hated this. Hated knowing. Hated knowing so little, but enough to alarm. "I don't know, Lenora. I only know that it will be a difficult birth and you should deliver in a hospital, not at home."

"So, maybe she'll need a cesarean section?" Annette asked.

"Yes, maybe that is it," I said, though I had no idea.

"My sister had a C-section with her youngest," Jacqueline said. "She was in labor for something like twenty hours and they finally had to do the cesarean to save the baby. She was born perfectly healthy. And at ten pounds, my sister was grateful for the scar. She doesn't even mind not wearing a bikini anymore."

And so the discussion turned to birth stories, both their own and their friends and what they'd heard, and Lenora calmed down. But I felt her eyes on me.

Something was brushing Holly's cheek. She opened her eyes to find Antonio's tail resting against her face. She'd fallen asleep, her grandmother's diary facedown on the rug. She glanced at the clock: 12:47 a.m. She turned off the lights and settled back under the blanket, wondering what became of Lenora Windemere's baby, if this was the same child who Francesca Bean had mentioned had died young, but not wanting to know at the same time. She had a feeing it was and wondered what her grandmother's connection was. Something she'd "foreseen"? Whatever it was, it was something Lenora had clearly held a thirty-year grudge over.

Just before she fell asleep, she also wondered if the fact that Mia was her apprentice would cause trouble with her new friend, a Windemere. She wouldn't be surprised if Madeline Windemere, of the "We're letting you in our exclusive M Club because we like your hair and your name starts with *M*," was as mean as her mother, Amanda, and her grandmother, Lenora.

She reached for her white satin pouch of stones and clutched it in her hand, hoping it would reveal something in her subconscious as she slept.

NINE

"Please, please, please let Daniel Dressler ask me to the Fall Ball," Mia wished into the mixture of ground beef, egg, and bread crumbs in the bowl on the center island. "Extra please with please on top," she added, measuring out a teaspoon of salt and tapping it in.

Class number two of Camilla's Cucinotta's cooking course was off to a great start, the meatballs and spaghetti to wow Simon's daughter (he planned to attempt it himself that weekend, when she'd be visiting), almost ready for their pots.

"Even though Madeline Windemere thinks he's a loser," Mia whispered in the bowl.

"Why does Madeline Windemere think he's a loser?" Tamara asked, once again in her meet-men uniform of a pencil skirt, fitted sweater, and knee-high boots. Someone definitely had a date tonight, Holly thought. She added the parmesan cheese and the half

184

teaspoon of pepper.

Mia bit her lip. "She said he thinks he's all Edward Cullen because he acts so serious and wears cool vests over T-shirts and carries around a book we're not even supposed to read for class. But those are three of the reasons I *do* like him so much."

"Should I be embarrassed that I know who Edward Cullen is?" Simon asked, winking at Mia. He and Juliet were on garlic mincing duty, and the smell in Camilla's Cucinotta was so delicious that Holly knew the meatballs would be a hit even before they were formed.

"Mmm, this smells so good and it's raw," Mia said, stirring in the garlic and watching the basil tumble in the bowl. "Daniel isn't some freaky weirdo, he's just a loner type and does his own thing. He doesn't care what anyone thinks about him. Isn't that awesome?"

"It is awesome," Holly said. "I'm beginning to see why you like this boy so much."

"He's so cute too," Mia said. "Today at school I almost crashed into the water fountain because I was staring at him. "*That* would have been embarrassing."

Tamara nodded. "I had a date last night, and the guy did just that while checking out another woman with huge boobs. Well, he

185

didn't crash into the water fountain, but into the wall on the way to the men's room."

"I assume there'll be no second date?" Simon asked.

"Definitely not. And anyway, I don't have time for second dates because I have a first date set up every night this week. I've decided to take back charge of my own love life. Not because my family makes me feel pressured and like a troll for being single — but because *I* want to find Mr. Right. And fine, there's no way I'm showing up single to my younger sister's wedding and having my relatives say, 'Maybe if you straightened your hair or stopped being opinionated, your prince would come too.' " She pulled her iPhone out of her bag and touched the little screen. "Tonight, Mark, nine p.m., the bar at 555 in Portland. Tomorrow night, eight p.m., wine tasting at Gem's wine bar. It goes on and on all week."

"Where are you getting all these dates?" Holly asked. "Fix-ups?"

"Ugh, no way," Tamara said. "Been there, done that. I'm engineering them myself on-line. At least I can decide — and usually wrongly — that I might be attracted to someone or have something in common with someone. My last blind date, my best friend Amy fixed me up with her boring accountant for two reasons only: he's single and he makes a lot of money."

"Why would your best friend fix you up with someone boring?" Mia asked. "Just because he has money?"

"I guess she's just trying to help, since he's a single guy and she's happily married and wants me to find what she has."

Mia rolled a meatball, squashing her first attempt but scoring on her second. "Well, my maybe best friend, Madeline Windemere, has a cute, popular boyfriend and thinks I should like his friend, Seamus, but I can't stand him. He's always bragging about how great he is and I've heard him say really mean things about girls in our school. I hate that Madeline thinks the guy I'm madly crushing on is a loser. I can't even talk about him with her because she'll just roll her eyes and say 'ew.' "

"Don't tell anyone I said this," Tamara mock-whispered to Madeline, "But the Windemeres don't get to decide who's a loser and who's not."

"That's right," Simon said. "My ex was a Windemere type and I think she's turning my daughter into one. Apparently I was right about why she doesn't want to stay over for our weekend. She told her mother that the room I made for her is all wrong

187

and makes her feel like she's sleeping in a hotel, even though it's her dad's apartment. I bought a pink blanket and put up a poster of Dora the Explorer, so I don't know what else to do."

"Dora's for three-year-olds," Juliet said, pulling her long cardigan tighter around her slight figure.

Once again, everyone was so surprised that Juliet had actually spoken that they all stopped what they were doing and stared at her.

"My daughter loved Boots, Dora's monkey best friend." Juliet burst into tears, her hands covering her face, and just stood there and cried.

Oh, no, Holly thought. *No, no no.*

"Why are you crying over that?" Mia asked, rolling another meatball, her gaze darting to Holly's.

Juliet took a deep breath. "Do you know what I wish?" she said, taking the plate of meatballs from the island and carefully placing them one by one in the pan on the stove, the hot oil pinging up with each drop. "I wish my daughter didn't die." Holly rushed over and took the plate of meatballs just as Juliet burst into tears again. She didn't run from the room; she just stood there by the stove, sobbing. "But I can wish all I want and it'll never change."

"Oh, Juliet, I am so, so sorry," Tamara said, taking her hand and rubbing it. Simon moved to the other side and took her other hand.

Juliet sucked in a breath. "I wish I could go home and find her in her room, playing with her stuffed Boots and singing the ABC song. I wish she was still here."

Mia glanced at Holly, then said, "Um, Juliet, is it okay if I ask how she died?"

Juliet pulled her sweater tighter against her and tucked her chin to her chest. "Something awful called bacterial meningitis. One day she was very sick and her little body couldn't fight it. She was only three."

Simon rushed over to the rolltop desk and grabbed a box of tissues and handed it to Juliet, who clutched it against her.

"That's so, so sad," Mia said, biting her lip. "I'm really sorry."

"We're all sorry," Holly said, taking Juliet's hand. "Would you like a cup of tea?" she added, as though that could fix anything.

Juliet stared out the window for a moment, at the huge oak with the trio of bird feeders. "I'd like a bottle of vodka. But I'll settle for a glass of red wine, if you have."

Holly nodded and reached into the cabinet where her grandmother kept her bottles of wine. She chose a red and opened it, pouring a glass for the adults and some soda for Mia. "Why don't we go into the living room and just sit and talk," Holly whispered to Juliet, her heart breaking for her friend. Holly knew how much the loss of a loved one could hurt. But she couldn't imagine the depth of the pain Juliet was in.

Simon nodded. "Yeah, we can finish up and call you in when it's time to try our masterpieces."

Juliet shook her head. "That's all right. I want to be here. Right here in this kitchen. I'm glad I finally said it aloud."

"What was her name?" Mia asked.

Juliet took a breath, her lips trembling. "Evie."

"Evie," Mia repeated. "That's pretty."

Juliet reached out and squeezed Mia's hand, then took a sip of her wine. "So, what's the next step?" she said, glancing at the spaghetti boiling on the stove. At that moment the timer went off, and Juliet laughed. "Well, who's on strainer duty?"

Tamara placed a large silver colander in the sink, then came over with two oven mitts to lift the heavy pot. Holly, Juliet, Simon, and Mia watched the steam rise before Tamara brought the spaghetti over to the center island and transferred it into a large bowl.

"I propose a toast," Juliet said, raising her glass of wine. "To this class. To cooking. To talking. To wishing and remembering, even when it's very, very painful."

Holly wanted to hug Juliet, but she sensed her old friend needed a bit of space, needed to move from the subject of her dear daughter, at least publicly.

All raised their glasses in the air.

"Can I try the wine?" Mia asked.

"I don't think your dad would appreciate my giving an alcoholic beverage to his tweenage daughter," Holly said.

Twice that past week, Liam had come in for pasta and sauce. Alone. No pink woman. He'd been friendly, but nothing more, didn't bring up their hour-long adventure of looking for Mia. Holly had thought there had been something in that final gesture of his outside her house, something in the way he held up his hand in an *okay, you're safe, I can go now* wave, but reading into a man's wave was ridiculous.

"Speaking of dads," Juliet said after a bracing sip of wine, "Simon, I think eight-year-olds are into Hannah Montana. A girlfriend of mine has a nine-year-old and she's nuts about Hannah Montana."

191

Mia nodded. "I was too. I still am, well, not so much Hannah Montana, but I like Miley Cyrus."

Simon let the garlic press drop on the counter. "I just don't know what I'm doing. I get the feeling that even if I go buy a Hannah Montana poster and hang it up, she'll walk in and look at it and then just sit on the bed and stare at the floor. It's not the room, you know? But it kind of is. I think if I could just get that right, *really* right, she'd feel more comfortable or want to be in there and then maybe she'd open up a little. She hates me since the split, and I'm not the one who left. I think my wife — my almost ex-wife, I should say — wants me to fail at this, wants Cass to hate me."

"That's sad," Juliet said. "And wrong."

"We'll help," Tamara said. "One thing we all are is girls. I'm an interior decorator. Show us your space, and then we'll descend on Target and whip you up a girly paradise bedroom on a budget."

"Really?" he said, clearly touched. "I do need help."

"Then you might want to never wear that shirt again," Mia said, eyeing his loud, plaid button-down. "I mean, my *eyes.*"

He laughed, and even Juliet smiled. And just like that, they had plans as a group to

192

meet at Simon's apartment the next night at six p.m., as though they were . . . friends. Holly liked that. A lot.

When Holly arrived at the Gellers' the next night to pick up Mia, her eyes were almost blinded by the shiny white Prius, with a Maine license plate reading JODIE, parked next to Liam's navy-blue SUV. Mia couldn't be happy about providing her father and the bobblehead — *Jodie,* Holly corrected herself — privacy for a couple of hours by having plans. And Holly had to admit her own heart had sunk at the sight of the name with its extra *e.* Everything about Jodie was extra.

Holly took a deep breath and rang the bell, three baroque chimes, and Liam answered the door, looking gorgeous in a dark green long-sleeved T-shirt and jeans. "Hey, Holly," he said. "Mia, it's time for your field trip," he called toward the stairs. He smiled at Holly, and for a moment all thought went out of her head except for an urge to kiss him. Full on the lips.

Until she heard a certain girly voice. "Now Mia, honey, are you sure you don't want me to write down my suggestions? Pink, pink, and more pink. Glitter too. My eight-year-old niece has a princess bedroom that's even been photographed for a local magazine, and I helped decorate it."

At the sight of Jodie coming around the corner with Mia, Holly felt a little gray cloud pass overhead.

Mia glanced at Holly and surreptitiously rolled her eyes. "Uh, thanks, but Simon said his daughter isn't really princessy. She's — Holly, what's that word?"

"Eclectic," Holly said, smiling at Mia. She turned to Jodie, as casually dressed as Liam, in tight, low-slung jeans that Holly knew would show the teensiet bit of thong in the back, and a tight pink mohair cardigan with a pink lacy cami peeking out. She hated to think what would go on in this wonderful little house by the bay after she and Mia left.

"Yeah, eclectic," Mia said. "She likes girl stuff, but she's also really into the planets and science."

"Well, isn't that nice," Jodie said with her too-bright smile, linking her arm with Liam's.

Mia slipped on a thick hoodie and wrinkled up her nose. "Bye."

"I'll have her back no later than eight, is that all right?" Holly asked Liam as she and Mia walked to the door.

"That is just fine," Jodie said before Liam

could open his mouth. "Have fun!" she added, opening the door and practically pushing Mia and Holly out. As they headed up the path to the driveway, Holly could have sworn she heard a "Now where were we?" in Jodie's girlie voice.

I don't care, she told herself. *I don't care. I don't like him. I shouldn't like him.*

Mia stuck her finger in her mouth and mock gagged. "I almost wanted to cancel on tonight and fake a barf attack so he'd have to cancel on *Jokie,*" she said, getting into Holly's car. "What I don't get is how he can stand her. She's so fake! I think her teeth were even bleached brighter white than the last time she was over, which was like the other day."

Fake, but pretty. And sexy. And probably a lot of other things, like good in bed.

"Well, that's the amazing thing about chemistry," Holly said, starting the car. "You can't help who you like, who you're drawn to. That's what's so mysterious and amazing about the human heart."

"Yeah, like if I were remotely attracted to Seamus, my life would be a lot easier. But lately all I can think about is Daniel."

Holly smiled. She remembered her first crush as a twelve-year-old. The boy's name was Ethan Walsh. Holly had liked him so much that she'd actually let her friend ask Ethan if he liked Holly back, and he'd said no, not at all, but she's good at Spanish, and nothing had gotten Holly to smile for two weeks.

"But now I have this huge problem," Mia said as they made a right turn onto Blue Crab Boulevard. Simon lived on the other side of the island, away from the water, in a new condo development that half the islanders had tried to prevent.

"What?" Holly asked, glancing at her.

"Well, the first part of my problem is great. But the second part is the problem. Here's the great part." She turned to face Holly, a big happy grin on her pretty face. "Guess who asked me to the Fall Ball today?"

"Daniel?"

"Yes!" she squealed. "After history, he asked if he could talk to me privately for a minute, and I thought he was going to ask if he could borrow my notes from yesterday, since we're having a quiz tomorrow, and I rock at every test in history, but he took my hand, *took my hand,*" she repeated, closing her eyes and sighing, "and led me over to this little space between the locker banks, and asked if I was going to the Fall Ball, and I said, 'Well, I *want* to, and he said,

'Well, would you like to go with me?' and I said, 'I would *so* like that,' and he smiled this smile I will never forget for the rest of my life."

Holly grinned. "That's great, Mia! I'm so happy for you!"

"I can't even believe it. Do you think it's because I wished it into the meatballs?"

Holly laughed. "Maybe so. Wishing can work. But I'll bet it's because Daniel likes you."

"Yeah, and that's the problem," Mia said as Holly pulled her car into the Blueberry Ledge Condominiums, double-checking the address Simon had scribbled down. "My friend Madeline said again that Daniel Dressler is *not* in our league and if I'm going to drool over weird guys who think they're cool when they're so not, I'll need to find new friends."

Good Lord. This crap never changed. "She said that?"

Mia gnawed her lower lip. "Yup. And the other Ms backed her up. And then Madeline said, 'Everyone knows the girl code is that your friends are supposed to come before some guy.' And that she hoped I knew that too or I wasn't M material."

Wow, the mini Windemere was tricky stuff. "Mia, there really isn't a girl code, but if there *was* one, it would be about friends supporting each other. If you like a boy, and your friends don't get it, they should still be excited for you. Especially if he asked you to an important school dance and you're so happy about that."

"So I don't have to tell Daniel I can't go with him?"

"Nope."

"Oh, good! Because I like him so much!" Her shoulders slumped. "But then I won't have any friends. Madeline and her clique are really popular. If they kick me out, I'll be like an outcast. And then what if Daniel dumps me for being a total loser?"

"First of all, you'll very likely find new friends. Friends without conditions. Friends that will back you up. Friends who are excited for you when you're happy and there for you when you're sad. And from how you've described Daniel, he doesn't make decisions based on what other people think."

Mia brightened. "And maybe there's a chance Madeline doesn't really mean it."

Holly would love to know what Jodie would say to all this. *Court the popular friend and forget the downer boy* most likely. Mia could just hear her use the twisted girl code to say: *Mia, sweetie, boys come and go, but friends are forever.*

"What do you think I should do?" Mia asked as Holly turned at the drive marked Condo Group B 1–12, pulling into a spot marked GUEST PARKING. They headed up the path to building B-6. The two-story white condos were identical, each with a little balcony and a black front door. A closed up pool dominated the grassy area in front of the building marked ADMINISTRA-TION AND MANAGEMENT, and a group of people, all of whom seemed to be holding Starbucks cups, stood in a long dog run, five or six dogs chasing happily after each other.

"I think you should do what feels right to you. And I sense that's saying yes to Daniel."

Mia's face lit up. "It is. Do you want to know a secret?" She leaned closer. "I don't even really like Madeline or her friends all that much."

You're gonna be okay, Mia girl, Holly thought as Mia rang the bell and Simon welcomed them in.

Despite the fact that Simon was a research scientist full of quirky personality, the apartment was devoid of character altogether and had just enough furniture that was required for basic comfort: a small sofa, a coffee table, and a wall unit holding the TV. Those vinyl miniblinds on the wall. No rug. The kitchen, with its fake wood cabinets, held a square table and four chairs. Simon's bedroom was equally boring, with bed-in-a-bag green-and-white striped bedding and a beat-up dresser with a picture of him and his daughter on it. Cass looked just like her cute dad, with her doe eyes and sandy blond hair. In the photo they were cheek to cheek, happier days, Holly figured, and likely the only happy cheek-to-cheek current photograph Simon had of himself and his daughter.

And then there was Cass's room. Just as devoid of personality, let alone girl or childhood, as the rest of the place. There was a twin bed jutting out under the window with a pink comforter and one pink pillow, upon which lay a stuffed rabbit with long floppy ears. More vinyl miniblinds on the windows. A wood dresser and matching desk and a small pink and tan round rug rounded out the rest of the furnishings. The only personal items were a wall calendar of the planets above the desk, two books about the solar system, and the entire hardback Harry Potter series. The closet door was open and Holly could see a bunch of light blue clothes. The room was perfectly okay, if a little standard and boring and unwelcoming. Especially for a little girl whose home life had just been upended and needed to feel like going to her dad's new apartment was just as much her home as her main one had been.

"Why didn't you just let her pick out what she wanted from Target and be done with it?" Mia asked, grimacing as she gazed around the room from the doorway.

Simon stood just behind them. "I did, actually. This is what went in the cart. I guess she didn't know what she wanted either."

"Well, it helps to be here," Holly said, "because now we have a sense of what appeals to her. She likes baby blue. And planets. And Harry Potter."

"I know!" Mia said. "A wizard's room, but in space. Like, if you had magical powers and could live among the planets or something."

Simon nodded. "That sounds great, Mia. She'd love that. The planetarium is one of her favorite places and she's crazy about Harry Potter. But I have no idea how to do that."

"Tamara's an interior decorator," Mia reminded him. "She'll know."

And she did. Tamara arrived, took one

look around, shook her head, and started making lists, then listened to Mia's ideas and scribbled furiously. They made a date to go shopping the next day. A half hour later the doorbell rang, and they were all surprised to see Juliet standing there.

"Wait till you see Tamara's ideas," Mia said, taking Juliet by the hand and leading her to Cass's bedroom.

As they all stood in Cass's bedroom, the larger of the two, Holly now realized, Juliet's gaze fell on the honey-colored stuffed rabbit on the bed, one of its long floppy fuzzy ears half ripped off.

"Are you all right?" Holly whispered.

"Not really," Juliet said, "but I'm trying." Holly slipped her arm around her shoulder and led her to the kitchen, where Simon had set out glasses and a pitcher of iced tea. "I don't even know if I'm a mother anymore," Juliet said. "Isn't that weird? I mean, I know I'm not because there's no . . . child, but there was one."

Holly gently squeezed Juliet's hand. "You'll always be a mother, Juliet. Just like you'll always be your father's daughter."

Juliet looked like she might burst into tears, but she nodded, and Holly was relieved to have said the right thing. She wondered what the situation was between

Juliet and her husband, but she'd wait until Juliet brought that up.

Simon offered everyone his famous nachos, so they all sat around the coffee table in the living room, enjoying the tortilla chips piled high with spicy shredded chicken and cheese and beans. Tamara told them about her date the night before with a man named Rick, who'd accepted three cell phone calls at the table. In an hour she was meeting a boat mechanic named Fred. Mia told everyone about her wish coming true about Daniel and the Fall Ball. And Juliet said the Maine air, being back on Blue Crab Island, had done something — even though it was just a little something — for her spirit that she thought was gone forever, as her husband had said it would.

"Is he staying with you at the Blue Crab Cove?" Tamara asked.

Juliet shook her head. "Things between us are kind of strained."

Everyone was silent for a moment. Holly was relived to hear the husband was still in the picture, that there was someone waiting for Juliet, strained or not.

And then it was time to get Mia home to finish her homework. Tamara, Simon, and Mia arranged a time for Tamara and Simon to pick her up at her house tomorrow and meet her dad, and then they all said their good-byes.

"If I get home and Fakie is still there, I'm going to scream," Mia said as she got in Holly's car and fastened her seat belt.

For her own sake, Holly almost hoped Jodie would still be there, so Holly could let go of her crush that came and went with the tide.

When Holly pulled up in the Gellers' driveway, the beagles yapping at the car door, the shiny white Prius with its JODIE plates was gone. Liam came out at the sound of the car pulling up.

"Stay for a cup of coffee?" he asked, slinging an arm around Mia's shoulder.

Say no.

She wanted to say yes. Just to sit on the same sofa with Liam Geller and smell his soap (Ivory, Holly would bet on it) and look at his face. But the man had a girlfriend. And a daughter Holly was getting a little too close to. And Holly had a lot of work ahead of her if she was ever going to succeed at something. "Thanks, but I'd better get back. I have a big tryout for a catering job in four days and I need to work on my saffron risotto."

Good for you, she told herself.

"God, I love risotto," he said. "I once had saffron risotto in Italy, actually, the summer I bummed around Europe after graduating from college, and though I've ordered it a few times in restaurants, it's never been that good again."

"You should be her tester, Dad!" Mia said.

He smiled at Holly. "A risotto tester? Sign me up."

"You could stop by tomorrow after work," Holly said, wanting to punch herself in the arm. What was she doing? Trying to create trouble for herself?

"I absolutely will," he said. "Sixish?"

"Oh, wait, Dad, I forgot to tell you, the other students in Holly's class invited me to go room shopping for Simon's eight-year-old daughter because her room is so boring, and I came up with this great idea for a wizard meets space concept, and Simon, that's the girl's dad, loved the idea, and Tamara's an interior decorator, so can I go? They said they'd come get me at six, six fifteen."

"Can you vouch for them?" he asked Holly.

She nodded. "They'll just head out to the mall for an hour and have her back by seven, seven thirty. Same as tonight."

"I'd like to be here to meet them when

they pick you up," he said. "So I'll stop by afterward," he added to Holly.

"Great," Holly said. "See you then. Have fun tomorrow, Mia."

"You too," she said without the slightest bit of a wink.

Oh, boy.

TEN

She couldn't keep fiddling with the risotto; the more she added pinches of this or that — a bit more Parmigiano-Reggiano cheese, or salt — the more slightly off it tasted (*what was she doing wrong?*), and if she kept it on low heat another minute, it would start to scorch, despite still being a bit too watery. At first it was too thick, and she added a bit more broth, but then it was too sticky. The bells jangled just when Holly scooped the yellow mush into a big serving bowl.

Liam stood under the archway in a leather jacket and jeans, his hands in his pockets. How was it possible that he looked hotter every time she saw him? Because she liked him more every time she saw him, she knew. He smiled that smile, slightly crooked, sincere, kind. "Risotto tester here for duty."

The fact that his smile, his face, his long, lean, muscular body managed to blink out the C-minus she'd given herself on the risotto said a lot.

Like that she was sunk.

"Come on in," Holly said, handing Liam a fork.

Keep your jacket on. Don't be planning to stay. Taste and go.

Of course, he took his jacket off and draped it over a chair by the window. Then he came around the center island and stood right next to her, leaned down, and breathed in the risotto. "Smells delicious."

It did smell good. And when she tasted it, it wasn't bad-bad, which was why she didn't give it a D, "I think it's missing something. Or not missing enough. I just can't seem to ever get it right."

He dipped in his fork and she watched it slide into his mouth. "It's good."

"Italy good?"

He took another bite. "Restaurant good. Which is saying something, Holly." As if to prove it, in went the fork for another mouthful.

She appreciated his honesty. He was hired as a tester. "Beer to go with it?"

At his "sure," she went to the refrigerator for the bottles of Shipyard beer she'd thought to buy just an hour ago for this very occasion. She popped the top and handed it to him. "Can you tell what it's missing?"

He took a swig of the beer, then set it on the counter. "Let's see the recipe."

She headed for the recipe binder on the counter on the other side of the stove, aware that he was watching her, watching her walk, watching her click open the binder rings, watching her walk back, watching her as she handed him the sheet.

"Well, I don't know anything about beef marrow broth or saffron threads, but I know about gilded coloring and your saffron definitely has that. One of my farmer clients wanted a gilded quality to the barns, inside and out, so that they'd shimmer and make the livestock happy."

"I didn't know livestock cared about shimmer," she said, hoping he'd keep talking about barns and move on to chicken coops and what made hens happy. She could barely take her eyes off his face. "Do architects have much to do with colors? I thought you guys only designed or took measurements, that sort of thing."

"When you're a one-man operation, you do it all. Last year I was hired to create a small farm for an eccentric woman who wanted all the structures to resemble tepees. Orange tepees. It was so ridiculous and near impossible that I earned a fortune on that project." He drank from his beer, glancing at the recipe again. "One sad memory, huh. Mia told me all about the special ingredients. I've never heard of anything like that. You know, maybe your memory for the risotto was too sad."

"Maybe, but I can't mess with the ingredients, even the ones you can't buy at the supermarket. My grandmother was an original. And if I'm going to keep her business going, I have to follow her recipes to the T. Wishes and memories and all. Has Mia shared her memories and wishes with you?" she asked before she could stop herself. It wasn't a fair question.

"She mentioned that one of her wishes into a bowl of ground beef involved my girlfriend accidentally falling off a cliff. Which I took to mean she wants Jodie out of my life, not so much dead." He took in a breath and let it out. "Who knew food could be so revealing?"

Holly smiled, deciding to keep her mouth shut.

"What was your memory for the risotto? Unless that's too personal," he added quickly.

She glanced at him, then turned her gaze to Antonio, then at her feet, then back at him, then at various bowls and jars and canisters lining the kitchen. "I thought about the man who broke my heart before I came here six weeks ago."

"Ah. Freshly broken heart, then. I'm sorry. I know what that's like." He took another forkful of the risotto. "It *is* good, you know."

To have something to do other than to fling herself into his arms, she tried the risotto herself again, and yeah, it was *okay*. But not Blue Crab Cove worthy. And it had to be. It had to be Italy worthy.

Liam looked at her. "Maybe the risotto's trying to tell you something, Holly. Like that you should stop thinking about this heart-breaker so much."

"A sad memory is a sad memory, isn't it?" Though she had to admit that the pangs she felt lately were more for Lizzie than John. He'd hurt her so badly, disappointed her so deeply, that lately she just felt anger when she thought of him. His face would float into her mind and she'd think, *Ass-hole. Jerk. Cheater.* Instead of *I miss you.* But the thought of adorable Lizzie and the way her corkscrew curls would spring side-ways after a nap, the way she'd shriek with joy when Holly pushed her high on the swings, how her soft little body felt in Holly's arms for a hug, these were the memories that poked at her heart, leaving tiny holes.

"Yeah, but some sad memories are bitter-sweet," Liam said. "Like when Mia started closing her bedroom door all the time. I know she needs privacy, of course. But it was upsetting to realize that our relation-ship had to change from little kid and dad to almost teenager and dad. Upsetting but prideful at the same time. My baby's grow-ing up."

Huh. He had a point. "That's pretty wise," she said. "I could go bittersweet. I do have several of those."

"So how badly did this guy break your heart?" he asked, picking up the bottle of beer.

"Bad enough to scare me from falling in love for the rest of my life."

He took a swig, staring at her pointedly. "I don't believe that."

She smiled. "Me either." He raised his bottle at her in solidarity, and she asked before she could stop herself, "So . . . how serious are things between you and Jodie?"

He glanced at the floor. Too personal maybe. But given how personal things got during the Mia hunt the other day, it seemed reasonable. "I don't know," he said, leaning back against the counter. "Some-times I think she's just what I need and then sometimes, like last night, I think she's from another planet. I thought she'd be so helpful with Mia, be able to give me the girl perspective, you know? But she's such a different species of girl than Mia is."

Holly nodded, secretly thrilled that he noticed.

He reached for the bottle of beer and took a drink. "Relationships are tough stuff, huh?"

"Like this glop," she said, gesturing at the risotto, and he laughed.

And then there was a moment, the tiniest of moments, but there nonetheless, when their eyes met for just a second longer. A kissable moment.

"I attempted the chicken Milanese, by the way," he said, the moment popping like a bubble. "I think I undercooked the chicken, though. 'Browned on both sides' doesn't necessarily mean cooked *inside*. So, because the chicken was still kinda pinkish inside, I decided to nuke it for a couple of minutes, but then it tasted like rubber." He stood up a bit straighter. "I'd like to take you up on that rain check, learn to cook a decent, easy meal instead of relying on takeout and pizza."

Or Jodie to teach him, she thought. Too happily. She could feel herself beaming. "Any time."

"Maybe . . . Thursday night?"

Thursday night. Three nights from then. And the night of her tryout at the Blue Crab Cove. That was good. If she failed miserably, she could use the comfort of a handsome man on whom she had a monster-sized crush. And if she did get the job, she would be clinking champagne with a man on whom she had a monster-sized crush. It was win-win. Except for the pink girlfriend.

During the next three days, there was nothing but food and bowls and pans and the kitchen, except for the occasional text message from Mia, who'd seen the dress of her Fall Ball dreams in a magazine and hoped she could find it at Forever 21 or Macy's in the Maine Mall. Mia reported in that she'd had a great time shopping for Simon's daughter's room and was sure the girl would never want to leave her new room, which she and Tamara and Simon had spent only a half hour setting up to utter space-wizard perfection.

Holly appreciated the connection to the outside world, since she'd barely left the cottage, other than to hit up the super-market or farmer's markets, worried that she was spending too much on expensive ingredients to ensure the best quality for the tasting. She had sold what came out well (and had heard rave reviews from the reference librarian that the spinach and three-cheese ravioli was exquisite) and dumped what was eh (another attempt at the risotto and yesterday's crabmeat gnocchi, though today's was delicious). She went to sleep each night with the recipes and menus scattered over her. And she'd wake at six in the morning, full recipes in her head, itching to get downstairs and make her little flour well, pouring in the egg to create her pasta dough.

She'd taken Liam's suggestions to heart. Into the white bean pâté she wished for luck, but into the spinach and three-cheese ravioli, she went for bittersweet rather than outright sad, recalling an unexpected weekend with her mother that had brought them closer (if only for a weekend) the summer she'd graduated from high school. Her mother had driven her up to Maine and pulled her own suitcase out of the trunk, which was unusual for Luciana, who usually couldn't wait to leave Blue Crab Island and Camilla's presence. But that weekend she'd stayed, seeming to need something from Camilla, which Camilla seemed to understand immediately. And in Camilla Constantina's wonderful way, she gave her daughter what she needed without a word about it. A fortune disguised as her opinion. A lamb chop and side of garlic mashed potatoes, her mother's favorite meal, without a pinch of Italian influence. And cup after cup of strange herbal teas that had soothing properties.

Holly hadn't gotten much out of her mother that weekend, but apparently there was trouble with Holly's father, who'd hurt her feelings in some caveman way. And when her mother's wish into the ordinary margarita pizza they were making was that she hadn't lost the two pregnancies after Holly, that maybe she would have been a happier person, like Bud Maguire had apparently bellowed the night before Luciana and Holly had left, Holly felt as though she understood her mother a little better. The wishing didn't seem to help her mother, who finally admitted she'd been devastated to lose the babies, but it had been Bud who'd pushed for a second baby and Bud who now accused her of not being happy because she didn't have the boy he always wanted.

After that, her mother had opened up some, and the three of them had talked and talked and talked, over food and wine and desserts that melted in their mouths. But the next time Holly saw her mother, when she'd come to pick her up after her month in Maine, Luciana Maguire was the same, as if the magic weekend hadn't happened at all. And all the prodding and remembering on the drive down to Newton didn't light a flicker.

Call her now, Holly told herself. You can't get closer to someone, feel closer to someone, without reaching out. Holly wiped her hands on her apron and called her mother.

"House burn down?" Luciana Maguire asked.

Why did her mother have to do that? Manage to dig at Holly's skills *and* be so cavalier about her own mother's house, the house she'd grown up in. All before even saying hello. Holly suddenly wished she hadn't called.

"I just wanted to say hello," Holly said, frowning.

"Oh. Well, I'm glad you called. I've been wondering how you're doing up there. Lonely?"

"Actually, no. I've made some friends — my students. And there's this guy," Holly dared to add.

"Ah, so that's why you're staying. I knew it couldn't be the cooking class and that snotty community." Her mother sounded so relieved.

Holly sighed. She and her mother would never understand each other, never be able to talk to each other, hear each other. Holly had no idea how to fix this, how to just say, *No, Mom, it's not the guy. It is the cooking class and the island, which isn't really all that snotty, except for the Avery Windemeres.* Her mother wouldn't understand because she'd been there, done that, and had been miserable for reasons Holly couldn't understand.

A constant stalemate.

"Mom, my ravioli is burning. I'd better hang up. Tell Dad I said hi."

Bittersweet, ha. Her relationship with her mother was just plain sad.

She cooked on, tasting, dumping, testing, perfecting. Aware that her mother was wrong. Being here, in this kitchen that made her feel so happy, so challenged, so safe, had nothing to do with a man and everything to do with herself.

That night before the tasting, though, Holly did wish into the saffron risotto that somehow, someway, she would have at least one amazing night with Liam, that she'd experience those lips on her, those hands on her, those eyes on hers. And when she dipped her fork in to try it, the risotto as perfect as can be, she was sure there was something to those bittersweet wishes and memories.

When Thursday dawned a bright, beautiful day, the sun lighting the yellow and orange trees outside her window like the flames under the various pots and pans that were her life now, Holly felt so positive. She had her menu, she had her recipes, and she had Camilla's Po River stones in her pocket. She set to work on the pasta dough, sure for the first time that she could do this, would do this. Even when Francesca Bean called to say that her mother insisted she include a veal marsala in the tasting, as it was her husband's favorite dish and most people liked it even if Francesca did not, but her mother had dismissed her as an eccentric. Francesca also reported that the two mothers insisted not a word be spoken at the tasting until they made all their notes and put their forks down.

Veal marsala? No problem. Notes like she was a contestant on the *The Next Food Network Star*? Fine. She was ready. She'd even hired an off-duty waitress at the hotel to help her bring everything over, set up, clear, and keep things moving smoothly for two hours.

And so, with Antonio watching her, U2 blaring on the iPod dock, and the garlic-

and-onion-infused kitchen irresistible even
to her after three days, she got to work.

ELEVEN

Holly peered out of the small kitchen attached to Banquet Room B to see Francesca Bean, her mother, and her future mother-in-law walking in and taking off their coats. The mothers both had perfectly highlighted Martha Stewart bobs and wore similar outfits of pants and flowy blouses with chunky necklaces. Holly was surprised they weren't sisters. A short, rectangular table had been set up by the inn staff, and the two mothers seated themselves, leaving the one in the middle for the bride to be. Francesca turned toward the kitchen and mouthed, *Good luck,* then sat down between the two tough cookies.

"You've got your work cut out for you with those faces," Sarah, the waitress Holly had hired for the occasion, said with a wink. "The scowling one is always here, complaining that the coffee isn't hot enough." At Holly's frown, she added, "Don't worry,

221

though, I've served steaks tougher than her. You'll be fine."

Oh, great, Holly thought. Just as Holly was about to tell Sarah not to say another word, a bell chimed. Mrs. Bean had come up with the bell system as she was clearly used to ringing a little bell when she wanted her housekeeper to dust a chair her flat tush was about to sit on. At the first bell, Holly was to come out and introduce herself, then return with the first course. The next bell would signal that they were ready to have their plates cleared for the next course, and so on.

Holly glanced down at her Camilla's Cucinotta apron to make sure it wasn't covered in marinara, pasted a smile on her face, and walked into the room, stopping in front of the table. "Hello, my name is Holly Maguire, and I'm thrilled to have this opportunity to cook for you today. I've created a tasting menu that I believe suits the happy couple, this beautiful venue, the groom's heritage and the bride's home state, and all of your special requests. I do hope you'll be pleased with the results."

Her little speech seemed to charm Mrs. Mariano, the groom's mother; she smiled in that *isn't that lovely* way to Francesca, but Mrs. Bean remained as snooty-faced as ever. Well, Holly planned to crack that constipated expression with one bite of the amazing mozzarella she'd found at a tiny Italian market in Portland. By the time the woman got to the veal marsala, she'd be breaking out into song.

Holly gave a little bow, then dashed back into the kitchen. Everything was ready, heated to just the right temperature, and the tasters were waiting.

"Everything looks amazing," Sarah assured her. "Go knock them dead. Well, not *really*," she added.

If only this were a weekend and Mia would have been available to help, Holly thought. She closed her eyes for a moment and sent a wish up to the universe to let her get this job, then came out with the first course on a large round tray and set down three small plates of her artfully arranged antipasto — delectable mozzarella, the most intense olives, and bruschetta, infused with olive oil and herbs and a topping of fresh tomatoes and bits of eggplant.

"Mmm, doesn't this look good!" Francesca said, as though she couldn't help it.

"Shhh," her mother admonished, slicing her fork into the cheese. The kitchen door was perpendicular to the way the table was set up, and the tasters' backs were to the

223

kitchen, so Holly couldn't see expressions, but at least no one had spit out anything with a "This is disgusting" like John Reardon had.

The spinach and three-cheese ravioli was on deck, and when a bell rang, Sarah came out to collect the plates and refresh their water glasses. Then Holly brought out the tray of ravioli, placing a plate before each woman.

Mrs. Bean poked at each of the three raviolis with her fork, writing something down on a little pad next to her as though she were a *Top Chef* judge. Mrs. Mariano simply scooped it up with her fork and put it into her mouth, her expression giving nothing away. Francesca forked a bite, and Holly could tell from her expression that she loved it.

And so it continued with the crabmeat gnocchi, the veal marsala, the tagliatelle Bolognese, which Holly considered her masterpiece, two kinds of vegetarian pastas, and an herb-infused sole that flaked just right.

And finally, Mrs. Bean dug her fork into the saffron risotto, which Holly would grade an A. Not an A-plus, not Camila Constantina's Italy, but Liam's perhaps. Good enough for the Blue Crab Cove, Holly thought.

Mrs. Bean took two more tastes of the

risotto, then scribbled on her pad. And finally there was napkin dabbing and bell ringing. All that was left for Holy to bring out was herself for the assessments.

"I'll begin," Mrs. Bean said, eyeing Holly under her glasses with all the disdain she could muster. "I enjoyed the veal marsala and the crab-stuffed gnocchi, but the Bolognese was too rich for me, and the risotto, I don't know, a bit *too* flavorful. Oh, I did love the mozzarella from the antipasto selection. That was exceptional."

Holly deflated a bit. Her only rave was on the one thing she hadn't made herself.

"Well, I *loved* the Bolognese," Francesca said. "In fact, I loved everything, except the veal marsala, which I found just a bit too heavy, but only because A, I don't like veal marsala and B, because I envisioned everything a bit lighter for a first day of spring wedding. I loved the risotto. Mmm, was that good. And the color was beautiful."

Holly's pride puffed back out a bit.

But the one Holly was most worried about, because of the Italian connection, half or not, was Mrs. Mariano.

The groom's mother cleared her throat and put on her reading glasses, which hung around her neck on a multicolored chain, then picked up her little pad. "I gave everything a solid B, except the tagliatelle Bolognese, which was an A-minus, and the risotto a solid A. Oh, and I agree on the antipasto selections. That mozzarella was magnificent."

Mrs. Bean smiled. "Unfortunately, dear," she directed at Holly, "A solid B with only two A dishes is not quite what we're looking for when it comes to the food for our baby's wedding. But thank you — Holly, is it? — with time and experience and a bit more seasoning, we're sure you'll be a fine caterer."

"Mom," Francesca said, her cheeks flushing.

Holly mustered a thank-you from the bottom of somewhere inside her. She offered Francesca a brief smile, then began collecting plates to have something to do and returned to the kitchen, where she hid against the side of the doorway and tried not to burst into tears. Sarah squeezed her hand and rushed in to collect the rest of the plates.

"Mom, I thought everything was great," Francesca said, her voice carrying loud and clear to the kitchen.

"I disagree, dear," Mrs. Bean said. "A few items were, yes. But the majority I'd honestly have to give a solid C. Even your father wouldn't rave over the marsala, and you know how he loves that dish."

Francesca shook her head. "Mom, the food was delicious. And I want Camilla Constantina represented at my wedding."

"I understand that. So we'll borrow one of her signature recipes and give it to Avery or the Portland company, and she'll be represented."

"It's not the same," Francesca said. "Holly's grandmother is the reason Jack and I are together in the first place. If she hadn't told me to take my paints and my questions to the pier every day for that week, I could be in California right now, dating a string of surfers."

"Surfers were never your type, Francesca. And stop being so dramatic about this."

As Holly scraped the uneaten food into the compost can, she glanced out the door to see Mrs. Bean slide back her chair and sling her purse over her shoulder.

"And besides, the fact that you and Jack are getting married already means she's represented, doesn't it?" Mrs. Bean said, glancing at her watch. "Let's move on, dear. We have an appointment to look at headpieces in less than an hour."

Francesca stood up and crossed her arms over her chest. "Mom, I loved the food. I want to hire Holly and Camilla's Cucinotta."

Mrs. Bean made a show of rolling her eyes and throwing up her hands. "Anna, talk some sense into this romantic daughter of mine."

Mrs. Mariano shook her head. "Oh no, I'm not becoming the classic mother-in-law and butting in." She smiled and picked up her purse as well.

"Mom, this is *my* wedding," Francesca said.

Mrs. Bean let out a heavy sigh. "Sweetheart, we had an agreement that Anna and I make the final decision about food. Unless you can come up with the ten thousand or so the catering will cost."

Francesca slumped down into her chair, turning toward the kitchen door, where Holly was standing, a plate of half-eaten risotto in her hands. Francesca mouthed an *I'm sorry* to Holly, then followed her mother and her future mother-in-law out the door.

Holly dropped the entire plate into the garbage and closed her eyes. All that work, all that wishing, all that money spent on ingredients. For nothing.

"Sorry, Nonna," she whispered to the air.

There was enough money to keep Camilla's Cucinotta going for another few months. After that, she'd have to find a job, a full-time job, doing who knew what, and she'd have no time to make the pastas and sauces for the little takeout shop. She'd have no energy to teach the class — or the daily practice required to become proficient at the recipes. And Camilla's Cucinotta would become a memory, like her grandmother.

Tears stung her eyes. And now in four hours she was expected at the Gellers', where she had to pretend she was qualified to teach anyone how to cook.

"Holly, right?"

Holly turned around, a bulb of garlic in her hand, to find Avery Windemere standing in front of her, her shopping cart containing what looked like a bottle of champagne.

"Yes, I'm Holly," she said, unwilling to let Avery know she recognized her.

Avery was beaming, her long, white teeth almost the same color as her white-blond hair, which Holly knew was natural. Avery was one of those pretty women who required no makeup to look polished. "I thought that was you! It's been what, ten years since we probably saw each other?" She ran her gaze over Holly's same old hair, which hadn't changed since she was five years old, long and straight to her shoulders with a fringe of bangs. "You haven't changed a bit."

"Neither have you," Holly said, barely managing a smile.

"Well I didn't have *these* ten years ago," Avery cooed, shoving her two-carat diamond ring and gold wedding band at Holly. "And I wasn't yet in the restaurant business. But now I'm happily married and own my own bistro, and did you see my signs, I'm offering cooking classes now."

"Yes, I saw."

"I'm offering an Italian segment, but a little healthy competition is good for people, don't you think, Holly? Will keep us both on our pretty pink toes."

God, she was sickening. Not only was she naturally pretty with gorgeous hair and good teeth, she had the ability to seem as though what she was saying was perfectly nice. It was how she'd never gotten into trouble as a rotten kid or mean bully of a teenager. "All I said was that if Holly let her hair grow out from that awkward length and stopped wearing green near her face, since she's so fair and it completely washes her out and almost gives her a green cast, you know like the Wicked Witch of the West from *The Wizard of Oz,* which we all watched as a family yesterday — isn't that the most touching movie? — she would look much better."

And the adult's comment was always, "We watched that last night too! Avery, you really should think about becoming a stylist. For television or magazines or films. You're so naturally gifted at fashion and beauty."

"Oh, and I hope it's not out of line for me to say I'm sorry about the Bean–Mariano wedding," Avery added. "I just heard that one of the caterers on their list of possibilities has been crossed off, and since I know you had your tasting today . . ."

Holly glanced at her watch. "Oh, it's almost five o'clock. I'd better get going. Nice to see you." She started to push her cart away.

Avery slightly blocked Holly's cart with her own. "I'm *so* nervous for my tryout tomorrow afternoon. But excited too." She glanced at her diamond-encrusted watch. "Oh, look at the time. My Madeline is due home from cheerleading practice. Better run."

Holly watched her high heels click away, but then Avery turned around. "Oh, Holly? You're welcome to sign up for my course starting next week," she said. "It's not Italian focused until the third week, but I'm sure the lessons will carry. What you got wrong at the tasting is about skill."

"Or something else, perhaps," Holly said and turned her cart around just in time to see the slight confusion in Avery's beady blue eyes as she tried to figure out exactly what Holly had meant.

Thank you, Avery Windemere, she thought as she set her groceries on the checkout table. *You just buoyed my spirits because you're so transparent and wrong. My not getting the job had nothing to do with my skills as a chef. I know I did well. I know it wasn't the food. And there are other catering jobs to court.*

That felt great until she hit the cool October air and reality hit her in the stomach.

TWELVE

"Uh-oh," Mia said as she opened the door of her house.

Holly clutched the brown paper bag of groceries to her chest. "Uh-oh is right. I didn't get the job."

Mia puffed out her lips in a frown. "How is that possible? Wasn't this Tamara's sister and mother? How could they not love your cooking? Did you make your tagliatelle Bolognese?"

"I did. And it was rated too rich."

Mia rolled her eyes. "*Whatever* on them. If they want mystery meat and rubber chicken like at our caf, I guess they'll hire someone else."

Holly smiled. "At least I have one fan."

Liam came down the stairs, and for a moment Holly's heart actually lifted, but then it sank again. He glanced from Holly to his daughter and back to Holly. "So I can see by your faces that we're not celebrating tonight."

Holly shook her head. "And the risotto was even Italy worthy, or at least I thought it was. I saved you some at the house, so maybe you can tell me sometime if I'm crazy and it was just as off as it was the other day."

"Sorry," he said, taking the bag from her. "I know this job meant a lot to you."

"It meant everything," she said. "I'm not sure how I'm going to keep the business going. But I could try and go after other catering jobs. If I get my confidence back."

"There will definitely be other jobs, Holly. It's just one wedding. And what, you've been at this for barely six weeks. If your risotto tastes that good after six weeks, imagine it after four months."

That did make her feel better. But if she couldn't get a catering job with the bride pulling for her, why would strangers hire her? Then again, perhaps off Blue Crab Island, where mothers of friends of enemies of her grandmother were not aplenty, she would not have the same issues.

Liam took one look at her face, which was clearly about to crumple, then took her hand and led her to the sofa. "Why don't you let us cook for you? We have the recipe. I have the ingredients. Just sit back and relax with a glass of good red wine and some music. I'm not saying dinner will be good, but since you've been cooking non-stop for days, it's your turn to be served."

Fine, make things even worse. Be wonderful, Liam. She leaned her head back against the soft leather and stared out the window, focusing on where the short strip of sandy beach met the dark water. She stared at a rowboat docked on the little square pier, *The Mia* written in dark purple paint across the side. The sight of it made Holly smile. This was a dad who loved his daughter.

As they disappeared into the kitchen amid lots of "No, Dad, you're supposed to coat it in flour first, *then* the egg, *then* the polenta" and "Daddy, the pan has to be *hot* first," Holly realized Mia had absorbed more than she would have thought in just two classes. A glass of red wine and a dazzling smile appeared in front of her, and as Liam returned to the kitchen, Holly took the opportunity to check out his butt in those worn jeans. Which also made her smile. The man was sexy.

She gazed around the room, taking in the décor, which looked like interesting items Liam had brought back from various far-away vacations, until she noticed a photograph of Mia and a woman on a city street, maybe New York City, on the long row of bookshelves by the window. Holly got up, wineglass in hand, and walked over, pretending great interest in the many sculptures on the shelf, but staring at the photograph. The woman had to be Mia's mother. They had the same hair color and texture, but the woman's was cut like Cleopatra's with a shock of bangs. She was sophisticated and elegant, wearing high heels and an interesting wrap type thing for what looked like sightseeing. She was beautiful too.

Holly had a quick vision of a younger Liam offering this woman that engagement ring however many years ago with all his loving heart. She wondered what that felt like, to be loved enough for someone to propose and hand over a diamond ring symbolizing forever and everything else those jewelry store commercials promised.

She took a gulp of wine and sat on the sofa and leaned her head back, staring up at the ceiling. Six, seven weeks ago she was in California, dreaming of one life, and now she was here, living quite another, here in this room with these people she hadn't known existed before September. Another father and daughter. And the father had a girlfriend.

Proceed with caution, she said to herself

slowly, enunciating just in case the wine had gone to her head, which she hoped it had.

"Dinner is served!" Mia said, coming through the kitchen doorway with a large plate of chicken alla Milanese that smelled delicious. Liam walked into the living room carrying a bowl of linguini covered in marinara.

They sat at the table, Liam and Holly across from each other, Mia regaling them with stories of teachers she liked and teachers she hated.

"Hey, this is great," Holly said as she closed her lips around a bite of the chicken. It was the slightest bit overcooked, but so flavorful. "And the linguini is cooked just right."

Mia beamed. "I mostly did both. Dad was on dredge duty."

"Aren't I always," he said, and Holly laughed.

Mia grimaced at them. "Why are adults so geeky?"

Liam pretend-swatted her with a breadstick, which Holly had bought from the bakery in town.

"We decided to not say our wishes aloud, but I know mine will come true," Mia said, smiling.

"I hope it does," Liam said, and Holly

wondered what *his* wish had been.

"So, Holly, can I ask you the biggest favor?" Mia said. "Now that I'm not exactly on good terms with Madeline, can you go dress shopping with me?"

Liam twirled a forkful of linguini. "Mia, I'm sure Holly —"

"Would love to go dress shopping with you," Holly finished. Had he been about to say that Holly was surely busy and that Jodie, clearly the fancy dress queen, would he happy to take her to all her favorite shops?

"Yay!" Mia said. "Can we go after school? I'll come over when I get home and drop off my backpack."

"Sure can."

"Is Holly the best or what?" Mia said to her father.

"She certainly is very kind," Liam said, winking at Holly.

Holly hated winks. Winks always seemed to Holly something people did when they wanted to take back whatever they'd just said. Or add an "I'm not really being serious."

And then Liam turned the conversation to the farm he was renovating for a couple from New York who'd decided to give up the rat race. Neither had ever milked a cow and suddenly they were making their own butter.

"That's sort of like what Holly's doing," Mia said. "Before she came here, she never cooked. And now she's a teacher — an amazing one. Why can't my teachers at school be like you?"

Holly smiled at Mia and wanted to hug her. And she did, since she'd been there for two hours and it was nearing eight o'clock and time to go.

Liam stood and started clearing the table. "Mia, if you'll finish clearing, I'll clean the kitchen and do the dishes when I get back from walking Holly home."

"Oh, you don't have to walk me home," Holly said, even though she liked the idea.

"I get out of cleaning and dish washing and all I have to do is clear the rest of the table? I'm so taking this deal."

"And start your homework immediately after," Liam added.

Mia scrunched up her face and stacked plates. "See you tomorrow after school, Holly. I'll meet you at your house at around three thirty, okay?"

"Perfect," Holly said and Mia carefully balanced dishes and glasses as she headed to the kitchen.

Liam leashed the dogs and they headed

up the path to Blue Crab Boulevard, commenting on the weather, which was still warm enough to barely require a light jacket, and how good the food was and how amazed Liam was that making a delicious and healthy dinner took no more time than waiting for Pizza Palace to make an extra-large pie with meatballs and peppers.

When they arrived at her porch, Liam sat down on the top step. Holly sat beside him, and for a moment they both stared at the moon, a perfect yellow crescent in the dark sky.

"Thanks for tonight," he said. "I've been looking for something to bring me and Mia closer and I had no idea it would be the teacher of her cooking class. I owe you more than I can put into words." He turned to face her. "Thank you."

He was sitting so close to her, his thigh so touchably close that for a moment Holly was rendered speechless. And when he leaned closer, as if he might kiss her, Holly felt goose bumps along her arms.

Good ones *and* bad ones, though. She leaned slightly away. "Your life seems kind of complicated right now, Liam. And I don't kiss guys who have girlfriends." Even if she was dying to.

"What about guys with former girl-

240

friends?" he asked.

She glanced at him. "You and Jodie broke up?"

He nodded and stared straight ahead. For a moment she didn't think he was going to say more, but then he added, "She asked where the relationship was heading, if I was serious about her, and I told her the truth. I told her what I told Mia. And she said that wasn't good enough for her, and a whole bunch of words later, she punched me in the stomach and left."

"Did she really punch you?"

"Yup."

Holly had no trouble envisioning Jodie punching someone. "Why?"

She said I acted like I liked her more than I obviously did and that I was a fraud, and then she wailed me in the gut."

"Did it hurt?"

He shook his head.

Which all meant Holly was free to fall for him and have her heart broken in five places. She should just feed him the *sa cordula* now and get it over with.

"Have you told Mia yet?"

"No. I will in good time." He held her gaze for a moment. "So, if you're interested, I thought I might take you on a real date. Actually, a date not involving food."

She was way too happy about this. "I'm sick to death of food."

A few minutes later, a day and time agreed upon, he and the beagles were headed back toward Cove Road. When he crossed, he turned and stopped, eyeing her for a moment before holding up his hand and disappearing down the path with her heart.

The next morning someone was ringing the doorbell like a lunatic. Holly glanced at the clock on her bedside table. It was barely eight o'clock. Mia, maybe? She went to the window to see if a car was parked in the drive, and there was a little red Honda with Maine plates.

She put on her robe and went downstairs as the bell rang again. And again.

"This had better be important," she whispered in the direction of the door.

More peals of the bell.

"Okay, okay," Holly said as she opened the door.

Francesca Bean stood there, beaming, in a pantsuit with a little filmy scarf wrapped around her neck. "Sorry about dragging you out of bed at the crack of dawn, but I wanted to come see you in person before I left for work. You're hired, Holly! You're catering my wedding!"

Holly's mouth dropped open. "What?"

"I had a long talk with Jack about the wedding and what this whole being bossed around because 'they're paying for it' means for every single moment of our future — get-togethers, family dinners, holidays — and how if I don't put my foot down now about my own wedding, my own life, I'll always be a doormat to them. And Jack backed me up."

"That's great," Holly said. "Good for you and him."

"I know! I was so proud of myself. So we sat our mothers down for our weekly breakfast checklist of where we are on the wedding and what's done and what needs to be done, and —"

"Wait, you have a weekly wedding meeting with your and Jack's mother?"

"You met my mother, Holly. What's not to understand?"

Holly laughed. "Go on."

"Well, we told them we'd decided that *we* would foot the bill for our wedding ourselves and have just a simple affair at the college in the English department's meeting room, since they had the nicest furniture with almost leatherlike Naugahyde green sofas and chairs, and all those old hardback books, and they both got the *funniest* looks of pure horror on their faces and agreed that *I* make all final decisions. They could put in their two cents, but I make the final call — on everything. So guess who's catering my wedding for sixty-two guests?"

Holly grabbed Francesca into a hug. "I don't even know how to thank you, Francesca. You really put yourself on the line for me. And for my grandmother. You're amazing."

"I'm the happiest I've ever been in my life, Holly. Because your grandmother sent me down to that pier. Yeah, I was happy enough before I met Jack, but what we have, how he makes me feel about myself, how comfortable and truly happy I am just sitting on the sofa with him at night watching *American Idol* or whatever — I've never had this kind of crazy, perfect, just-right relationship before, Holly. My love life sucked until Jack."

"I know what that's like."

Francesca squeezed Holly's hand. "And so does my poor sister, who's dating herself into a total depression just to have a date to the wedding. Nothing I say is getting through to her, so maybe you can tell her she can't force it. Yeah, she doesn't have someone with magic stones telling her that her guy will turn up in the supermarket in the peanut butter section, but it's like she thinks she's going to miss him if she doesn't date every guy in Maine."

"I think she just wants what you have. She wants what everyone wants."

Francesca glanced at her watch. "Oh, God, almost eight thirty. I'd better get going. But I don't want to forget to tell you that my mother even admitted your work was more an A than a B and she was only thinking of her 'dear friend Amanda Windemere and Avery, who are *such* good friends of the family,' blah, blah, blah. So forget all the nasty stuff that was said. We'll hook up again closer to the date to plan the final menu, but don't let anyone else hire you for the first of spring."

"No weekly meetings to plan the menu?" Holly asked with a smile.

"Those are history too. And, really, it's thanks to you, since the big confrontation was over you. Okay, gotta run. Bye!"

Holly closed the door, happiness pinging from her toes along her entire body.

She did it.

"I did it! Antonio," she shouted, scooping up the grumpy cat and twirling him around kitchen — the place where *she* felt comfortable and truly happy and with which she

245

was having a crazy, perfect, just-right relationship.

THIRTEEN

After champagne (white grape juice for
Mia) and clinking of glasses all around,
Holly and her four students began chopping vegetables for *minestra maritata,* Italian
wedding soup, in honor of Holly's victory.
Camilla had two versions of the hearty soup
in her recipe binder, one that took hours for
the various meats to simmer, and one
quicker version, and Holly chose the quick.
The recipe once again involved meatballs,
but since last week's spaghetti and meatballs
was such a hit, especially with Simon's
daughter, Holly had come to think of
meatballs as good luck charms.

As Juliet crumbled the ground beef and
Italian sausage into the bread crumbs and
eggs in the large metal bowl on the island,
Mia was sniffing the start of the soup, the
classic Italian *soffrito* of sautéing onions,
garlic, celery, and carrots in a large pot on
the stove. Simon and Tamara were on chop-

ping and mincing duty, an array of colorful vegetables and herbs awaiting Juliet's knife and Simon's grater and mincer, from basil and bay leaves to leafy green spinach and thyme.

"I always thought orzo was rice," Tamara said, pouring in the cup of undercooked barley-shaped pasta to the fragrant pot of broth and vegetables. "Which reminds me of my moronic date a couple of nights ago — a monologue on whether couscous is a pasta or a grain. I wanted to jump on the table and shout 'Who cares?' at the top of my lungs. This guy went on and on in these fifteen-minute monologues about his deep thoughts on everything."

"I can't even imagine dating ever again," Simon said, taking a sip of champagne. "I can barely figure out what I'm supposed to do as a person now that I'm suddenly not living with my wife and daughter. Every day I feel like I'm living someone else's life."

Holly was reminded of her conversation with Liam during the hunt for Mia a couple of weeks ago. "I feel like that sometimes. Like I'm trying to be my grandmother when I'll never come close to filling her shoes."

"You got a very big catering job on your own merit," Juliet said as she ripped spinach into a wooden bowl. "That's major. You used your grandmother's recipes, but *you* got the job."

Everyone raised a glass, and Holly walked around and clinked every last one, unable to believe how far she'd come in these two months. From sobbing with the blankets pulled over her head to leading this class with something close to confidence.

As Simon and Juliet formed the little meatballs, Holly said, "The soup calls for a happy memory, and mine is the last day I spent with my grandmother, right here, watching her crank the pasta machine and eye the stretch of dough with such love as though it were the first time she was making pasta. Seventy-five years old, and she still loved what she was doing even though she'd been doing it her entire life."

The meatball Mia was rolling slipped out of her hands and onto the floor. "Oops," she said. "I was just thinking my happy memory into that one. Does it still work if I start over with a new one?"

"Your memories will always be your memories," Holly said. "So yes."

Mia scooped up the dirty one with a paper towel and tossed it in the garbage, then sat back down at one of the island stools and began rolling another. "My happy memory is two years ago when my mom came for my birthday. My dad kept telling me not to get my hopes up, that she might not be able to come, but she'd left a few months before that and I'd only seen her once since, and I did get my hopes up, and when I woke up in the morning, guess who was sitting in a chair by my bed?"

Holly envisioned the sophisticated, beautiful woman with the model hair and high heels in the photograph at the Geller house. She was such a different type from Holly. Holly, drawn to jeans and riding boots and cozy sweaters and ponytails, rarely wore a dress, let alone heels. And her only piece of jewelry was a delicate gold necklace, a chain with three tiny dangling discs that her grandmother had given her for her sixteenth birthday when she'd finally shared Holly's fortune. On each disc was an initial of Holly's name, HMM, Holly Marie Maguire.

Discs. Holly reached her hand up to her necklace and walked over to the entryway, where a beautiful round mirror was hung over a side table holding explanations of pastas and sauces. She stared at the necklace. The tiny circles were meant to symbolize the Po River stones. Why had she never realized that before?

"And guess what else?" Mia continued, rolling another meatball. "My mother said she'd been sitting there for over an hour, just watching me sleep. My birthday is this Friday and I know she's going to come. I haven't seen her in almost six months, and the last time was for only a couple of days."

"That must be hard, not seeing your mom very often," Tamara said. "My mother is a total nightmare, but she's my mother . . ." Tamara stopped talking, eyeing Mia, who was looking at her expectantly. She'd seemed to realize she was talking to an almost twelve-year-old and not an adult and that this was a very sensitive subject. "It'll be exciting to see her. What's her name?"

"Veronica Feroux. Isn't that pretty? It's French. Her maiden name was Smith. And then Geller when she married my dad. And now that she's married to René, she's French. It's too bad Daniel's name is so boring. Dressler. Not that I'm marrying him."

"Daniel Dressler. I like that name," Simon said. "You'll never forget it, either, since he's escorting you to your first dance."

Mia beamed. "This week is going to be my best memory ever. First my birthday and my mom and the next night, the dance with Daniel. You should see my dress. Holly took me shopping after school this past Friday. It's a sparkly lavender and has the coolest

251

neckline."

"We want pictures next Monday," Simon said. "Oh, I almost forgot to add my happy memory into the soup. The expression on Cass's face when she opened the door to her bedroom and saw what we'd done. She'd been so . . . dour a moment before and then she lit up and turned to me and said, 'This is mine?' And she walked in so slowly and looked around, taking in every little thing, every star on the ceiling. And then gave me the fiercest hug of my life. She almost knocked the wind out of me and she's just eight."

"Awww," Tamara said. "I love that. I'm so happy our great plan worked."

"Thank you all," he said, raising his glass to everyone.

Juliet took a sip of her champagne and set down the glass. "I have a happy memory to put into the soup. A few weeks before my daughter passed away, it was her third birthday, and her father and I threw her a party, just the three of us, and it was the most complete day of my life. We were in the park with a duck pond by our house, and we were throwing bits of bread at the ducks and she was laughing." A smile lit her face for a moment, but then tears filled her eyes. "I can remember being so thankful.

Now that she's gone I don't know how to go forward without her. My life was complete with her; how can it ever be without her?"

"Does it help to remember that day at the duck pond, when she was laughing? Or does it just make you sad?" Mia asked.

"Both," Juliet said.

Mia bit her lower lip. "Then maybe that's how. By remembering the happy and the sad. Seriously, that's how I deal with my mother being gone. A few days ago, one of Madeline's friends said she'd heard my mother *abandoned* me. Can you believe she used that word? First of all, she didn't *abandon* me, she just moved across the country. If she lived closer, I'd see her all the time. But she lives half the time in Europe. Anyway, sometimes when I really want her, when I wish she was here, I think that maybe she did abandon me and I get really upset. But then I'll try and think about something that makes me think good thoughts about her, and I feel better. That's what my dad told me was a good coping mecha-something."

"Mechanism," Holly said. "A coping mechanism."

"Smart man," Simon added.

And smart girl, Holly thought, her heart

going out to Mia.

"Yes," Juliet added. "That is smart. Thank you, Mia. I don't want to forget Evie. So I can't *not* think of her. But when I do think of her, I just get so overwhelmed by missing her."

"Doesn't your husband make you feel better?" Mia asked, and everyone turned to stare at Juliet, curious to know what their story was.

"He tried, but I guess everyone grieves differently. Or at least, that's what the shrinks said. I found it hard to be comforted by him when he wasn't grieving the same way I was. And he was getting tired of being accused of not caring that Evie was gone."

Holly watched Juliet's face crumple. "Oh, Juliet."

Juliet sniffled. "I was thinking earlier today about when I was your age, Mia, or a little younger, and taking boats out on the Blue Crab Bay with Holly and talking about our futures, how I'd become a marine biologist and marry a whale specialist, and Holly would become a famous playwright and marry her leading actor. And now here I am, everything so . . ." She shrugged her slight shoulders and stared at the floor.

"Did you marry a whale specialist?" Tamara asked.

"He's an attorney like I am." She smiled. "I never thought I'd become a lawyer. Or marry one."

"Do you miss him?" Mia asked. "Since he's . . . where? In Chicago?"

"Sometimes I do, but sometimes I just want to stay here by myself."

"I think that's how my mother feels," Mia said. "Like she misses me, but she wants to be in France and California with René. That's my stepfather. I've only met him twice. Isn't that insane?"

"Why does life get so complicated?" Tamara asked.

"Seriously," Mia said.

Five glasses raised in the air.

Since that coming Friday was Mia's birthday and Saturday the dance, which Liam was chaperoning, they'd chosen Thursday for their date. Liam had called earlier and asked her to meet him in his backyard at six o'clock — and to wear something warm.

Since they'd agreed on a no-food date, it couldn't be a picnic. Staring up at the stars? Night bird hunting?

She'd spent a half hour going through her closet and her too-many pairs of jeans, discarding any that would require pointy high heels, and chose a comfortable pair that managed to look both semi-sexy and worthy of a hike in the Maine woods. She went through her shirts and sweaters and came up with a white cotton camisole with a slightly lacy edge, a thin heathered V-neck sweater that both hid and clung, and her favorite heavy tie-wrap cardigan. Her comfy brown cowboy boots, her grandmother's Po River–stones necklace, and the tiniest dab of one of Camilla's perfumes, and she was ready.

She glanced into the floor mirror in the corner of her bedroom. She hardly looked like the woman in the photograph in the Gellers' house. Or Jodie. Liam clearly liked the sophisticated type who wore lipstick. But Holly was a jeans and sweater girl who might slick on some scented lip balm. And since he'd leaned in for a kiss the other day, he had to be attracted to her on some level. *Whatever,* as Mia would say. She was who she was.

And besides, he was taking her on a date involving a backyard and the need for warm clothes.

She took a deep breath and left her house, walking down the path to the water. It was so peaceful and quiet, the only sounds the occasional swoop of a seagull or a child's voice from a backyard. At Liam's house, she headed to the backyard, where she found him standing on the little square dock, wearing that sexy black leather jacket, his hands in his pockets, the breeze blowing his hair.

He waved her over, and as she got closer, she saw the rowboat docked next to him had two cushions on the seats, and the metal holders attached to each side, near the oars, held a bouquet of wildflowers in one and a bottle of wine and two glasses in the other. An old-school boom box was set at the bow, softly playing what sounded like blues jazz.

All the tension in her shoulders slid out at the perfect simplicity of it, the innocent romance of it all. The last time someone had taken her out on a rowboat she'd been a gawky thirteen-year-old with braces at summer camp, and the boy, who she'd had a big crush on, had actually fallen in the water because he'd freaked out when he saw a snake.

"Hey," he said. "You look great."

She smiled and accepted his hand up onto the dock, then down into the boat. "I love this."

His hand was so warm. "I had a feeling you would."

She liked that he'd planned this with her

in mind. She'd spent the past two years going to events and parties at which people stood around talking about futures and securities and stock indexes. Since there weren't many events and parties for dog walkers and waitresses, Holly had been free to attend all of John's events, and she'd been glad to, thinking she'd learn something by osmosis and that eventually she'd be able to make small talk about the Dow Jones, something she still didn't understand. "You shouldn't try to talk about what you know nothing about," John had once whispered harshly into her ear when she'd embarrassed him by trying to join a conversation in which she'd stood by his side like an idiot for twenty minutes. She'd stayed too long at the party — literally and figuratively speaking.

Liam sat across from her and took up the oars, rowing out toward the middle of the bay yet staying in line with his house. The bay at this end was surrounded by huge oaks and evergreens and a rocky cliff on both sides, as private as if the stretch of water belonged to him.

"This is so beautiful and peaceful," she said, listening to the hum of cicadas and crickets, the moon above an almost perfect crescent.

"I row out here a lot for that reason. I take Mia out when I need to talk to her without her being able to escape, but of course once she was so mad at me that she jumped right in the bay, out here in the middle too."

"I'm crazy about that girl," Holly said before she could stop herself. It wasn't the thing to say to "that girl's" father while she was on a date with him. It sounded so . . . Jodie fake. But it was true, she realized. She was crazy about Mia.

"Me too. And I'm worried about her. She's so sure her mother's coming Friday for her birthday, and who knows if she will or not? I've emailed Veronica twice to ask if she's coming and even called her chateau or whatever she lives in in France, and she doesn't respond. Mia's texted her and emailed her too — three times and same thing. No response." He shook his head and stared out at the water.

"Is this typical?"

"Unfortunately."

Holly couldn't imagine having a child and being so out of touch, out of the child's life, living in another universe, basically. And not responding to emails and texts.

"And so instead of her birthday being exciting for her, she'll be a wreck all day at school on Friday, half-expecting her mother to show up during English or history or lunch with a completely inappropriate and overly expensive present."

"Would she do that?"

He shrugged, then started rowing again, the movement of his muscles almost mesmerizing Holly. "She's capable of anything. And she likes grandiose gestures."

"And if her mother doesn't come?" Holly said. "How upset will Mia get?"

"She'll be a wreck for a good couple of weeks. And then she'll talk herself into a rationalization that she can live with, that makes her feel better, and that makes her mother some kind of mythical creature instead of a neglectful parent."

"That must be so hard on both of you," she said, wishing she had something more insightful to say. But she didn't understand the situation at all. How did a mother just walk away from her child like that? Calling every now and then? Sending expensive gifts as though it made up for her presence, her love?

"It's only hard on me because I can't do anything about it. I can't make her mother act like a mother. I can't give her that."

"But you're a great dad," she said.

"I hope so. Sometimes I feel like I don't know what the hell I'm doing. Especially now that she's turning twelve and everything's changing. Everything — her body, her interests, our relationship. A few months ago I was in the drugstore picking up toothpaste and shaving cream, and I realized there were some items Mia would need soon, and there would be no one but me to get them for her, so I bravely marched into the aisle marked 'feminine' and couldn't even handle standing in front of the hundreds of boxes of tampons. I wouldn't have known what to get even if I wasn't embarrassed about being there."

Holly smiled. "Did you buy the wrong thing or something?"

"I got overwhelmed and bolted. And so I just asked Jodie to pick up the basic necessities that a girl going through puberty would need. She came back with two big shopping bags."

"Of what?"

"I don't know — a lot of brightly colored boxes. Pink deodorant. Mouthwash. Shaving cream in pink canisters. Pink razors. A couple of things I had no idea what they were."

Holly laughed. "It's very clear that you deeply love your daughter and that you're devoted to her. You're doing just fine."

Liam slowed the boat and slid over on his

261

seat. "Come row with me?"

She smiled and set her cushion next to his, taking the left oar. They attempted to row together, but it took a while to get their motions in sync.

"Why don't we drift for a while and open the wine," he said, reaching for the bottle and a corkscrew.

She held out the glasses and he poured each glass half-full with the red wine. "Thank you. This is really nice." And *nice* was just the word.

"I know I said this would be a foodless date, but I couldn't resist getting some good French bread and my favorite cheese." He slid a small cooler from the stern, taking out the crusty loaf and setting the cheese and a tiny knife on a small wooden cutting board.

"What didn't you think of?" Holly asked, her heart pinging with how touched she was. This entire date was romance at its sweetest and purest. A boat. The water. A good-looking man whom she was dying to kiss. Good red wine, a hunk of Gouda, and a loaf of crusty bread.

"I didn't think of how I would attempt to make out with you without knocking the oars into the water."

She laughed. "Actually, isn't that the classic smooth move? The guy 'accidentally' lets the oars slip into the water so the woman is his captive?"

Liam held her gaze, his handsome face so close to hers on the wooden seat, and then he leaned forward and kissed her, soft and warm on the lips, letting his lips linger on hers before pulling back to look at her — and looking at her like she was beautiful. He kissed her again, full and deep, his hand reaching up to pull her closer against him.

"Your hair smells like flowers," he whispered into it.

"Not garlic or Bolognese sauce?"

He laughed. "Flowers. And that perfume is driving me crazy."

She might have whispered "good," because he shifted her onto his lap so that she was straddling him, and they were kissing so passionately she was surprised the boat didn't tip over.

FOURTEEN

Holly felt like she was floating the next morning. She woke up smiling, all because of a perfect date on a rowboat under the stars, quite possibly her favorite date of all time. Even if it ended way too soon. The wind had started to blow and it had been nearing eight thirty, when Liam expected Mia home from a hockey game at her school, and so they'd rowed back together, and Liam had walked her home, the beagles scampering ahead of them. And on her porch he kissed her again, the kiss as sweet as it was passionate, and Holly knew that night had been the start of something.

She came downstairs all lazy and happy in her robe and noticed something slipped under the door, another card in Mia's strawberry-scented stationery. But this was in Liam's handwriting.

Holly,

   Thank you for an amazing date. Can't wait to do it again. And again. And again.
                                    Liam

She grinned and pressed it against her chest, then tucked it in her robe's pocket and floated into the kitchen, where she gave Antonio an extra liver snap. She couldn't shake her goofy smile all day, even when she realized she'd forgotten the dry white wine for the Bolognese sauce, which she'd only discovered when she'd tasted it after wishing for even just one more perfect date with Liam. She'd made stupid, my-head-is-in-the-clouds mistakes all day, but didn't mind a bit. And she had to admit that she liked that she was able to tell she'd forgotten the wine.

Though earlier in the week Holly had offered to take Mia out for lattes and treats at the bakery after school for her birthday, Mia had said no, she didn't want to miss her mother in case she came to pick her up at the house. So at four o'clock that afternoon, Holly wrapped up Mia's gift (her grandmother had a closet devoted to various wrapping paper, bows, and cards for all occasions), pretty dangling earrings with tiny purple beads to match her Fall Ball dress, and headed to the Gellers' house.

Halfway down, she could hear someone running toward her, and then Mia's excited voice calling, "Mom?" And then there was Mia, out of breath, the disappointment on her face that it was "just Holly" heartbreaking.

"Oh," Mia said, the excited gleam in her eyes dulling. "I thought you were my mother."

"So she's coming this afternoon? That's wonderful!"

"Well, I don't know for sure. I haven't heard from her. But I assume she is. She probably wanted to wait till after the school day. You know how parents can be about school. I'm sure she'll just come straight here from the airport any minute now."

Holly hoped so. Really hoped so. Her mother coming for her birthday clearly meant so much to Mia. And Holly could certainly understand why. If there was any special day, for her mother to show that she actually did care, this was it.

"Did you see anyone on Blue Crab Boulevard looking for the turnoff to this road?" Mia asked, straining her neck to see around the bend in the road where the trees obscured the view of the path. "Maybe my mother is having trouble finding it?"

"It's pretty well marked," Holly said gently. "And she could ask anyone in town. She'll find the road no problem." If she was coming. "Why don't we head back to the house?"

Mia searched the road again, but there was nothing but the occasional squirrel and bird. Her face fell and she trudged up the porch steps and sat down, wrapping her arms around herself.

"Want to go inside?" Holly asked. "It's getting pretty cold."

"No, I'm okay. I'm just so excited about my mom coming. I mean, I'm sure she'll come. It's my *birthday.*" She zipped her hoodie up to her chin. "And the mail came and there was no birthday card from her, so that must mean she's planning to be here. There's no way she wouldn't send a card *and* not come in person, right?"

Oh, hell. Holly hoped not.

"Well, here," Holly said, handing her the gift as she sat down beside her. "Happy birthday, sweetie."

Mia brightened. "Wow, thanks." She undid the ribbon, ripped away the wrapping paper, and opened the box. "Oh, my God, Holly, these are gorgeous! She held up the pretty earrings in the light. "And they'll match my dress perfectly. Thank you so much," she added, leaning over and hugging Holly. "I want to wear them right now, but I feel like I should save them for the dance."

Holly smiled. "I totally agree. And you're welcome. I can't wait to see pictures of you in your dress — with your cute date."

Mia's blueberry-colored eyes twinkled. "Me too. I'm so excited. Just one more day."

"So tell me more about this cute Daniel Dressler," Holly said, and they sat there for another hour, talking, glancing up at every sound, but by five o'clock Mia's mother hadn't arrived. At five thirty, an hour and a half of sitting outside, a car came down the path and Mia jumped up and ran toward it, but it was the navy SUV. Just Dad.

Mia burst into tears. She stood there, tears running down her cheeks as Liam got out of his car. "She's still not here, Dad. Is she going to come? Did she leave you a message?"

Liam's expression basically said *Oh, shit.* "I'm really sorry, honey, she hasn't left any messages for me. I did call her and email her a few times, and I tried again this morning, but I haven't heard from her."

Mia's face crumpled. "Then she must be on her way." She sat back down on the steps, brightening a bit at the new hope

268

she'd given herself.

Oh, Mia, Holly thought, sighing. For a moment Liam looked like he wanted to kill someone, namely his former wife, but she wasn't exactly around. He glanced at Mia, and his expression softened.

"Have you been sitting out here since you got home from school?"

Mia nodded. "Holly came down around four o'clock with a present for me. Look how pretty these earrings are. They match my Fall Ball dress perfectly." The excitement in her eyes lasted for just a few seconds.

Thank you, he mouthed to Holly. "Mia, let's go in. I'll order a pizza with your favorite toppings. And I have a present for you. Something you've been begging for since your last birthday."

"I just want to wait out here for Mom," she said, kicking at the step with her foot.

"Honey —"

"I want to wait out here, Dad."

He stared up at the sky for a moment. "I'll take it from here," he said to Holly. "Thanks for staying with her," he added in a whisper.

"Of course," she said. She walked over to Mia and gave her hands a squeeze. "Happy birthday, Mia. And don't forget that I want to see pictures from the dance, okay?"

"Okay," Mia said, then resumed her foot scuffing, her head popping up with every minor sound.

Holly didn't want to leave, and she wasn't quite sure if Liam had asked her to go or just gave her the option of going. Awkward. She wanted to stay and try to be a comfort to both of them, but this was a family matter. Holly needed to go and let Liam handle it the way he wanted.

"Okay, well, bye," she said.

Liam offered a brief smile and then sat down next to his daughter, his elbows on his knees.

She hoped they wouldn't be sitting out there too long. But when she reached her bungalow and opened the door, she still had not seen a car turn down Cove Road. She heated up one of that day's pastas, the penne in vodka sauce, which even in her goofy-brained state that morning she hadn't been able to mess up, then ate on the tasting bench, one eye out the window. She never did see a car turn down Cove Road.

For Mia's sake, she hoped she'd missed her.

A bit after midnight, Holly's cell phone rang. She was in bed, the fluffy down comforter so warm and cozy on the chilly night, her grandmother's recipe binder on her lap. She'd been working on menus for the rest of the cooking class sessions, but she'd been unable to concentrate on anything other than the Gellers, one tall, dark, and hot, the other an adorable tween, both whom had gotten inside her heart. She grabbed the phone, figuring it was one of them.

Liam. "Because it's midnight, Mia finally gave up," he said, his voice angry, despairing, hurt. "She just went to bed, sobbing. I'm at such a loss to know what to possibly do to make this better."

Oh, hell. "I'm so sorry," Holly said. She scooped up the three Po River stones, hoping they'd help her find the right words, but she had no idea what to say — and didn't want to say the wrong thing.

"Holly, I — I don't know. I don't know what I want to say. I just want to take care of my daughter. That's all I want to do."

He was silent, so Holly waited a moment and said, "You do what you need to, okay?"

"Okay."

So maybe there would be no perfect second date. Liam was right to focus on his daughter, not his love life. She respected him even more for it.

"It's just that you're the first person she's

271

trusted in a long, long time, Holly. You're such a good role model for her — a female role model. I don't want to screw anything up with that. If I mess this up —" He sucked in a breath. "Am I making any sense? I have no idea what I'm saying, or what I mean."

You're saying that if we start dating and things go bad, Mia loses me. Holly got it, and she understood, but it still . . . poked at her heart. "I completely understand, Liam. You just want to protect your daughter, who just got her heart broken in a way you can't fix. And you want to make sure you don't do anything that could make things worse."

"That's exactly it. I told her that Jodie is out of my life, and that perked her up, but not for very long. So maybe we can take this very slow?"

The poking stopped. Very slow was not *stop.* "Very slow is good. Very slow is a sweet date on a rowboat that ends in an amazing kiss and nothing more."

"That was some good-night kiss, huh? And the ones preceeding it were hard to top." He was silent for a moment, then said, "I'm not too sure I want Mia's date for the school dance to end with an amazing kiss. Do twelve-year-olds kiss?"

She smiled. "Innocent kisses. Anyway,

you're chaperoning. And I'm glad you are. It's a big night for her, something she's so excited about, and maybe having that to look forward to will help take the edge off this disappointment. It's great that you'll be right there. She might not say so, but I'll bet it means a lot to her."

"Unless I embarrass her by trying to moonwalk or something."

Holly laughed. She wanted to run down the road and hug him and then come right back to the safety of this cottage, but she stayed put in bed, Antonio curled in a semicircle at her feet.

All day Saturday, Holly was dying to call the Geller house and ask if Mia needed anything for the dance, if she needed help getting ready. Holly might not have gotten along so well with her mother during her own tween and teen years, but Luciana Constantina Maguire had always been there, with that box of Tampax when she first got her period, when she needed a strapless bra for her 32AA-sized chest for her first school dance, when she'd been betrayed by friends or hurt by boys. Her mother wasn't exactly warm and fuzzy, but she'd been there.

Holly couldn't even imagine what it was

like to be a girl with a mother who basically gave her up for a new husband and a glittering life three thousand miles away in California with constant trips to Europe so that Mia wasn't even sure where she should call if she wanted to reach her mother. Two years of that had to have taken its toll on Mia — and Liam. No wonder he'd had such high hopes for head-to-toe pink Jodie with her pretty highlights and focus on which colors best suited which complexions. There was a superficiality there that wouldn't interfere in the two-ness of the fragile Geller family, yet there was a supergirliness that Liam thought would make up for a total absence of a mother. Holly didn't have to wonder if Jodie missed Mia. She'd seen the lack of real warmth when Jodie had inquired about the cooking class. But Jodie would have come in handy tonight as Mia was getting ready, not that Mia would have let Jodie anywhere near her.

Holly would love to see Mia all dressed up in her sparkly lavender dress with the dangling beaded earrings. But she kept her hands off the phone. She had agreed to take things very slowly, which included not busting in on Liam's first experience with his daughter's first school dance. He could handle whatever came up. Like telling Mia she looked beautiful in a cracking voice that would assure her he meant it.

On a day when she could keep herself distracted by rolling out pasta and trying a new shape, like tortellini, which seemed very intricate to Holly, she'd barely spent any time in the kitchen at all. She'd sold four containers of the penne and six jars of the vodka sauce from yesterday, and then found herself standing in the middle of the living room and taking stock of the furniture and decorations, as though she suddenly realized this was her home now, hers to change if she wanted. Like the depressing-to-look-at oil painting of a stern-faced older man walking with a cane, Camilla Constantina's own grandfather. And the lamp, on the beautiful side table by the window with the See No Evil, Hear No Evil, Speak No Evil three wise monkeys sitting around the base, creeped her out. Holly took down the painting and removed the lamp, then went upstairs and pulled down the creaky attic steps, bringing the painting and lamp, one at a time, up with her. The small attic was very clean and spare, but there were a few lamps and several paintings and an entire bookshelf of books, most in Italian. Holly spent an hour going through everything, filling a large basket with things she loved, like three little sculptures of the human figure, a man, woman, and a child, and four small paintings, one of Antonio, looking cranky and bored, as always, one of the house Camilla had grown up in in Italy, one of this bungalow, and one of Camilla sitting on a stone bench near her tomatoes.

Holly brought her treasures down, happy with the idea that she could make this house more her own. Now that she'd gotten the catering job and there was the potential to go after other affairs, especially between now and the wedding, she didn't feel so much like a guest in her own home anymore. She could start thinking of this cottage as hers, her home, and put herself into it. She liked her grandmother's romantic, ornate style, her love of the Tuscan colors and European influences. But with the pretty beaded lamp in the living room and a painting of a perfect olive tree where the dour-faced grandfather had been, the living room was a place that Holly would want to spend time in, reading a novel or just staring into space.

Once she was satisfied with the living room, she got out the cleaning supplies and spent the next couple of hours vacuuming, dusting, and polishing, enjoying every minute of the work she usually found tedious. After a long, hot shower, she dressed in soft yoga pants and a long-sleeved T-shirt and stood in her bedroom, surveying the décor for what she wanted to change. The thick white polyester curtains on the window would have to go. Something floaty and sheer in its place, with perhaps some dark green velvet drapes. She'd ask Tamara for help with that.

The phone rang and Holly lunged for it. It was just after seven forty-five, and the Fall Ball had started at seven, so it wouldn't be Liam or Mia asking her to come down and see how pretty Mia looked. Which, she had to admit, was a call she'd been hoping for during her cleaning frenzy. It was Tamara, and Holly was glad, because she could use a girlfriend right then.

Tamara launched into a funny blow-by-blow of the date she'd gone on last night, a good second date with a sports reporter named Cameron. He'd arranged the evening, a dinner cruise around Casco Bay, from which, Tamara noted, there was no escape, so he must have really liked her on their first date.

"He barely talked about sports the entire night," Tamara said. "And he's so funny! And smart and so, so hot. Holly, you should see him. He has incredible green eyes. And great guy hair, dark blond and kinda wavy. And every time I told him one of my funny stories about decorating someone's office or house, he really listened and asked questions. And he drove me home and gave me the kiss of my life at the door without even one lame attempt at getting inside. I was so close to inviting him anyway, but something just told me to hold off, not rush things, and he asked me out for a third date right then and there. Oh, God, Holly, I think I'm in love. Can you be in love after two dates?"

"Definitely yes. And he sounds wonderful. I'm so happy for you, Tamara."

"He's gonna look so amazing in a tux," Tamara said, and Holly knew her friend was envisioning herself in her sister's bridesmaid dress, green-eyed Cameron in his tux at her side. "I can't believe how much I like him after two dates. I'm even thinking he'll be getting some third-date sex."

Holly laughed. Third-date sex. She could quite possibly have a third date with Liam any day now. If she counted dinner with the Gellers as a first date. But third-date sex was not going "very slow." It was the opposite of slow.

"Just when I thought I was destined to spend every wedding, holiday, special occasion, and Saturday night — not to mention the rest of my life — alone, I meet this guy. Don't you love the name Cameron? And guess what, Holl? I'm cooking for him on Wednesday night. I'm thinking your tagliatelle Bolognese, some bruschetta with the tomatoes and eggplant, and a bottle of great red wine. And for dessert, maybe tiramisu — in goblets."

Holly was touched by the "your tagliatelle." Not "your grandmother's." Not "Camilla's Cucinotta's." *Yours.* "That sounds perfect, Tamara. Romantic, sexy, light, yet full of mystery."

She laughed. "Oh, good, because that's *exactly* what I'm going for."

Holly thought about telling Tamara about her own date, but she wanted to keep it private for a while, keep it all hers.

The doorbell rang just as Tamara was saying good-bye. Holly headed downstairs, glancing at the grandfather clock at the foot of the stairs. It was just past eight. Juliet, maybe? Francesca, stopping by to tell her she had to take it back, that the wedding job had gone to Avery Windemere after all?

But it was Liam, looking pale and nervous and furious. Just past eight o'clock meant it was only one hour into the school dance he was supposed to be chaperoning.

"Liam? Why are —"

279

"Her mother showed up. One minute the band's playing Miley Cyrus, and the next they're singing 'Happy birthday to you, happy birthday dear Mia,' and there's Veronica, standing onstage holding long-stemmed red roses and looking like a rock star in some trendy outfit."

That was unexpected. Or maybe not. "Wow. Mia must have been thrilled."

But Liam clearly wasn't. "Of course she was. She was so shocked she didn't move for a moment, and then she rushed up for what seemed like the staged hug of the year."

That seemed a little cynical. "It must have meant the world to Mia, though."

"Her mother has done this twice before. Not seen her for months, then just blows into town like a fucking tornado and swallows her up and spits her out on her way out of town."

"Come in, Liam," she said, her hand on his arm. "I'll make you some coffee. Or maybe you want a drink?"

He stepped inside but didn't take off his coat, didn't answer her. "She misses her birthday, makes Mia cry all day and night, then shows up three songs into her first school dance, barges in on her first date, and makes it all about her, how she couldn't 'bear another minute on this earth without seeing her baby.' Right. Mia barely said good-bye to her date. Or me."

"I can imagine how excited she must have been, though, Liam. This was her dream."

He stared at her. "Her dream. Her dream to see her mother? Every six, eight months? Whenever Veronica is feeling low or gets into a fight with her husband and needs somewhere to hide for a while? So she suddenly remembers she has a daughter and her sudden fake love and fake concern fills her up for a good few days until she's feeling so much better that she's ready to go back to her jerk of a husband."

"Liam, I don't know what to say. I don't know this woman. I can't speak about her motives. I just know that she's Mia's mother."

"*Barely* her mother. And when she's tired of Mia, when Mia starts actually demanding things from her, needing things from her, like *love,* Veronica will leave and break her heart into a million pieces, and it'll be me sweeping up again. Until the next time this happens. I'm sick of it, Holly."

She didn't know what to do, what to say, so she opened her arms and he hesitated for a moment, then stepped closer and let her wrap her arms around him.

281

"I can't do anything either," he said, his arms resting heavily on her shoulders. "I'm completely powerless in this. I have to just let what happens happen. That sucks."

"Maybe things will be just fine," Holly said, her voice almost a whisper since his ear was so close to her mouth. She closed her eyes for a moment, the feel of him against her so nice. She hoped she had the right things to say now that he needed her, needed her to say something that would make this okay. "Maybe her mother will stay for the weekend, treat Mia like a princess, then go home on Sunday night with promises to come back soon. And maybe that'll fill up Mia till the next time. That her mother crashed the dance probably made her so happy. And everyone saw Veronica make a big fuss over her birthday."

"Yeah, a day late."

Holly hugged him a bit tighter. "Mia's happy right now, right?"

"Yeah."

"So go with that. She's happy. Her birthday wish, a day late or not, came true. She's with her mom. Go with that and try not to think of what might happen. Because what might happen is likely that she'll go home tomorrow night, leaving Mia feeling loved."

He relaxed against her but didn't say

anything. Just held her. "Your hair smells like flowers again."

"I just took a shower."

He was silent again for a moment and then he kissed her, a kiss that seemed to contain every emotion he was feeling, from anger to despair. But there was something in that kiss that didn't feel very "go slow." And so she took him by the hand and led him into the kitchen where they sat next to each other on the island stools and she fed him cheese and grapes and a crusty Italian bread until he seemed calmer.

So calm that he leaned very close and kissed her. "I'm a wreck."

"Maybe I can help," she whispered. She got up and stood behind his chair, careful not to get closer than she needed to, massaging the back of his neck, his strong shoulders. She could feel the knots and dug in deep to work them out.

And then he stood up and kissed her. Not a kiss like before, where he wasn't looking at her. A full-on stare-into-her-eyes-and-then-kiss-her kiss. She kissed him back, so overwhelmed by emotion and the desire to feel his hands on her, anywhere on her, that she could barely process thought. Somewhere, the imaginary little shoulder angel and devil were having a conversation on their respective sides, the angel offering a gentle warning that this might not be a good idea, given all the drama, the complications. But the little devil, with its pudgy belly and pointy ears, was so comical that Holly almost laughed when he rolled his eyes at the angel and whispered, *Oh, whatever.*

So when Liam picked her up like he was Richard Gere and carried her upstairs, she briefly, vaguely thought of saying something like *Maybe this isn't a good idea. This isn't very slow.* But when she opened her mouth to speak, nothing came out, and he took the opportunity to kiss her as he carried her up the stairs. She trailed her tongue up the side of his neck to his ear, and when he brought her to a bedroom, what was now truly *her* bedroom, and laid her down on the iron bed with the Po River stones, she decided it was fate, that the stones were offering their blessing.

And she still said nothing as he slowly lifted her T-shirt over her stomach, over her breasts, where he spent a good few moments before slipping the shirt over her head and tossing it off the bed. She did the same to his shirt, kissing her way down as she unbuttoned. She loved the sight of their shirts in a messy heap on the floor, then her attention was completely taken by the feel of his hands and mouth making their way across various bare expanses of her skin until she was completely naked, her yoga pants and lacy white underwear and his gray pants and black boxer briefs, Calvin Klein, she could see from the waistband, joining their shirts.

And then for a good long while, there was nothing but sensation and the delicious cool air blowing through the slightly open window.

Liam turned back into a pumpkin around ten o'clock, which was Mia's bedtime and when he figured her mother would bring her back home.

Holly's bed, so warm a moment ago, seemed so big and cold without him. He was dressing, his features tightening with every button, every zip. "I'm not even sure if Veronica's bringing Mia home or keeping her for the weekend or what," he said, buttoning his shirt over that rock-hard chest that she'd felt and kissed every inch of. "I wish I could stay. I wish I could stay the night with you."

"Me too. But I understand."

She put on her little satin robe and tied it tight around her, ready to walk him downstairs. At her bedroom door he turned suddenly, untied her robe, and pulled her against him in a fierce hug that stole her breath, then reached up with two fingers to touch the side of her face, her jawline. He tied her robe again, smiled briefly, and put his arm around her as he led her downstairs.

If she were making ravioli or mushroom risotto, she would wish he could stay, that circumstances were different. *And yes, yes, yes, Tamara, I can now personally attest to the fact that you can fall in love on your second date. You could fall in love on a brief visit, a knock on the door at eight o'clock.*

In the kitchen, she found his jacket lying on the floor where he'd shrugged it off when he'd first kissed her. And then she walked him to the front door. "Call me if you need to talk, okay?"

He nodded, then leaned over and kissed her, both sweetly and passionately, on the lips, and opened the door. She watched him walk across the road, his shoulders seeming stiff again. When he crossed, he stopped and looked back, holding up his hand the way he had the last time, and Holly held up hers.

FIFTEEN

In the morning, when Holly opened the front door to get the Sunday newspaper, there was something wrapped in white tissue paper on her welcome mat, a note atop it. Holly breathed in the cool early November air, picked up the large, round, flat package, and flipped open the card.

H — Couldn't sleep for a bunch of reasons, but mostly because I can't stop thinking about you, about last night. I'm the type of insomniac who makes things, so I made this for you. L.

What was it? she wondered, her goofy smile back as she removed the tissue paper to find a wooden sign in the shape of a tomato, HOLLY'S KITCHEN carved into it in beautiful script.

She stared at it for a moment, ridiculously happy. No matter what, there was feeling in this gift, in what it meant and represented.

She hung it next to the stove and stepped back and looked at it. HOLLY'S KITCHEN. She smiled, picked up the phone, and pressed in Liam's number, but she got voice mail, so she left a message thanking him — for the incredible gift and last night. She made a pot of Milanese coffee, opened the last package of her grandmother's favorite Mulino Bianco breakfast cookies, and, her eyes on the sign, sat at the breakfast nook where her grandmother had told so many fortunes.

Holly would not serve Liam Geller *sa cordula*. She would not even think about it.

In the afternoon, as she prepped for the next day's class, he finally called back. Mia was staying with her mother at a hotel in Portland for the weekend, Veronica would drop her off Monday morning, and Mia had sounded so excited over the phone that he'd held his tongue and said fine. And apparently he and Veronica had spoken for quite some time. His ex-wife had dropped some bombshells that had made Liam's head spin, he'd said, and though Holly was dying to know what, Liam didn't want to get into the particulars until he'd digested them himself.

"I need a manual for how to deal with

this," he said. "Blueprints. And a really strong drink."

Ditto, she thought.

It was almost six on Monday. Holly wondered if Mia would come to class that night. But at five forty-five, the door blew open and Mia came running in, her smile bigger and brighter than when she'd told Holly that Daniel had asked her to the dance. She wore clothes Holly hadn't seen before, tight jeans tucked into knee-high brown riding boots, a long multicolored scarf tied around her neck, its long swatch hanging down to her silver belt buckle. And her hair, her perfect, long chestnut hair was now cut into a sophisticated style, with sideswept bangs and long layers. She looked like she was sixteen.

Liam had to be furious. If he'd even seen her yet.

Mia twirled her way into the kitchen, three pirouettes, and came to a stop, laughing. "Look at me, Holly! Aren't I totally all glam? My mom took me shopping and to a salon. Look at my eyebrows!"

Her eyebrows had been perfectly fine before, but now they were perfect slashes above her beautiful blueberry-colored eyes. At least she wasn't wearing makeup. Except for some sparkly lip gloss. That was new too. But Holly could live with the sparkly lip gloss. Even if it was probably Chanel.

"All my wishes came true, Holly! My mom came to the dance and picked me up and we went back to her hotel and we had the most incredible weekend. And then this morning, she dropped me off at my house, and my dad flipped, of course, at my new clothes and my haircut. Hello, I'm *twelve*. Not ten. Why do I have to have little-girl do-nothing hair that just lies there? My hair is no different than Madeline's or Morgan's now. And big deal, I'm wearing jeans tucked into boots. I do that all winter."

Twelve-year-old-girl-appropriate jeans tucked into L.L. Bean duck boots wasn't exactly the same thing, but Holly knew this conversation wasn't about the clothes or the hair or the eyebrows. It was about Mia's mother in her life. And she had to tread very carefully.

"You should have *seen* Madeline Windemere and her M friends' faces when I walked into school this morning. And Daniel couldn't stop staring at me in history. He asked if we could go out again this week, and I said sure, but I didn't know when because my mom has us totally booked for like every night. Oh, my God, Holly, could my life *be* any better? Yes! Because guess what the best part is? She's staying! I mean, she's actually moving back here! She's going to rent a house for us in Portland, either on the Eastern or Western Promenade or maybe one of those condos right on the harbor in the Old Port, until she finds exactly what she's looking for for us. And she said I can have veto power over the house she buys!"

Whoa. "She's moving back? With her husband?"

"*That's* actually the best part," Mia said, taking both Holly's hands and jumping up and down. "She said she's getting a divorce!"

Double whoa. This was happening very fast. And very swoopish, like Liam had said. No wonder he'd been so worried.

"And do you know what that means?" Mia asked, spinning around again.

"What?"

"That my mom and dad will get back together. I know they will. You should have seen his face when she showed up at the dance. She was onstage when they were singing 'Happy Birthday' to me, and I looked around to spot him and he was staring up at her and I haven't seen him look like that in a long time. He's never looked

291

at Jodie that way."

Like he wanted to kill her? Holly wondered.

Or had there been a moment, before the anger and fear set in, when Liam had looked at his ex-wife and felt something much softer?

"Oh, and Holly, is it all right if I don't stay for the class tonight? My mom is taking me to an art exhibit at a gallery. Isn't that so cool?"

"Of course it's okay."

"I mean, I still plan to be your apprentice, even though our mission is done. We got rid of the fake-o bobblehead! My mom is a great cook, so it's not like I need to learn anymore, but I really like the class. And we had a deal, right?"

"Right," she said, squeezing Mia's hand, her mind working to take this all in and not focus on any one thing. Like Liam looking at his ex-wife with love and tenderness.

"Okay, well, I'd better get home. My mom's picking me up in like fifteen minutes. And now I have an amazing outfit to wear! Thank you for everything, Holly. If it wasn't for you, Jodie would still be in my dad's life and that would have totally complicated everything. Now he's back to being single and is totally available to get back together with my mom."

Holly managed a smile, a smile that actually felt genuine because she cared about this girl, a lot more than she realized, and for her, she wanted this fairy tale to end happily.

But it couldn't, right? No way, no how? Because Liam was way over his ex-wife, didn't even *like* his ex-wife. And because he and Holly had had a perfect date on a rowboat that had ended with an amazing kiss and then they'd shared Gouda cheese and grapes and Italian bread and had made love.

Because Holly was in love with Liam.

"Where's Mia's tonight?" Juliet asked, glancing around the big kitchen for her. Mia was such a bright, boisterous presence that the lack of her, especially with only worried Holly and grieving Juliet, made her absence all the more noticeable. Tamara had called, sounding very congested, and said she'd come down with a nasty little cold and couldn't make the class, and Simon, Holly was happy to see, had just come through the door.

"She's with her mom," Holly said, holding up a hello hand to Simon as she placed the copies of the recipes on the center island. Maybe she'd bring down Mia's copies later, just to have a reason to knock on the Gellers' door. *Uh, you're not falling back in love with your ex-wife, right? Preposterous, right?* And he'd say, *Holly, silly woman, how could I feel anything for any woman other than you after the past few times we were together? I carved for you, didn't I?*

Hardly likely. Though he did carve for her.

"That makes me very happy," Juliet said. "For Mia's sake. But I just don't get her mother at all. How do you just leave like that, start a new life as though you don't have a child somewhere? It makes me crazy, especially because I'd do anything to be with my daughter for one more minute, and here someone just up and left her ten-year-old daughter for a man, coming back for every-now-and-then visits."

Simon tied on an apron. "I know. Those first few weeks of not seeing Cass every day, having to call her if I wanted to hear her voice, find out about her day, was so hard. It's almost impossible to imagine a parent who's able to go for weeks or months without seeing her own kid's face. I don't get it either. Mia must be overjoyed, though. Her wish into the wedding soup came true."

Wedding soup. Holly had almost forgotten the wedding soup. Maybe she'd helped set up this family reunion without realizing it. A Camilla Constantina moment.

She had to remember that this was a happy occasion for a child, that a girl's wish had come true. And how often did that happen? And this wasn't just any girl, but Mia, whom she'd come to adore. For the past few weeks Mia had shared her hopes and dreams with Holly — when Mia had no one else with whom to share them — and now Holly was going to be the interloper?

She needed to take a giant step back.

"You two have put things into perspective for me," Holly said. "Without even realizing it. Thank you."

Juliet smiled. "I'm not that self-absorbed, actually. I know you've got a serious thing for Mia's father. And I also know that things happen that you have absolutely no control over. Like love. And loss."

"So you're saying I should be on guard? Or that I need to let him go?" She wondered what he was doing right then. Walking with Mia and her mother along the windy beach near Mia's favorite lighthouse in Cape Elizabeth? Sitting down to dinner at Liam's house, the three of them talking about old times when they were a family?

How could she wish into tonight's risotto that Liam would choose her instead of the opportunity to put his family back together?

How could she?

"Holly, I'm just saying that you can't control everything. Anything, really. Like the food we've been making. We can follow the recipe exactly as your grandmother wrote it, do everything exactly — or almost exactly — as she had, and the dish can come out so-so instead of amazing. Or it can come out amazing when you were expecting very little."

Simon nodded. "You're very wise, Juliet."

"Hardly. I'm just trying to make sense of Evie's death for myself. I come up with something like I just said, and I think I believe it, but then the next day I'm back to the crying, back to the anger that makes me want to hit something, back to the total despair that makes me want to smash my car into a brick wall."

Holly stared at her, then at Simon, then back at Juliet. "But you wouldn't, right?"

Juliet shook her head and tears filled her eyes. "No, I wouldn't. Not that I haven't thought about it, when I've been behind the wheel and sobbing and there have been a few brick walls looming ahead. It would dishonor Evie's death." Her face crumpled, and where a moment ago she'd been so strong, Holly could tell her knees would give out if she didn't sit down. "Right?"

Holly led Juliet over to the breakfast nook and sat her in one of the cushioned chairs. "Right, Juliet. Very right. It's what my grandmother would say, I know it."

"And Ethan needs me. I know he does. I'm just not interested in being needed by him. I know how cold that sounds."

Simon poured a glass of white wine and handed it to Juliet. "Not cold. Everyone grieves their own way. How long has it been since your daughter died?"

"Almost six months. At first I stayed in the house with Ethan. I tried. I tried to let him comfort me, but when he started going back to work after two weeks, *two weeks,* I started to hate him. And he'd come home from work, full of stupid, who-cares conversation about a corporate takeover case he was working on, and I started hating the sound of his voice. I shut myself in Evie's room, sleeping in there, which I guess made things worse. And eventually he stopped talking to me, would just walk around me. And I finally felt like I could leave. And I came here."

Holly squeezed Juliet's hand. "Oh, Juliet. You've been grieving the loss of your husband just as much as your daughter."

She shrugged, her slight shoulders barely rising. "Here I go again, sucking all the air out the room like Ethan accused me of. I don't want to turn this class into some depressing sob story. You two go create amazing risotto. I could use some fresh air, anyway."

"So let's all just go sit out on the porch with the bottle," Simon said, taking two more glasses from the cupboard. "I'm bone tired from work today. No energy to mince garlic, let alone deal with beef marrow."

"Me either," Holly said. "A glass of wine and two friends sounds just like what the doctor ordered for all of us."

And so the three headed outside to the side deck and lay in the chaise lounges facing the evergreens and the beautiful swing between the oaks, sipping their wine and talking about love and loss until Simon started to snore.

Juliet laughed, a welcome sound.

Holly was in bed with her grandmother's diary in her hand and Antonio curled at her feet when her phone rang. For once, she didn't lunge for it. She almost didn't answer. But of course she did.

"Hey," Liam said.

"How are you?" she asked, holding her breath.

"I'm okay. Except for the fact that my

head feels like it's going to explode. Mia's mother has thrown a few curveballs, and" — he stopped for a moment, and she realized she was holding her breath — "and suddenly things are . . . *complicated* when they weren't a few days ago."

Complicated. Her least favorite word.

She lay back down and stared up at the ceiling. "I know. Mia stopped by before class tonight. She told me everything. I don't think she left a single thing out."

"Ah. That's probably a good thing."

Or a very bad thing.

"Veronica says she's really staying, that she's going to look for a house — to buy. She seems to really mean it."

This was good for Mia, Holly reminded herself as worry crawled back inside her. "So she just left her husband, just like that?"

"That's her M.O."

This was so confusing. She had left two husbands. And Holly was supposed to root for her to take one back, the one Holly had fallen in love with?

You're supposed to root for Mia, she told herself. *For a fractured family that could have a second chance.*

Not that they were a family. Veronica was an *ex*-wife. Ex. She chose to leave. Holly supposed she could think her away around this in circles forever and never know what was right for her to feel.

"I'm sorry that I kind of defended her the other night, for Mia's sake," Holly said. "I can see why you're so worried about her mother's intentions. But I guess if she's serious about staying, that is a good thing for Mia, right?"

"Have you seen her jeans? Her eyebrows? She'll be getting a tattoo next. I don't know how good it is."

Holly had no idea what to say to this, to any of this.

"Listen, Holly, I might make myself a little scarce for the next few days, just until I know what's really going on, what Veronica's intentions are, if she's serious."

"Could she be?" *And are you part of those intentions?*

"I guess. She was serious enough about leaving me and Mia for a life in Santa Barbara and Paris with the husband she's now leaving. If she left us, I'm sure she could leave him too."

"So maybe there's another man in the picture?" Holly asked. *Not you,* she added silently. Meanly. Selfishly.

"I wouldn't be surprised, but I don't see her going from an international banker with houses in four countries to a Maine lobsterman. We're meeting tomorrow night to talk, so I'll find out everything then."

Meeting. As in getting together. At Liam's house, most likely. No, most likely at Veronica's hotel, so they could talk privately.

She tried to remember Juliet's words about not being able to control everything. But she would do anything for a magic wand or her grandmother's gift of *knowing*.

The kitchen couldn't get any cleaner. Despite not even holding class earlier, Holly had scrubbed the stove, refrigerator, counters, and floors. She was out of things to scrub. And the one thing that did need a good scrubbing was her brain, to get Liam and Mia out.

"What's going to happen, Antonio?" she asked the cat, who stared at her from his cat bed. She held out her hand with his favorite liver snap and he waddled over, his little belly pooch swinging from side to side. He gobbled it up and wound his warm body between her legs.

At least she'd won him over. Even if it took liver snaps.

"Come, Antonio. I'm going to take a long, hot bath. You can curl up on the fluffy rug."

And indeed, the cat followed her up the stairs and sat in the doorway, then came in and lay down on the gold rug beside the tub. Holly ran the bath, pouring in bath beads, large mother-of-pearl ones that smelled like baby powder and comfort. She headed into the bedroom and picked up the diary from where she'd left it on her bed, then undressed and slid into the hot water, holding up the composition book so it wouldn't touch a drop of water. She needed to exit her life for a little while and perhaps she would find some lesson in her grandmother's experiences about how to deal with the unexpected.

The moment she read the first sentence, though, she closed the book, not sure she wanted to find out just what happened to Lenora Windemere's poor baby. But she adjusted her little bath pillow and took a deep breath and began to read.

May 1964
Dear Diary,
   Lenora Windemere did not have her baby at home with a midwife. When the contractions started, according to Annette, Lenora began timing them, and then when she knew it was time, Richard grabbed her bag and off they went to the hospital.
   It was a difficult birth.
   And the baby, sickly and underweight,

was born with a hole in its heart. "The baby would not have survived if you'd had him at home," the doctor told Lenora. "Thank God you had the sense to deliver in the hospital."

But the baby, named Richard after his father, did not get better. Given weeks to live, then perhaps months, little Richard Windemere died just after he turned a year old, in his little bassinet at the pediatric intensive care unit at Maine Medical Center, where he'd spent the past several weeks fighting for his life.

The morning of the funeral, I cooked and packed a week's worth of dishes I knew the Windemeres liked and would freeze well. Then I bundled up Luciana in her good wool coat and drove across town to the Windemeres' mansion on the water.

"Remember, Luciana," I said as we waited for someone to answer the door. "You do not need to say anything while we are here, but please use your best manners." Luciana is now six and has lovely manners, yet I worried because I was afraid the gathering of solemn faces in black, the crying, would bring back memories of her own father's funeral, and she might start to scream. I did not plan to stay long, for that reason. A funeral is not a place for a little girl who's already experienced the loss of a parent.

Martha, the Windemeres' live-in housekeeper, opened the door and said that Lenora and her friends were in the formal living room, having coffee.

The moment I stepped across the threshold, I felt it. The anger. It swirled in violent slashes of black and purple in front of me, like tiny floaties before my eyes that would not go away. I held tighter on to Luciana's hand, not quite sure that I should even go in, yet I was there, with the food and my sincere condolences. I would stay just a minute or two.

The anger grew stronger as I entered the living room. Lenora sat on the camelback sofa, flanked by Annette and Jacqueline, two older women, Lenora's mother and grandmother, whispering on the sofa across from them. Lenora held a white handkerchief under her eyes. Annette was holding on to her hand.

"Oh, Lenora, I'm so —" I began.

"Get out of my house," Lenora screamed at me. "You should have let well enough be. I should have gone with my instincts and had the baby at home with the midwife. I hate you!"

Luciana gasped and I felt her stiffen. I

tucked her closer against me.

"But Len, he would have died minutes later," Annette said, rubbing Lenora's shoulder. "He wouldn't have made it to the hospital."

"Yes, that's right," Lenora screamed. "And the past year wouldn't have been a living nightmare, always waiting for him to die. You made the last year hell, Camilla. My little boy would have died peacefully as a newborn. Instead he had a life of pain! Surgery after surgery! And it's all your fault. You're a disgusting witch. Get out of my house."

Luciana started to cry. In shock, I dropped the bag, which thudded to the floor. I just stood there, unable to move, unable to think, as though Lenora's hatred had blocked everything inside of me.

"Get out!" Lenora screamed again. "It's your fault!"

She was crazy with grief, I knew. She needed someone to take her pain and anger out on. And I was that someone. There was nothing I could possibly say. I held on to Luciana's hand and hurried out and down the steps, tears stinging my eyes.

That was the end of my relationship with Lenora Windemere.

Yet it was the beginning of my fortune-telling business taking off. The sad story of the poor Windemere baby spread all over Blue Crab Island and the nearby towns. How I had saved the baby's life by telling Lenora to deliver in a hospital instead of at home with a midwife. That the baby had died was like a sad afternote to the story that went around; what people cared about was that the baby had lived for a year, had had a fighting chance. And my phone began ringing with appointments. To save my sanity, I limited fortune-telling to one client per day and I charged twenty-five dollars.

But things between me and Luciana were never the same, not since that terrible day in Lenora Windemere's living room. When she called me a witch. A disgusting witch. And threw me out of her house.

When Luciana had questions, concerns, fears, dreams, she turned to her teacher, a lovely woman who looked like a princess with blond hair and blue eyes and a very sweet manner. She insisted on being called Lucy and refused to answer to Luciana. And she looked at me with something like suspicion in her eyes. As if I could do something bad to her.

So I turned even kinder, and for a while things were better. But only for a while.

The entry finished, Holly closed the book and realized her hand was shaking. *Oh, Nonna,* she thought, trying to imagine that moment in Lenora Windemere's living room, her mother as a frightened six-year-old hearing all that, being a part of it.

She got out of the bath and slipped on the thick blue robe her grandmother always had hanging on the hook for her, went into her bedroom, and called her parents' house in Newton. It was almost eleven p.m., and her mother and father were likely watching *Law & Order* in bed, getting ready for the news, after which they'd watch a little of *The Tonight Show* and then turn off their bedside lamps.

Her mother answered on the third ring, as always. She could be sitting right next to the phone and reading *Good Housekeeping* magazine, but always waited for the third ring so as to seem like she was busy and leading a full life, a phone call just one of her many activities.

"Hi, Mom. How are you?"

"Holly? What's wrong?"

"Nothing's wrong. I was just getting ready to head up to bed and wanted to say hi and see how you are. How Dad is." *And to somehow transmit through the telephone wires that I'm sorry about what happened that day in the Windemeres' living room. You must have been so scared.*

"Oh, well, we're fine. Same old, you know. I won a contest at the library and am getting a signed copy of a mystery author's book. And your father's cholesterol check was much better this time. If I could just get him to stop it with those disgusting cigars already. He's like an eighty-year-old man, your father."

Holly could hear her father muttering, "Oh, please, Lucy." She laughed, picturing Bud Maguire with his almost bald head and auburn fuzz on his ears puffing on his cigar and absently watching TV while flipping through his favorite magazine, *Popular Mechanics.*

She thought about telling her mother what she'd read in Camilla's diary, then decided against it. If she brought it up, her mother would stiffen and go silent. She knew her mother that much. It would not be a conversation that would bring them closer; it would only widen the gulf. Holly was choosing to take over the life her mother couldn't wait to escape.

"So you're still teaching the cooking class?"

"Yes, and in fact, I just had my fourth class tonight." Not that they'd actually cooked anything. "Once I started calming down and just following the recipes, really paying attention to the ingredients themselves instead of how much work was before me, I got pretty good."

"Well, to be honest, I don't know how you stand it up there. But you were always a decent cook. Remember that prime rib you made your father for his fiftieth birthday when you came to visit a few years ago? And the garlic mashed potatoes? He loved those. He always asks for the garlic mashed when we go to Olive Garden. You could sell the house and open a diner."

Holly smiled. Now that she knew more about her mother's childhood, why she was so negative about the island, Holly didn't quite attach an attack to everything her mother said. "Well, I'm committed to Camilla's Cucinotta, so maybe you and Dad could come up sometime and try my risotto alla Milanese. I've almost got it down. In fact, I'm going to be catering a local wedding at the Blue Crab Cove. Was that here when you were growing up?"

Luciana was silent for a moment, then

said, "Oh, yes, that's been around forever. Well, isn't that something, Holly. I suppose you're all right then, up there?"

Except for my worried heart, yes. "I'm more than all right, Mom. I feel like I belong here. I feel bad saying that to you because I know how much you hated it here."

"You're your grandmother's granddaughter," she said. "You always were. Tell you the truth, Holly, I was always a bit relieved about the special relationship you two had. My mother and I never saw eye to eye, but I loved her. And I respected her, even if I didn't like the fortune-telling. I didn't have an easy time of it growing up, but I've always felt bad about all but estranging myself. It helped to know she had you. And that she still does."

It must have been awful — and at six years old — to hear your mother being called a "disgusting witch." And from what Holly read in the diary, that was only the beginning. "That means a lot to hear you say, Mom."

Lucy Maguire was silent for a moment. "I've always wanted you to be happy, Holly. And you never did find your place. Maybe Blue Crab Island is it. Maybe it's always been it for you."

"I think it is," Holly said, picturing the

sign Liam had made her. HOLLY'S KITCHEN. "I think this is where I belong, Mom."

"Well, I'm sure your grandmother is at peace. And I'm glad you called, Holly."

"Me too." And then after a bit of small talk and a say hello to Dad, Holly hung up, her heart feeling slightly soothed.

Holly bolted up in bed, having awoken from a strange dream she couldn't quite remember, except that Juliet was in it and that there was something Holly wanted to tell her, but Juliet kept floating behind a cloud with the word *hospital* carved into it (dreams were odd that way) every time Holly tried to get her to listen.

Yes. There was something she needed to tell Juliet.

She glanced at the clock. Almost two a.m. She picked up the phone anyway and called her friend, who she doubted was sleeping.

She answered on the first ring.

"Juliet, it's Holly. I'm sorry for calling so late, but there's something I need to tell you."

Juliet was silent for a moment, then said, "Okay."

"I've been reading my grandmother's diary about teaching her first class. One of her students was pregnant, and Camilla knew that it would be a difficult birth and cautioned her to deliver in the hospital and not at home with a midwife, as she'd done with her first child."

Juliet said nothing, but Holly could feel her listening. Waiting.

Holly got out of bed and walked over to the window and stared out at the few twinkling stars, at the almost full moon. "The baby was born sick, a hole in his heart. But he lived because of immediate medical attention. But then just after his first birthday, he died."

"Why are you telling me this, Holly?"

"Because the mother of the baby blamed Camilla for her grief. She would rather have lost the baby at birth than loved him and lost him a year later. I just read all this tonight and it's so heartbreaking and —"

"She would rather have lost him at birth?" Juliet repeated. "I can't imagine thinking that for a moment about Evie. I had three precious years with her. Three years I wouldn't give up for anything, not for this unrelenting pain and black grief. No, I wouldn't give up those years for anything."

"I didn't think so," Holly said, gazing at the perfect white stars in the night sky. It seemed that once again, her grandmother had managed to help Juliet.

SIXTEEN

Over the next few days, Holly kept busy by making lists of local gourmet shops and then surreptitiously dropping in to make notes on their offerings and what might complement their menus. She set up seven appointments to bring in her pastas and sauces, and today she was determined to work on a couple of pasta salads, something her grandmother had never been a fan of. But Holly could live on cold pasta salads with olives and sun dried tomatoes, and it seemed a safe way to start making Camilla's Cucinotta a tiny bit her own.

Twice, once on her way out and once on her way in, she'd seen Liam's navy SUV turning down Cove Road, a dark-haired woman in the passenger seat. She wished she knew what was going on. She missed Mia. She missed Liam. She missed that brief few hours when she'd given in to how she felt about him and had allowed herself to be excited about a new romance, a new relationship.

Nothing soothed her and distracted her as much as making fresh pasta. And today she was determined to make her own rotini, a spiral pasta, for her cold pasta salads. She measured out the semolina and durum flour onto the wooden work surface and cracked in the eggs, mixing and kneading until it was beautifully elastic, when the bell jangled and Liam appeared under the archway. Looking serious.

She glanced at the clock. Almost ten. "Taking the day off today?" The question was so light and banal that no one would guess she she'd seized up inside at the sight of him, her stomach full of those butterflies. And knots.

He looked at her so intently, with a mixture of what seemed like confusion and surety at the same time. "I'm actually taking the week."

"I can understand that. You want to be around and available while Mia's mother is in town. Just in case she up and leaves again, despite all the talk about buying a house." She was rambling. "How is everything going, by the way?"

He stared at her for a long moment, then took a deep breath. "Holly, I —" He ran a

315

hand through his hair. "Veronica, Mia's mother, she's very convincing."

Holly could feel her stomach drop. "Convincing?"

"About how she feels. What she wants. Mistakes she made."

"About you?"

He leaned his head back for a moment. "Yeah. About me. About Mia. What she gave up and what she's supposedly learned."

"Supposedly?" she asked, hating the hopeful note in her voice. Hopeful that he was putting air quotes around the "supposedly."

"She wants a second chance."

Holly turned away for a moment, tears filling her eyes. She blinked them away. "And what do you want, Liam?"

He was silent on that.

If only she had the gift of knowing. If only she were even 30 percent psychic so she could have seen this coming and could have stuffed Liam's mouth with the cheese and grapes and then sent him home instead of to her bed.

Do not burst into tears all over the pasta, she ordered herself, tightening her lips.

He closed his eyes and shook his head. "I thought I *hated* her. For what she did to me. To Mia. To our family. My family was everything to me, and she shattered it without a thought to me or her own daughter. And now she's back and she's asking for a chance, and at first I told her I'd never take her back — never. And then she talked and talked and talked, and after a while I found myself listening, and —" He stopped and glanced out the window. "And this part of me thought, maybe she *has* changed, got what she needed out of her system, realized what she really wanted." He took a deep breath and let it out. "I don't know if I'm the biggest idiot in the world or what the hell I'm doing. What I'm *supposed* to do."

He sounded so distraught that she wanted to go to him and put her arms around him and tell him everything would be okay, but of course she couldn't. She had no idea what "okay" meant in this situation.

"And this morning, to see Mia so full of hope, so happy, so completely wrapped up in this fairy tale that her parents will get back together —" He glanced down. "It's powerful, Holly. All of it is very powerful."

For a second she was so overcome with emotion that she could only nod. "I can understand that."

"But you know what else is powerful?" he said, holding her gaze. "This amazing thing between us. I have strong feelings for you, Holly. I don't know what the hell to do."

She looked at him, searching his eyes for something to hang on to here, but not knowing what that was. Was she supposed to try to pull him over the line to her side? It would be wrong.

"I have strong feelings for you too, Liam. And I have strong feelings for Mia. So . . . if there's a chance for you and her mother to get back together, to become a family again, you owe that to yourself and to Mia to at least try, right?" How she managed to say that without bursting into tears was amazing.

He took a deep breath and let it out, his hands jammed into the pockets of his leather jacket. "You think so?"

This time she couldn't even nod. The tears stung and she started to cry. "Yes. I think so. Don't you?"

He was silent for another moment. "I'm so sorry," he said, stepping toward her and reaching his hand out.

She shook her head. "No, don't. Just . . . go do what you have to do."

He stared at her and she looked away. "I am sorry. I hate to hurt you, Holly. I mean that more than I mean anything else."

She glanced at him but was so afraid to burst into wracking sobs that she nodded and managed some kind of rueful smile.

"I believe that, Liam."

"You're an important person in Mia's life. I hope she can still . . . take the class — if you think that's all right. You mean so much to her."

"Of course she can still take the class. Just go and be with your family," she said, the tears burning.

The moment the door clicked closed, the bells stopping their jangle, Holly slid down against the wall and sobbed.

The next night, Holly sat at the kitchen table, facing the view of oaks and bird feeders instead of the sign Liam had made for her, writing out a binder copy recipe of her first own creation: Fusilli alla Holly, with pine nuts and black olives and sun dried tomatoes in a creamy pink sauce. She'd spent last night and today making several iterations until she got the measurements just so. Cooking had helped heal one broken heart and would have to work overtime on another.

The bells jangled and Tamara came in, uncharacteristically dressed in jeans and a long-sleeved T-shirt and sleeveless puffy vest. She looked as though she might burst into tears at any second, and then she did.

"I got the 'It's not you, it's me' bullshit."

Tamara's shoulders slumped and she dropped down in the chair beside Holly. "And what makes it even worse? I didn't see it coming. I *always* see it coming — you always know when a guy is only half there, or even three-quarters there. You know when there's the slightest thing wrong. But this time, after that amazing third date, amazing third-date *sex,* he dumped me. Apparently sleeping with me made him realize he still loves his ex-girlfriend and that maybe he is ready to commit to a future with her, after all. Do you believe this?"

Yes, Holly did. She filled in Tamara on everything that had happened between her and Liam, including the bad-timing speech she'd gotten the day before.

"Oh, Holly, I'm so sorry. Men suck."

"Love sucks," Holly corrected.

"And even love is great until it falls spectacularly apart, though. I'm never dating again. I've had it. I'll happily go to my sister's wedding alone."

"At least you'll have some good Italian food," Holly said, trying to smile.

"Let's make something right now. Something gooey and fattening." She stood up. "I know. Let's make tiramisu. If I don't take it back for myself it'll forever be ruined for me. I made it for that jerk on our third and

320

last date."

"My grandmother always said tiramisu was the Italian version of chicken soup and could cure anything."

"Do you happen to have a hundred ladyfingers in the cupboard?" Tamara asked. "Because I need at least ten servings."

Holly squeezed Tamara's hand. "Let's go shopping. We can pick up a good bottle of wine and a tearjerker movie to make us feel better about our miserable love lives."

Ten minutes later they were at the supermarket across the bridge in Portland, their cart full of mascarpone cheese and *savoiardi* ladyfingers.

"So all this with Liam happened yesterday?" Tamara asked as she selected a white wine. "I wished you would have called me. Not that I have any good advice for getting over anyone."

"When he left and I was all cried out, I thought about calling you, but I didn't want to heap all that on you when you were so happy. I just threw myself under the covers and stayed there for a while, and then I got this sudden urge to make something. I wrote my first recipe — just a pasta salad, but I wrote it out and put in the binder."

"That's great, Holly! What's the final ingredient? A wish?"

"Yeah. Just a plain old wish. And after I added the delicious sausage to the pasta, I wished that I'd wise up."

"You're plenty wise, Holly. You fell in love with a great guy. Not that that's gonna make you feel any better." She laid their groceries on the checkout table. "I guess mine wasn't such a jerk either. Oh, who the hell knows. Maybe he *was* being honest. Maybe sex with me suddenly did make him realize how empty and nothing sex with someone you barely know can make you feel and maybe it did make him realize what he had with his ex. I actually have been through that myself. It's just so hard to know what's real or not, what's a bullshit excuse for 'I'm just not that into you.'"

"Well, I like thinking that they were being honest and we just got caught in the fallout. Makes me feel better than being all cynical."

Tamara nodded. "I think we should double the tiramisu recipe so we can stuff our brokenhearted faces all night."

"Agreed," Holly said, grateful for her new friend.

When they walked back into Holly's cottage, Tamara said, "Hey, something's different in here." She glanced around. "What is it?"

"I took down that big brass mirror that was on the wall by the kitchen nook and put up a bunch of smaller oil paintings. Antonio. That sweet little one of this house. And those two above the kitchen table. Look how vibrant the colors are. Oh, and there's that sign," Holly added, staring at Liam's gift.

"Holly's kitchen," Tamara read. She smiled. "This *is* your kitchen. But were you afraid to change anything? Like maybe some of your grandmother's magic would leave with it?"

"I think I was afraid to change anything at first, but now I'm feeling more comfortable making this place mine. And the business too. I still can't believe I wrote my own recipe. It may not seem like such a big deal, but it never occurred to me that I *could*." Holly glanced at the recipe for tiramisu and made the espresso, using Camilla's stash of Italian Lavazza.

Tamara opened the wine and poured two glasses. "You're so lucky to have this place. I've been thinking of going into business for myself as an interior decorator but I'm not sure I could develop enough of a client base. If only I could have a list of clients as long as ex-boyfriends and third-date guys who blew me off. I'm beginning to think I shouldn't even expect a guy to fall in love with me and that I should just settle for Mr. Okay."

The espresso was done, so Holly poured it into a bowl and set it aside to cool to room temperature. "I don't think settling is the answer either, though."

"Then what is? It's not like I have this stupid list of what I want in a husband. I just want a real connection. Someone I can talk to for hours, you know, like everyone says of their first date with the person they ended up marrying. And, yeah, I want to be wildly attracted to him. But that doesn't mean he has to be gorgeous, just that I'm dying to jump his bones." She got up, glanced at the recipe, and then added the unsweetened cocoa and then the cognac to the espresso. "I just wish I knew when the guy was the right one."

Holly sighed, taking another bowl and using a mixer to beat eggs and sugar, adding the mascarpone and another shot of cognac. "Me too." She was beginning to think she should learn to make *sa cordula* and carry it around in little containers with her, so if she met a guy, she could say, "Would you mind letting me know if you like this?" Ha. It was going to be a while — a long while — before she even thought about men again. For now, there was food to think about. Dessert. In another bowl, she beat egg whites until they were fluffy, her hand about to go numb, then gently blended the egg whites into the other bowl.

They took turns dipping the ladyfingers into the bowl of espresso, careful not to soak the delicate ladyfingers, laying each in a pretty serving bowl, then spreading a layer of the mascarpone mixture on top, then more espresso-dipped ladyfingers, then more cheese and then a fine sifting of the cocoa. The tiramisu was supposed to refrigerate for a good four hours, but Holly made coffee and added some cognac and they settled on one hour.

They sat at the kitchen nook, where her grandmother had told hundreds of fortunes. Where Camilla had reiterated Holly's several times. They sipped their coffee and glanced out at the darkness, the almost crescent moon casting just a bit of light on the yard.

Tamara sighed. "I *really* wanted to bring my serious boyfriend to my sister's wedding. Pathetic as that sounds."

"It doesn't sound pathetic at all. Hey, why not just ask Simon? He'd go and have a wonderful time and make great small talk with all your relatives. He could even pretend to be your serious boyfriend to get everyone off your case."

Tears glistened in Tamara's eyes. "That's the thing. I don't want to ask a friend, much as I like Simon. I don't want some random date. I don't want someone to pretend to be my loving boyfriend to impress everyone and make me feel okay in this annoyingly coupled world. I want my own love. Why is this so hard? Why is it so easy for everyone else? I wish you could tell fortunes like your grandmother. I'm ready to *know*."

"I don't think I do want to know. Imagine if you *did* know, you'd never leave your bed. You'd just order in and watch TV and call it a day."

Tamara laughed. "You're probably right." She glanced at her watch. "Okay, it's only been a half hour, but I want that tiramisu."

And so they dug in, talking men, love, family, and broken hearts long after neither could eat another delectable bite.

At the farmer's market on Wednesday afternoon, Holly saw Simon walking with an adorable girl with his same sandy-blond hair. She wore a school backpack with her initials monogrammed on front. He looked so flustered, trying to unwrap the tight cellophane from the lobster-shaped chocolate lollipop he'd just bought her from the chocolate vendor, one of Holly's favorite booths. Her heart went out to him at how hard this all must be, seeing his daughter every Wednesday after school and alternate weekends a month, trying to earn the girl's fragile trust when he hadn't been the one who'd broken up the marriage, the family.

"Simon, hi," she called out, waving, just as he slid down the knotted cellophane and handed the treat to his daughter, who took a big bite out of the lobster's claw.

When he spotted her in the crowded market, he waved back and brought his daughter over. "Cass, this is one of the very talented people who helped me decorate your room. My Italian cooking teacher, Holly Maguire."

His cute daughter smiled up at her. "You taught my dad how to make the spaghetti and meatballs?" she asked, her lollipop pratically covering her face.

"I did. Hope they were good."

"So good. Last night for dinner we made meat loaf out of them, using my grand-mother's recipe, and it was so amazing. And we even had spaghetti on the side. Have you ever had meat loaf and spaghetti? It's awe-some."

Holly laughed. "I haven't but it sounds

delicious."

Cass nodded. "Tonight we're making a castle out of the recipe and using the spaghetti to make the moat."

Holly stared at Simon. "You could be writing your own cookbook for kids. Meat-castle and spaghetti? Brilliant."

"I didn't even know my dad knew how to make this stuff, but we got a kids' cookbook out of the library, and we've been making everything," said Cass. "And we're going to make a spaceship out of construction paper and hang it from the ceiling. Isn't that cool?"

"Very," Holly agreed.

"Dad, there's my friend Amy. Let's go say hi." She was pulling him away, no sign of the unhappy girl he'd described four weeks ago.

"See you in class," Simon called out as his daughter proudly marched her father over to her friend.

Happy for Simon, Holly watched them for a moment, then got out her list and examined the tomatoes and looked over the asparagus with the eye of someone who knew what she was doing.

"Hey, Holly," said Robert, who was always here on weekends with his artisan breads.

She was so touched that she knew so

many of the vendors now, that many knew her and would call her over, sharing a particularly good-looking basket of onions or garlic or tomatoes. She was a regular. And she liked being a regular.

She drove home with her ingredients, the sight of her round breads and eggplant and gorgeous tomatoes cheering her up. Perhaps she would offer a cooking class for kids, like Simon's daughter. Meatballs and spaghetti. Macaroni and cheese. Pizza.

Or maybe not. Kids liked to talk, liked to tell you every thought that was going in inside their heads, and once again, she would get emotionally involved and get her heart smashed, somehow, some way.

At home, she unpacked and made herself a cup of tea, then scooped up the leftover tiramisu and sat down in the living room. The beautiful painting of the olive tree was so much nicer to look at than her great-great-grandfather's stern face. And since Holly had come from the roots of that olive tree in Italy as much as her great-great-grandfather's bloodline, she thought the swap more than reasonable. She loved this room now, loved sitting on the brocade camelback sofa, the kitchen barely visible. This was a good room in which to think. Especially because Liam hadn't spent any time in it.

Her grandmother's diary rested on the end table and she picked it up, then put it down. Sometimes reading about her grandmother's life was too painful, especially when it concerned her mother. But sometimes her grandmother's words and experiences and lessons were like a soothing balm, and perhaps Holly'd find some comfort.

October 1964
Dear Diary,

I haven't written in a while. Not since that awful day when Luciana came off the big yellow school bus crying, tears streaming down her face. I kneeled down beside her to ask what was wrong and she screamed at me.

"Amanda Windemere says you're a witch and that she's not allowed to play with me anymore!"

It was a week after the funeral of Amanda's baby brother, the first day the girl had gone back to school.

I glanced up at the children on the bus. They stared out the window at me, some pointing and making phony faces of fear, some looking truly frightened.

Oh, Luciana.

"Anyone who wants to be Amanda Windemere's friend isn't allowed to be friends with me," Luciana screamed through her tears. She was about say something, but then just stood there and sobbed.

I picked her up, and though she fought me for a few moments, she finally relented and went limp in my arms, throwing her arms around my neck and sobbing into my shoulder. But then she stiffened and screamed, "Put me down! Let me go!" and ran inside. I heard a door slam.

I knew, deep down where the knowing began, that I would lose my daughter, that she would not be able to bear being the daughter of the island witch who lived in the apricot-colored bungalow in the thicket of evergreens. I thought about moving, selling the cottage and leaving this all behind, taking Luciana and starting over somewhere fresh, somewhere no one knew. But you are who you are, and you are where you go. I knew I wasn't meant to leave. That feeling was stronger than anything else. I was meant to stay. Leaving would reinforce for Luciana that there was something wrong with her mother, that her mother had to run away. And that she, Luciana, had something to be ashamed of. Which is not true. And so I stayed, hoping by doing so, I'd teach my daughter something important.

The women of Blue Crab Island still came, of course, wanting their fortunes told, now that everyone knew I did have the gift. Lenora had to stop blaming me because she'd been ordered by her husband to say that of course she was grateful to have had the year with her son, that of course she hadn't wanted him to die at birth instead.

And so my reputation was restored — and made. Luciana was once again invited to play, invited to birthday parties. Amanda Windemere continued to snub her and it was Luciana's mission in her life, unfortunately, to gain her friendship, despite what I tried to teach her about people, about being who she was, about being herself, and about self-esteem.

Lenora's friends no longer took my class, of course, but they did consult with me privately to have their fortunes told. And I continued to tell the truth, what I knew, when I knew it was right to do so.

"Why don't you just stop telling people's fortunes," Luciana yelled one day. "That's why everyone thinks you're a witch in the first place."

"Luciana, I am not a witch. But I am a fortune-teller. I don't know everything, but some things I do know. And I know it's important and right to share it."

"What do you know about me?" Luciana asked, her dark brown eyes full of hope. "Will Amanda Windemere invite me to her birthday party?"

"That I don't know for sure," I said, which was usually the right answer in so many regards.

"Well, then there's hope," Luciana said.

That was all anyone really wanted, I knew. Whether it was right or not. The hope.

Holly closed the diary. There were only a few more entries in the notebook, and she wanted to savor it, read it when she needed to hear her grandmother, spend time within her voice.

She was so glad she'd called her mother last week. Before bed, she would call her again. Just to say hello, to let her mother know she was trying, that she cared. That she loved her.

It was so true about the hope.

SEVENTEEN

The next day, Holly had driven all over Portland and a few of the towns just north and south of the city, introducing her pastas and sauces. Four gourmet shops had ordered a two-day trial, and one had even taken a week's worth of penne in vodka sauce and her spaghetti Bolognese. The four had also ordered a trial of her original pasta salad, Fusilli alla Holly.

That night, when she was looking through the menu for the previous course her grandmother had taught and looking over the notes she'd taken, she thought it was definitely time for the class to tackle the risotto alla Milanese, since they hadn't cooked at all last week. But when she went to get the recipe binder, it wasn't in its usual place next to the big bowl of fruit. She looked around the kitchen for it, on the table, on a chair, on a stool that had been slid under the center island, but the big white binder was nowhere to be found.

She searched the living room, under the sofa, under the cushions, behind the low rows of bookcases, not that the thick binder could have possibly fallen in that narrow space. She checked under her bed, under her old bed, in drawers, thinking perhaps she'd put it away with the diary, but no.

How could such a large, blinding white binder with the Camilla's Cucinotta label go missing in such a small house? It wasn't in the bathroom on the stool beside the tub, though Holly did find the *Cooking Light* magazine she'd been looking for yesterday. It wasn't in her car, not that she ever took the binder anywhere. It wasn't on the porch, on the tree swing, in the cabinets next to the boxed pastas, or in the refrigerator, where she'd once put it in those early weeks after her grandmother had died, thanks to a combination of exhaustion, fear, and grief.

An hour of fruitless searching led Holly to one conclusion. The binder wasn't anywhere. It was somehow . . . gone.

And tomorrow she had five pounds of pasta and eight quarts of sauces to deliver to her new clients. A class to teach tomorrow night.

And no recipe book.

■ ■ ■ ■

By the time class was set to start, Holly had cobbled together a few recipes with the help of old brochures and her grandmother's middle diary notebook, which turned out to be twelve handwritten recipes, none of which she'd used for the class so far. All was not lost.

Ha. All would be lost without that binder.

What had happened to it? She'd spent hours retracing her steps, going over the last time she'd held it. And every time she thought she'd figured out one last place it could possibly be, like the attic, it wasn't there.

She'd managed to lose a twenty-five-pound binder of her grandmother's life and legacy. It had to be somewhere in the house, somewhere she'd overlooked.

At the library she made copies of the diary recipes for veal scallopini and a fried asparagus that sounded scrumptious, then picked up the necessary ingredients at the supermarket across the bridge.

At five forty-five, when Holly realized Mia would be bursting in the door at any moment, full of stories about her mother and father and how they were back together,

Holly went outside to the swing and sat, facing the evergreens, trying to brace herself. "I really liked him," she whispered into the air, into the trees, trying to let it go, let *him* go.

At the sound of footsteps coming from across the road, Holly stood up, and there was Mia, in her tight jeans and knee-high boots, layers of slim-fitting T-shirts and earrings.

"Holly! Oh, my God, I have so much to tell you!" She wore mascara, Holly could see. And her dangling beaded earrings, which had morphed from dress-up earrings to everyday. Mia looked nothing like the girl Holly had met one month ago. She looked like one of those sophisticated tween stars on the Disney channel. Which was fine, but just not Mia.

On the way inside, Mia barely took a breath as she described how happy she was in ten different ways. "And it's all thanks to you, Holly! You helped me get rid of the fake bobblehead and because of that, my dad was totally single when my mother came back. Thank you, thank you, thank you." She squeezed Holly into a hug in the entryway, the very place she'd first met this heart stealer.

"I'm glad you're happy," Holly said, attempting a smile as she handed Mia an apron. Simon and Juliet walked in together, followed by Tamara a moment later, and Holly was relieved to turn her attention to them. "So, I have a bit of a problem, everyone. Actually a big problem. My grandmother's binder, with hundreds of her recipes, is gone. I've turned the house upside down looking for it. I managed to cobble together a menu for tonight and next week from some handwritten recipes I found, but without that binder, I'm sunk."

"Well, at least we have the copies of the recipes of the dishes we've already made," Tamara said. "And I'll bet some others you can re-create yourself, just by memory. Like the risotto alla Milanese you've made, what, a hundred times?"

That was true, Holly realized. She could probably close her eyes and re-create some of the recipes that way. The risotto. The gnocchi. Her spaghetti Bolognese and the penne in vodka sauce. Her Fusilli alla Holly and her new Heartbreak Rotini and Sausage Pasta Salad.

"And based on tasting, you can add what seems to be missing as you go along," Juliet added.

"You know, I really think I could do that," Holly said. "Amazing. Two months ago, I was afraid of a bowl of uncooked rice."

"Yup, it's amazing what time and experience can do," Simon added.

"That is so totally true," Mia said. "Because of time passing and the experience of not having each other and being with the wrong people, now my parents are getting back together."

"That's great, Mia!" Simon said, offering up a high five.

"So what's on the menu tonight?" Tamara rushed to ask before Mia could say one more word about wrong ex-loves.

Holly shot her a quick thank-you smile. "Tonight, we'll make a classic veal scallopini and a side that sounds delicious — fried asparagus."

"Yum, that even sounds good to me and I'm not crazy about vegetables," Mia said.

Holly handed out the recipes and they set to work, Mia and Juliet on the asparagus, and Holly, Tamara, and Juliet on the veal.

Mia glanced at the recipe on the island, then went to the cabinet for a large bowl and began snapping the ends off the asparagus. A stalk in her hands, she paused and said, "My wish is that my mom and dad will get remarried."

Tamara and Juliet glanced at Holly, then got busy opening the packages of veal and grabbing plates and bowls. They took turns lightly seasoning the veal with salt and pepper and rolling the pieces in flour. Holly crushed garlic cloves, each slam making her feel slightly better. And then worse.

"I bet they will," Mia said, reaching for a pot and filling it with water. Simon added salt it to and Mia turned on the burner. "I heard my mom say something about marriage last night when I woke up in the middle of the night and came down for a glass of water. They were on the couch, all lovey-dovey and totally making out. And I know I heard the word 'marriage' come out of my mom's mouth."

Just like that, Holly thought, her heart freshly breaking. One minute he was eating grapes out of her hand and carrying her upstairs, and the next he was making out with his ex-wife. And talking about marriage.

Simon checked the water, which wasn't yet boiling. "That's great that your folks are together again. I used to hold out hope that my wife and I could get back together, but I know it's not possible. And I know it's my daughter's fondest wish too."

Tears stung the backs of her eyes as Holly lay the veal in the frying pan with the crushed garlic and butter and olive oil. She blinked them away and kept her back to the class, watching the veal brown.

"Can't you try?" Mia asked him.

Holly removed the veal and placed it in a baking dish, and Juliet added the wine and mushrooms and onions to the pan. Holly's mouth began to water. She'd been so crazed trying to find the binder today and figuring out a menu for tonight's class and collecting the ingredients that she'd forgotten lunch. At least she had an appetite. That was a good sign. When she'd first arrived in Maine back in September, she couldn't eat for a week. Not even her grandmother's amazing breakfasts.

Simon dropped the asparagus in the salted boiling water. "A month ago, I would have tried if she were willing, but even if she were, I'm not sure my heart would ever be in it. Sometimes someone just takes a sledgehammer to your heart and even if you still have feelings for them, you can't ever quite feel the way you used to. The innocent part is all gone."

Huh. Holly had thought that was how Liam would feel.

Mia swept the asparagus ends into a paper towel and threw them in the compost bin. "I can see that. Like if Daniel broke up with me for someone else, I can't see taking him back as my boyfriend. Not after humiliating me. Like Jack Lourents did to Annabelle Martinour. He dumped her in the middle of Spanish class and then left the class holding hands with Angelina Casper. And then Angelina dumped him three periods later for someone else, and he tried to get back with Annabelle, and she totally took him back."

Tamara carefully poured the sauce from the pan onto the veal, scraping the bits, then slid the baking dish into the oven. "Sometimes people have to do that, try to forgive, give a second chance because they can't go on either way. And maybe it'll work and maybe it won't, but at least they know they tried."

Holly nodded at that. Not that it made her feel better.

"What if you don't want to try?" Juliet said. "What if you can't forgive or forget? What if you don't want to offer a second chance?"

Everyone stopped and stared at her for a moment.

"Then I guess you end up bitter and alone like Madeline Windemere," Mia said, "who won't take back her boyfriend, even though he's begged. And now that she wants him back, he's with someone else now."

Juliet stared at her. "No one wants to end up bitter and alone."

"Yeah, but people do," Mia said. "Because they don't know how to forgive."

"How did you get to be so smart at only twelve years old?" Simon asked, draining the asparagus. He and Mia took turns dipping the stalks in a mixture of beaten egg and milk, then coated each in bread crumbs and laid them in the pan of sizzling olive oil.

"Probably because I haven't had my heart smashed to smithereens yet," Mia said, sniffing appreciatively at the frying asparagus. "Oh my God, that looks so good. Anyway, I know my parents are going to get married and live happily ever after. How cool is it that I'll get to be in their wedding? I can't wait to do all that wedding stuff. Oh my God, Holly — you can cater the wedding!" Mia beamed at Holly and gave the asparagus a poke before flipping each stalk.

Maybe it was a good thing Holly had managed to lose the binder of recipes. Because that way she couldn't cater the wedding of the man she was in love with.

Over the next few days, Holly created a new binder of recipes. She'd typed up all her grandmother's handwritten recipes and added them, plus the ones she'd already handed out at the four classes so far. The binder was pathetically thin. She realized she could make a list of locals who'd taken the course in the past year or two and ask if they had held onto the copies of recipes, then copy them and add them. Her grandmother kept a ledger of her students dating back to the first class in 1962.

Holly flipped to the first page. Lenora Windemere. Annette Peterman. Jacqueline Thibodeaux and Nancy Waggoner. The last page contained twenty-five names with telephone numbers and a red stamp marked paid next to their names. Holly recognized seven of the names going back the past two years. Catherine Mattison and Julia Kentana were librarians at the tiny Blue Crab Library. Dale Smythe was the retired lady who now worked at the checkout counter in the general store. Margaret Peel managed the bookstore, and the Colemans were three generations of a family, grandmother, mother, and daughter who owned the bakery and café. Holly tried to imagine her grandmother, her mother, and herself working side by side in the kitchen on a daily basis.

Phone calls to everyone resulted in good news: everyone still had their recipes.

That afternoon Holly stopped at the bakery to collect the Colemans' recipes. Maeve Coleman, the grandmother, had taken the class on her own three years ago, then she and her daughter had taken it together two years ago, and last year the three Coleman women had taken it, resulting in over fifty recipes from the six-week course.

"What was it like, taking the course together?" Holly asked as Maeve delivered a mug of mochachino with a heart swirled in chocolate.

"Very revealing," Diana Coleman said as she set down a white chocolate and raspberry scone she insisted was on the house. "I learned a bit more than I wanted to about my mother and grandmother. And I learned how to make a great lasagna. I can't make risotto to save my life, though."

It amazed Holly that her grandmother had touched so many lives in so many different ways. Maeve and Diana sat down beside Holly and shared a story about the first Camilla's Cucinotta class they'd taken together, when they'd started arguing over something stupid and Diana had actually picked up the raw veal cutlet she'd been about to dredge and shoved it against her mother's chest with an angry, "Fine, do

345

everything *your* way!" Camilla had calmed them down and gotten their wishes into another pricey piece of veal and by the end of the class, the mother and daughter had each learned something about the other. Something that had set them on a path to opening the bakery together.

"I love hearing these stories," Holly said, sipping the delicious mochachino.

The door opened and in walked Liam and Mia. Holly froze, glancing behind them for Mia's mother, but she wasn't there.

"Hey, it's Holly!" Mia said, coming over to the table. "Oh, awesome, you're collecting recipes."

Holly managed to smile. She glanced up at Liam, afraid to let herself look at him too long.

"Hey," he said to Holly, holding her gaze. As if aware that Mia was watching them, he quickly added, "We're here for the Colemans' killer blondies."

"I won't keep you any longer," she said to Diana and Maeve, collecting the sheets of paper and tucking them inside her purse. "Thanks so much for your help." She turned to Mia, who was ogling the pastries in the display case. "Bye, Mia," she added. She shot a quick glance at Liam, and he was staring at her intently again with that

346

expression that said he was thinking ten things at once. She swore she saw *I miss you* there, and *I'm sorry.* And an *I still think about you.*

Holly rushed out and was halfway down the block when she heard his voice calling her. She stopped and turned around and he walked up to her. Right in front of Avery W's. She glanced in and Avery and her awful friend Georgina were in there, staring at them.

Look all you want. Nothing to see anyway, she thought, bracing herself for whatever he wanted to say. More *I'm sorry.* More *I didn't mean to hurt you.*

She took a deep breath and waited for Liam to say what he came out to say.

"I —" He just looked at her. "You look so pretty."

"I'd better go."

"Wait," he said, touching her arm. "How are you?"

"How am I?" she repeated like an idiot.

God, this was awkward. Awkward and painful and she had to go. Right then.

"Did you just want to ask me how I am, Liam?" *No, idiot, he came out to propose to you.*

His dark blue eyes were so intense on her. "I came out because I . . . it's good to see

347

you, Holly." He started to say something, then apparently decided not to.

She stared at him for a moment, then turned and hurried away, aware that he was standing there and watching her walk away.

She started to cry when she reached the bungalow. She scooped up Antonio to have something warm to hug against her. Then she blinked away the useless tears and set herself to work, re-creating the risotto the best she could, writing down what she did and what she thought she was supposed to do. It didn't taste half bad, even with canned broth. She checked her work against a few recipes online and realized she'd forgotten the white wine. But not the wish: that once again, she wouldn't let her grand-mother down.

Within a few days, Holly had added over a hundred recipes to the binder.

EIGHTEEN

Holly was making a béchamel sauce for her grandmother's famed lasagna, whisking the scalded milk into the roux of flour and butter, when she heard the knocking at the door again. She'd heard it earlier and thought someone was there, but it was just the November wind rolling off the bay and banging the screen door against the frame. She had to get that fixed. She went to make sure the screen door hadn't flapped open again, and Liam was standing there.

She was so surprised to see him that she was speechless for a moment.

"Can I come in?" he asked.

"Sure." She stepped back and wiped her flour-dusted hands on her apron, reminding herself to look everywhere but at him.

"Something smells amazing," he said as he walked into the kitchen. He glanced at the pots and pans on the stove, at the bowls on the center island, then stared out the window for a moment before turning to face her. "I'm afraid I'm going to say this wrong, so I'm just going to say it. I've come to realize something over the past couple of weeks."

"What did you come to realize?"

"That as much as I wanted to make Mia's dream for us come true, I can't. I got pulled back in by Veronica's big pronouncements of wanting to stay, wanting to be a family again, wanting back what we had before. I think I fell for that for a number of reasons, including the fact that I was afraid of what was starting between us."

She stared at him. "So you and Veronica *aren't* planning a second wedding?"

"No. I just don't have those feelings for her anymore, Holly. Two years is a long time to be on your own, raising a child — and one with a lot of hurt and anger over the divorce and her mother's abandonment. I've changed too much. Veronica tried very hard to create this new romance between us, and I tried too, but I don't love her, Holly. I don't know if it's because I really can't forgive her for how she's treated Mia these past two years or because I have changed. Probably both. I know there's no love there anymore. And that I have very serious feelings for someone else. You."

She finally let out the breath she'd been holding. "Liam, this is very complicated stuff. Suddenly I'm coming between you and your ex-wife, and Mia is involved —"

"No, Holly. You're not coming between us. My ex-wife came between *us* — for a little while."

"Does Mia know?"

He shook his head. "I just came from Veronica's hotel. I told her how I feel and I thought I'd just go home and sleep for two days, but instead of turning down my road, I pulled in your driveway. This is where I want to be, Holly. If you'll even give me another chance."

"I don't know, Liam. I don't know if I can believe in this, if I can handle how messy this is."

"Can we go back to the start of taking it slowly, then?" he asked.

"I really don't know."

"Then let me say this. I want to be with you, Holly. And not for any other reason than the fact that I'm crazy about you."

I'm crazy about you too. "I need to think about all this, okay?"

He stared at her, his blueberry-colored eyes so intense, so serious. She wanted to fling herself into his arms and take him upstairs, but she wasn't going to be stupid about this. He'd just been through something very emotionally heavy and adding herself to it didn't feel right. If a week or two passed and his feelings were the same, if he still believed what he'd said, then maybe she'd give this all a chance again. Maybe.

When Liam left, Holly dropped down on the living room sofa, mentally and physically exhausted. Antonio jumped up and lay his head on her thigh. She sat there for a good half hour, unsure and afraid. Then she called Tamara, hoping she'd be around for another tiramisu and talking session, but her cell phone went directly to voice mail. The moment she set her phone down, it rang, but it wasn't Tamara, it was Juliet.

"Holly? Are you busy?"

"Not at all."

"Can I stop over? I'm so confused. I'd really like to talk to you."

"Jump in your car and come right over," Holly said. "And I'm glad you called me."

"Me too."

In fifteen minutes, Juliet was sitting on the sofa next to Holly, a pot of lemon zinger tea, Juliet's favorite, on the coffee table in front of them.

"I did it," she said, her pretty hazel eyes

worried and tense. "I called Ethan and told him to come. But now that he's here, I'm . . . all shut down again. I picked a fight with him and he stormed out, booked a room of his own, and said he's flying back home in the morning, that he's tired of the false starts and has had it."

"And what did you say?"

"Nothing. I just let him go."

"Do you want to let him go, Juliet?"

She burst into tears and Holly put her arms around her, then went into the kitchen for a box of tissues. "When I saw him, when he appeared in the doorway of my room when he first arrived, what I felt was relief. Like, here's here, everything is going to be okay. But then he asked if I was ready to come home, and I said I wasn't sure, and he got upset and started pacing and telling me that he lost our daughter too. And that then he lost me and it wasn't fair, and it turned into a fight. And then he said he was booking a room and leaving in the morning."

"Can you imagine your life without him?" Holly asked.

Juliet sniffled and shook her head. "But I'm not ready to go home."

"Will you ever be ready?"

"I can't see how. He said we could move,

buy a new house near the lake so that I'll be reminded of here, yet get a fresh start. But how can we start fresh? I don't want to forget Evie."

"Maybe he just feels that a new home, one without her nursery, will help you begin to start living again."

"That's what he said. That I need to let Evie's memory become a part of me instead of something that keeps me in perpetual grief."

"That sounds right to me, Juliet. I know it's not the same thing, but it's close to what my grandmother said when your father died. How his memory would become a piece of you and when you needed him, needed to feel him with you, you could make his favorite dish and just the making of it, the eating of it, the putting the memory into the food, would bring you comfort."

"And it did. But this is different."

"Let's try, Juliet. Let's try making her favorite thing to eat. What was it?"

"Cheerios and scrambled eggs with a sprinkling of cheddar cheese."

"I assume the Cheerios weren't mixed in?"

She smiled. "No. She just liked to carry a baggie of Cheerios whenever we went out."

"So let's make her favorite meal, right now. We'll write up your recipe, exactly how you made it, and you'll decide on the final special ingredient."

She took a deep breath, nodded, and followed Holly into the kitchen. And for the next five minutes, there was the cracking of eggs and whisking of eggs and scrambling of eggs in a pat of butter. And just before the eggs set, Juliet stood over the pan and said, "I love you, baby girl," and then sprinkled on some cheddar cheese.

Holly took the pen and wrote *Sprinkle cheddar cheese.* And below that she added the final ingredient:

One true statement

They ate the eggs, which were delicious, and after a bracing cup of Camilla's espresso, a slightly stronger Juliet took the recipe and went back to the Blue Crab Cove, where hopefully she knocked on her husband's door.

One true statement. A perfect final ingredient.

Alone in the bungalow, too many thoughts racing through her head, Holly decided to create her own recipe for lasagna, since she finally had to admit she didn't love ricotta cheese and that for years lasagna was ruined for her because of that cheese. She would use a different kind, find the right one, and add the final ingredient of One True Statement, and another recipe would be hers.

I love Liam was one true statement that she didn't want to utter right then, so she stopped herself from thinking about him, about Mia, if he'd told her that he wasn't getting back together with her mother after all, that Mia would not be her mother's maid of honor.

She put away the flour and eggs and closed the recipe binder. *I'll lose myself in your life instead, Nonna,* Holly thought, pouring herself another cup of the espresso and settling on the sofa with it and her grandmother's diary.

October 1965
Dear Diary,

For years after little Richard Windemere died, Lenora Windemere tried to get rid of me. Someone from the health department would knock on my door to make sure my kitchen was spick-and-span, as I sold packaged foods. Someone from the town hall stopped by to discuss whether my home was properly zoned for business purposes, and I had to go through some rigmarole to get all the proper paperwork. But at least now all of that is in order. I am officially a business.

And then there were the rumors. Lenora's mother supposedly got food poisoning after trying the takeout dinners that I started selling. One of her friends almost choked to death on a bone — in the veal parmigiana she ordered special. Luckily, most people know that cutlets are *boneless.*

But still I stayed. This is my home. This is where I'm meant to be. And lately I've had this new feeling, that someone is meant to come home here. I have no idea what this means. Or for who. A cousin, maybe, from Italy. Luciana herself, when she's older?

Though, no, that's not it. Luciana will live a happy enough life far from Blue Crab Island; I know that with certainty.

But someone will come live in this house after me. Someone near and dear to my heart. Someone who'll love it here as I do.

"Me, Nonna," Holly said, her gaze on the painting of the olive tree. "That someone is me."

Just before midnight, Holly's cell phone rang. She grabbed it, hoping it was Juliet to say she wouldn't be at class on Monday, that she and her husband were leaving

357

together in the morning.

But it was Liam.

"Hey," he said, and she could picture him sitting on the back deck with a Shipyard beer beside him, the beagles scampering in the yard over their squeaky moose toy. He'd be resting his elbows on his knees and staring out at the water.

"Hey."

"I just wanted to say good night, Holly. And that I was thinking of you. I don't know how to exactly do this, if I'm supposed to give you space or what, but if there's one thing you can count on with me, I'm an honest guy. So I'm just going to tell you honestly that I'm sitting here thinking about you and wishing you were here. And one more thing. That I'm really sorry for hurting you."

Her heart pinged and she sat up in bed, hugging her knees up to her chest.

"I'm thinking about you too," she said. But she wouldn't say more. That she was scared to believe in this. That she wanted to run down Cove Road and sit beside him, watching the dogs, watching the water, watching their hands entwined.

"I'm glad you called," she said. "Very glad." And left it that.

"Sweet dreams," he said.

"Sweet dreams."

She put the cell phone back on the table and slipped the Po River stones out of the white pouch, holding them up to her face. "Can I trust this?" she asked as if the stones were a Magic 8 Ball.

Ask again later was the response she gave herself before turning off the lamp and snuggling back down under the covers, the stones in her hand.

NINETEEN

The next morning, Holly was having her own personal cheese tasting, from three kinds of blue cheese, including the king of cheese, Stilton, to a few different cream cheeses, trying to figure out which would work best as replacement for ricotta in the lasagna, when the bells jangled.

"Hello?" called out a woman's raspy voice, the kind affected by a lifetime of smoking.

Holly headed into the entryway, where a beautiful elderly woman, who indeed smelled faintly of clove cigarettes, stood holding a black and white canvas tote bag that read: *Friends of the Blue Crab Island Library.* She looked to be around her grandmother's age, seventy-five, perhaps even eighty. And she was also somewhat familiar, but Holly couldn't place her until she realized she'd noticed the woman at her grandmother's sparsely attended funeral. Her hair was luminous silver in a bun high atop her head with two diamond-encrusted pins poking out of the top. She wore black pants with a long white sweater, a sheer red silk scarf at her neck.

"My name is Lenora Windemere," she said, and Holly almost gasped. "I knew your grandmother. I took a cooking class here over forty years ago." There was no emotion in her voice, no nostalgia. This was not about reminiscing.

Holly smiled and held out her hand, and Lenora took it in both of hers for a moment and then let go.

She reached into the tote bag, her many gemstone rings, including an enormous diamond, sparkling on her fingers. "I found this in town." She pulled out the Camilla's Cucinotta recipe binder and handed it to Holly.

Holly did gasp this time. "The recipe binder! Oh, thank God! I've looked every-where for it. Where did you —"

"I found it in town," she repeated, her hazel eyes steady on Holly's.

You found it in your granddaughter's bistro, in the kitchen, most likely, as Avery prepared for the "Italian segment" of her own cooking class. That Holly knew with Camilla Con-stantina certainty.

She clutched the binder against her chest,

so relieved to have it back.

Either Avery Windemere or a friend of hers had stolen the binder. And Lenora had either found out or come across it and brought it back. She was telling Holly that her granddaughter didn't need to resort to crime to get rid of the competition, or that Holly *wasn't* any competition, or possibly, that the binder *belonged* to Camilla Constantina and now her granddaughter — and belonged in this bungalow. Regardless, Lenora was saying something.

"Thank you," Holly said, holding her gaze. "Very much."

Lenora stared at her for a moment, perhaps seeing Camilla in her features, in her dark eyes and hair. She glanced around for a moment, stopping at the blackboard menu noting today's pastas. She opened her mouth to speak, and for a moment Holly thought she might buy one of the pastas, but she just eyed the case and walked out.

The moment Lenora Windemere left, Holly went to a copy center in Portland and made two copies of the binder. The original would always remain in the kitchen, where it belonged, but she'd have the copies up in the attic just in case Madeline Windemere grew up with notions of stealing the recipes one day. It was almost comical to think about, but Holly wouldn't put anything past those Windemeres. On the way back, as she drove past Avery W's bistro, she thought about stopping in with the binder and confronting Avery somehow. She knew Avery was the thief — and there was only one reason why Avery would feel threatened by that binder. Because Holly's previously dissed skills were serious competition, after all. But the fact that Lenora Windemere knew Avery had stolen the recipe binder — whether to use it for her own Italian segment or to simply leave Holly recipe-less, or *both* — was all the satisfying justice Holly needed.

Back at the bungalow, Holly was layering the lasagna (she'd used store-bought sheets of pasta) when the bell jangled. There was no way she was leaving her béchamel to turn into sludge another time, so she called out, "Come on in."

Two animated young women, one with striking white-blond hair and the other with a mass of auburn curls practically to her waist, stopped under the archway. "Hi, we heard you offer a basic Italian cooking class?" said the blonde.

Holly finished whisking the white sauce and layered it on, then added another layer of meat sauce. "That's right, I do. My name is Holly Maguire, and I inherited Camilla's Cucinotta from my grandmother, who taught the class for decades. The fall course is in session right now, but the winter course will start in January."

The redhead said, "We heard she used to be called The Love Goddess and told fortunes. Do you tell fortunes too?"

Holly added the final layer of pasta, sprinkled on just a bit of Parmesan, having learned the hard way that too much would turn bitter. "No, I didn't inherit my grandmother's gift of fortune-telling, but I did inherit her gift of cooking."

Well, well. She'd said that with a straight face. Holly smiled. It was true. She *had* inherited her grandmother's gift. In her own way, her own style. She belonged in this kitchen.

"Oh, too bad," the blonde said. "We both just got dumped by our boyfriends. Well, not boyfriends so much as jerks we were dating and thought were our boyfriends. We were hoping we could learn to cook our favorite kind of food *and* find out what was in store for us."

Holly smiled. "Sorry about that. There's no fortune-telling in class, but if you read the brochure, you'll see that each recipe calls for special ingredients, like a fervent wish or a happy memory. It seems that wishing and hoping and dreaming and remembering can be even more helpful than knowing what's going to happen."

The pair looked at each other and smiled. "I love that. So can we sign up for the class? We're roommates and seniors at USM and we're totally sick of ordering Chinese food. We'd love to learn to make that, for instance. Lasagna? It smells amazing."

"It just so happens I'm planning to put this lasagna on the first week's lesson for the winter/spring course, which will start the first week of January."

"Awesome. Sign us up."

As the girls handed over checks for $120 each and wrote their names and telephone numbers in Camilla's old ledger, Holly realized she'd done it, she'd officially signed up two total strangers for the course. Herself.

"If you don't mind my asking, where did you hear about my course?"

"We were having lunch in DoodleBop's Café in Portland, and I had the most delicious pasta salad with sausage and sun dried tomatoes, and when I raved about it, the owner mentioned that a woman on Blue Crab Island makes it and that she also offered an Italian cooking class and that your information was up on the bulletin board. So here we are. Do you have any of the pasta salad today? I'd love to take a container home."

Holly slid the lasagna into the oven, then accompanied the young women into the entryway and showed them the pasta menu. They each bought a pasta salad.

And she'd earned these students with her own cooking. With her own recipe.

Thank you, Nonna, she said silently up to the ceiling.

Liam called that night. And the night after. Each time they had the same conversation, nothing more and nothing less. But his voice was becoming familiar to her again.

On the third night, she stared at the old-fashioned alarm clock on the bedside table, willing it to turn to ten o'clock, when he usually called, and anticipating the chimes of her cell phone. But it was the doorbell that rang.

And there he was, standing on her porch in his leather jacket and jeans, his hands shoved in his pockets, his expression saying *I need to be with you.*

She pulled open the door and he stepped inside, then she took his hand and led him upstairs to her bedroom.

As they stood in her room, standing across from each other holding both hands, Holly asked, "When will you turn into a pumpkin?"

"Not till tomorrow at three thirty, when Mia's bus pulls in. She's staying at her mother's hotel tonight. I told Mia that her mother and I would not be getting back together, and she was upset and furious and crying, and then her mother came and picked her up to assure her that she was staying this time, that even though we weren't getting back together, she was committed to being her mother, to living in Portland. I don't think Mia believes that. I think she needed the wedding to believe that."

"I can understand that. Poor Mia. This has to be very difficult stuff to go through at twelve. I'm just glad her mother is committing to her. Do you think she'll really stay?"

"She did buy a house. That's something. And it's one of those deals in which she'll lose a chunk of money if she backs out. She's serious."

"Well, I'm very happy to hear that, for Mia's sake."

He held one of her hands up to his face,

then kissed her palm. "I've missed you, Holly."

"I've missed you too."

He pulled her against him, and Holly closed her eyes, happiness flooding her from the tips of her toes to her brain, which wasn't saying anything but *okay.* Even her warring shoulder angels hadn't made an appearance.

And in less than a minute, their clothes were once again a tangled heap on the floor.

Holly woke at three a.m., likely because a strong arm was slung across her stomach. She was startled for a moment at how unexpected it was to find Liam beside her, in her bed. She stared at the fringe of dark lashes against the tops of his cheeks, noted the way his dark wavy hair tousled over his forehead. She leaned over and gently kissed his slightly stubbly cheek, taking in the utter gorgeousness of him.

She tried to sleep but it was useless, so after a half hour of tossing and turning and fearing she'd wake Liam, she got up and went downstairs to make a cup of chamomile tea. She brought it into the living room and picked up her grandmother's diary.

May 1965

Dear Diary,

I have a boyfriend. Oh, how silly it feels to use that word. His name is Fredward Miller. He is not Italian. He is not Armando, not even close, but I like putting on my lipstick and perfume and being taken out to a restaurant on Saturday nights. After dinner, he likes to take me to the beach and stroll along, skipping pebbles in the water. He talks a lot about how the ocean is so vast that it reminds him to dream big. He's a candy salesman, of all things. He supplies chocolate bars and lollipops and those Necco wafers I just love to accounts all over the New England area. You can imagine how much candy is in the bungalow for Luciana. She hasn't met him yet; I'm not sure I want to introduce them. Right now, I like my Saturday nights, and he's away selling his candy most weekdays.

Fredward thinks I'm exotic, but I'm not. I suppose for here, I'll always be the Eye-talian from Italy with the heavy accent. I'm so at home here on Blue Crab Island that I don't feel so different from everyone else, until of course, I feel someone's eyes on me, and I'll find Lenora Windemere staring at me from across the street or up the aisle in the general store.

I know how things will eventually end with Fredward. I also know that I'll have many other boyfriends and that none of them will be anything like Armando either. But I am not looking for love, just companionship. I have this feeling, although Luciana is only seven, that she will seek something other than a great love. She will look for companionship, in lifetime form, and that is okay. I know that Luciana will be fine. Fine for her, which is all that matters.

What I know about love is this: when you have it, you know it.

I know it, Nonna, she thought, *but I'm scared of it.* What if Liam changed his mind again? What if he went back to Veronica? What if, when Mia learned that her father and her beloved cooking teacher were involved, that she never forgave Holly?

What if, what if, what if?

Holly set the notebook down on the sofa and patted the space beside her for Antonio, who'd waddled into the living room. He jumped up and sat down practically on her lap, resting a paw and then his little gray chin on her thigh.

She had no idea her grandmother had had

boyfriends. It wasn't something Camilla had ever discussed. And the few times Holly had asked her if she'd ever thought about dating or getting married again, Camilla had said she'd had her great love and there would never be another like Armando and she'd never settle for a lesser love. Though she'd been widowed so young, Camilla Constantina had never remarried. But she'd had her boyfriends, her companionship, her heart full of her memories of her Armando.

It was scary to think that Holly would have married John Reardon and been living a completely different life in California, had he asked, of course. She would not have met Liam Geller. Actually, she likely would have. She would have come to Blue Crab Island when her grandmother died and she would not have been able to sell the house and let Camilla's Cucinotta go. She would not have done that, John Reardon or not. Not that she had any idea how all that would have worked. But it was a moot point, anyway.

And what she felt for Liam was different than what she'd felt for John, even in the beginning, when she'd been so madly in love she'd uprooted herself three thousand miles away. She'd been crazy about John. But Liam was inside her heart in a different way that she couldn't quite explain to herself.

" 'Night, Antonio," she said to the cat, giving him a pat on his head.

And then she headed back upstairs to her bedroom, where Liam lay sleeping, his arm up over his head. She crawled in beside him, took his hand, lay it back across her stomach, and closed her eyes.

TWENTY

The next day, instead of floating like last time, Holly felt her feet were firmly on the floor. There was something very eyes-wide-open about last night. And this morning, after they made love again and showered together, steaming up the shower door more than the hot water. She made him Juliet's scrambled eggs, which he pronounced delicious, and gave him two strong cups of Camilla's espresso, and then he left to go home and get dressed for three-quarters of a day of work. He wanted to be home when Mia's bus arrived, unsure what her mother may have told her.

Her one true statement into the eggs: *I hope Mia will be okay.* Holly wasn't sure if she'd turn up for the class that night or if she'd rage at her father for the evening instead.

At six o'clock, Tamara and Simon arrived — giggling. Holly mock-narrowed her eyes at them and said, "I noticed you arrived together last week too. Is something going on I should know about?"

"Oh, something is going on, all right," Simon said, taking Tamara's hand and kissing it.

Well, well, indeed. Holly smiled. "You make a fine couple."

"We're taking things very slow," Tamara said. "Not rushing in like fools."

"Even if I *was* invited to a family wedding three months from now," Simon said, grinning.

"They don't call this The Love Goddess' Cooking School for nothing," Tamara added, smiling at Holly.

My cup runneth over, she thought. Until Juliet walked in, a tall, handsome man beside her with world-weary eyes. Her husband. Now her cup had tipped. "Hi, Juliet."

Juliet was not wearing gray. Or black. Or dirty-beige, as Tamara called khaki. She wore an almost iridescent lavender-colored sweater over dark jeans, her feet encased in brown suede boots and not her usual gray skimmers. "Hi. Holly, this is Ethan Frears, my husband. Ethan, Holly Maguire. And this is Simon March and Tamara Bean."

Hellos and handshaking later, Juliet asked

if Ethan could audit the class, since they were leaving the next day, going home to Chicago, and Juliet wanted Ethan to meet the people who helped give her back her spirit.

"Oh, Juliet," Holly said, running up to her and squeezing her slight body into a hug. "I'm so, so glad. And, yes, of course you can stay for the class," she added to Ethan, who was holding on to his wife's hand.

Holly glanced at the clock. Almost six fifteen, and no Mia. She collected the recipes for tonight's class and handed them out.

"Lasagna," Ethan said. "I've always wanted to know how to make that."

"And it's my special recipe," Holly said. "With a little help from Juliet on the final ingredient."

Holly noticed Ethan's gaze slide down the recipe. One true statement. He squeezed Juliet's hand.

And so for the third time that week, Holly set out to make her lasagna. She didn't have to go over the steps for making the pasta; she heard Juliet teaching her husband how to make a well in the pasta and crack in the egg. Once he had his ball of dough, Simon, who joined the pasta team in his delight at having another guy around, showed Ethan how to knead it, to fold it and twist it until it was elastic.

"So you're leaving tomorrow?" Simon asked the Frears. "Which is worse, the Chicago winters or the Maine?"

Juliet smiled. "Chicago by a landslide. But we're not going back to Chicago to stay. We're subletting our house and Ethan is taking a leave of absence from the law firm and we're traveling around Europe for an entire month. First stop, Milan, Italy."

Holly smiled. "Land of Camilla Constantina. Send me a postcard?"

"You bet," she said, the most hopeful of smiles on her face before turning back to the pasta, which her husband was having a heck of time sliding through the pasta machine. Simon came to the rescue, an old pro now.

Tamara was on the béchamel sauce, whisking the scalded milk into the roux of flour and butter, and Holly on the signature Bolognese when the front door slammed open against the frame and Mia came rushing in, stopping under the archway, tears streaming down her face. She stared at Holly.

"I hate you. I hate you. I hate you! I just want you to know that!"

"Mia, I —"

"My dad told me everything," she

376

shouted. "This is all your fault! How could you steal him away from my mother?" Tears fell down her cheeks and she stood there for a moment just sobbing. But when Holly stepped forward, Mia screamed, "I hate you!" And then she went running out, the screen door slamming behind her.

Holly excused herself to call Liam and rushed upstairs with her cell phone, bursting into tears the moment she walked into her bedroom and closed the door. She dialed his number and he picked up on the first ring.

"Mia?"

"Holly. She just left. She ran in sobbing and yelling that I betrayed her and that she hates me, and then she just ran out. I was hoping she went back home, but clearly she didn't."

He was silent for a moment. "I'll go look for her. You stay put."

This time she wasn't the comforter. She was the Jodie.

"Holly — everything will be okay. Okay?"

She burst into tears again, trying to keep silent. "Okay," she managed. She dropped down on her bed and took a deep breath, picking up the white satin pouch. "Please let this work out okay," she said to the stones, and she set the pouch down on the bed and went back downstairs.

For the next hour, the two couples cleaned up every speck of the kitchen while Holly paced the living room, coming in every few minutes to help, but being shooed back out with a glass of wine. With the twenty-fifth assurance that she'd be all right, Holly walked both couples to the door.

"I promise to stay in touch," Juliet said. "You'll be getting that postcard from Milan."

"I'd better," Holly said, hugging her tight. And after goodbyes all around, Juliet in her lavender sweater and her husband, his arm around her shoulder, were gone, heading up Blue Crab Boulevard.

"It's a nice night for a romantic walk," Holly said absently as Tamara and Simon put on their coats, hoping Mia was safe and sound at home and not in one of her four places — three places, Holly corrected, as the swing on her side yard was not going to be one of her safety zones tonight. Tears stung her eyes and she wiped them away.

"She'll be okay," Tamara said, rubbing Holly's back. "It may take some time, but she'll be okay."

"She thinks I betrayed her, though. And she's twelve."

"A twelve-year-old who's going through her first romance and who's been talking about betrayals and breakups for weeks," Simon said. "She'll come to understand that you didn't betray her."

"I hope so."

Simon put his hand on Holly's shoulder. "If my daughter can come around, anyone can, trust me. And wait till she finds out I'm dating the mastermind of her space-wizard bedroom."

Holly offered a brief smile and squeezed his hand. "Thanks for everything tonight, you two. Now go. Make out or something."

"Or something," Tamara said, a gleam in her eyes as she and Simon headed out, hand in hand, toward his car.

Holly waved as the car left the driveway and then she sat down on the porch, wrapping her sweater tight around her and straining to hear down Cove Road, as if Mia's voice could carry that far.

An hour later, no call. Which meant Liam hadn't found Mia yet. He'd call to assure Holly that Mia was safe, Holly knew that. But just when she was about to call him, her phone rang. He'd found Mia in their unfinished basement, which they used for storage and the washer and dryer. She'd been lying in her sleeping bag, which she'd dusted off and unfolded next to the dryer. Liam hadn't even thought to go down there, since Mia was usually scared of the basement, but when he'd heard the dryer, he went down and found her, leaning against it for company and warmth. She'd been there the entire time.

"She's so exhausted and upset that she didn't push me away," Liam said. "She let me hold her for a half hour without saying a word. And then I picked her up and carried her to her room and stayed with her for a while till I thought she was asleep, but as I was tiptoeing out, she broke my heart."

Holly braced herself. "What did she say?"

"She sat up in bed and said, 'Daddy? I'm really sorry about all the stuff I said. I just wish things were different.' And I said, 'I know, sweetheart.' And then we talked for another half hour about how you can care about someone very much but just not love them the way you once did, and she started crying again and said she was afraid I'd feel that way about her, and I assured her I never would, that it didn't work like that with parents and kids, and she finally let it all out about her mother having left for those two years, that she was afraid I'd up and do that too one day, that that was why she wanted us back together so bad, so that she'd at least have one of us at any given time."

"Oh, Mia," Holly breathed. "What a thing to have to worry about."

"Give us a few days, okay? I know I keep saying that. I guess I might be saying that a lot. But I'm not going anywhere, Holly. And if you need me, I'm here. Okay?"

"Okay."

The last time he needed a few days, he was full of I'm sorrys for hurting her.

She wondered if anyone in the state of Maine knew how to make *sa cordula.* She should just get it over with now. In her dreams, he would like it and she'd know he was The One, her great love.

But Holly was beginning to think that there was no real Great Love. That maybe there was just love. And like her grandmother had written, when you had it, you knew it.

That night Holly and Antonio curled up on the sofa, both of them staring into the fire that Holly had dared start in the stone fireplace. So far, the house had not burned down. Her heart feeling like it might burst any second, Holly reached for her grandmother's diary to read the fourth and final one, hoping to lose herself in Camilla's world, find comfort in her voice.

June 1966
Dear Diary:

I always knew I had the gift of knowing. As a child, I would suddenly get a notion, so strong, such as a man proposing, and sometimes it would be accompanied by the image of a man I couldn't quite see, on one knee, a ring proffered in a velvet box. And then I would actually see Adrianna, my mother's young sister, slipping into the yard from the chicken coop, her cheeks flushed, her eyes full of love and hope. And if I watched for a full five minutes, I'd see Guiseppe, the neighbor's son, sneak away in the opposite direction. And I'd know that a proposal was coming. Sometimes I would see more in my mind, sometimes less. And sometimes there would be nothing. I realized the nothing was fine too.

I can remember having the flashes as a little girl of three — seeing things with my mind's eye that hadn't happened yet. Such as Daddy coming home from the war. Such as our married neighbor kissing our other married neighbor. I was so young and the flashes sometimes so confusing.

In one of the flashes, I was picking stones from the shore of the Po River, so when we went there on one of our many family picnics, I chose the three I remembered in the flash. They were just there, set in a semicircle at the water's edge, waiting for me. When I picked them up, I remember feeling a tingle in my hand. I slipped them into the pocket of my shorts and they've been with me ever since. They are not the source of my knowing, of course, but I was meant to choose them for a reason. I believe they heighten my knowing. As I would hold them and look at someone or think of someone, I would sometimes feel something very strongly when I otherwise would not.

Anyway, the more I started telling fortunes, the more I used the stones, since people responded to them so well, as though they were crystal balls. That made it easier for people to accept. Especially Luciana. She could blame the stones for my "witchery," not me.

She will go her own way as I went my own way, off to America with Armando at twenty-two, saying good-bye to my homeland. My daughter has never gotten over being different from the other girls in Maine and that never changed. But all the flashes

I've gotten about Luciana have been fine. That she'd settle down with the dull man, *si*. But she would be happy. And she would not have a dull child. No.

The child, my grandchild, will be *mine*. It won't be obvious. The child will not have my gift of knowing. She will not be able to scramble eggs without sloshing the egg out of the bowl. She will not be full-blooded Italian like her mother and grandmother and great-grandmother. She would be half of what I started by coming to America. But she will be mine. There will be an unbreakable bond that will carry on. Of that I am sure as I am of anything.

The diary left Holly with the urge to look through Camilla's photo collection, so she headed upstairs to the beautiful mahogany wardrobe in her bedroom for the stacks upon stacks of albums. Holly had looked through them over the years. Black-and-whites of Camilla as a young girl, with shiny black hair so long it almost reached her waist. Polaroids of Camilla and Armando having great fun, in the yard of the house Camilla had grown up in. In front of quite possibly every lighthouse in Maine, one of Armando's weekend missions. Snapshots of Camilla pregnant in her maternity dresses, achingly beautiful. Way too many shots of Antonio doing nothing more than staring at the camera looking very bored. And album after album of Luciana growing up, reading books in the very living room Holly had been sitting in. Helping her mother cook in the kitchen that had changed Holly's life. One album was devoted to shots Camilla had taken at Luciana's wedding. And there were more than twenty devoted to Holly, of visits down to Newton, Massachusetts. Of summers spent on Blue Crab Island. There were several of Holly and Juliet in flowered bathing suits and sunglasses. In Holly's favorite, they were jumping off a low cliff into the ocean, holding hands. Holly would scan it and email it to Juliet.

And there was a final photo, Holly's favorite, that she'd looked at every time she sat down at the dressing table to put on a little makeup and blow-dry her hair. The photo was tucked inside the mirror's beveled edge. Camilla had taken the photo with the digital camera Holly had bought her for her last birthday. She'd held it out at arm's length and snapped the picture of her and Holly on the porch, the night before she died.

"I miss you, Nonna," she said to the photograph, picking it up and kissing it before putting it back. She was about to put the albums away when she heard the doorbell ring. She glanced at the clock. Almost midnight.

It had to be Liam.

She hurried downstairs, opened the door, and there he was.

"I just needed to see you and give you this," he said, pulling her into a hug. Then he kissed her, full on the lips, looked into her eyes, and squeezed her hand before turning to walk away. At the other side of Blue Crab Boulevard, he stopped, turned, and held up his hand, and she held up hers.

TWENTY-ONE

"Give us a few days" turned into a week. She had not heard from Liam since his midnight hug last Monday night. She'd spent the time creating more pasta salads for her gourmet clients, signing up *three more* students for the winter course, working on the lasagna, going back to ricotta cheese but using less and making up the difference with Stilton and adding a touch more garlic. She'd also received a call from an old high school friend of Francesca's who was planning a wedding in Portland next summer and scheduled a tasting, which Holly celebrated by taking Tamara and Simon out for Mexican food. She'd been eating so much pasta, so much Italian food, that she'd almost forgotten there were other cuisines. The three of them made a vow to go out to dinner once a month, a different ethnicity every time. Next up was Indian.

Holly was so busy — so happily busy, with

her own work, her own life — that she'd barely given her love life a passing thought. Well, in between recipes and the call for a wish or a memory or a true statement. And then how much she cared about the two Gellers would flood over her, sometimes so much that she'd have to sit down for a second and a take a deep breath. She also had strange dreams of both of them. In one, she and Mia were in the rowboat, and Madeline Windemere and the M Club and Daniel Dressler were suddenly in the boat too, and then there was Liam, swimming in the ocean, away from them. Her grandmother had once told her that dreams were impossible to analyze and seek deep meaning from, except for the classic taking-a-test-you-forgot-to-study-for or going-to-school-without-pants ones.

Just before class was about to start Monday evening, Holly saw something slide under the door. It was one of Mia's strawberry-scented envelopes. She held it up to her nose for a moment, then hurried to open it.

Dear Holly,
     Sorry about the stuff I said. I don't really hate you. Can I still come to class? If the

388

answer is yes, just open the front door.

Love, Mia Geller

Holly's heart lurched and she pulled open the front door. Mia stood there, biting her lip, her dark blue eyes worried yet full of hope. Holly opened her arms in a hug. Relief flooded Mia's face and she rushed over, squeezing Holly tight.

"Are you mad at me?" Mia asked, looking up at her.

"No. I understand why you were so upset."

Mia came inside, leaving the door open for Tamara and Simon, who had yet to arrive. "I still am. What was the point of all that wishing and remembering if what I wanted didn't come true?"

Holly took both her hands and held on to them. "What I've learned, Mia, and what my grandmother always said, is that the whole point is the wishing and remembering — not if what you want happens, not if remembering hurts. Because when you wish for something, you're asking. And when you ask, you're trying. And all anyone can really do is try, right?"

She shrugged a bit. "I guess. I just wouldn't mind getting what I want."

Holly smiled. "That goes for everyone."

"Well, the good news is that my dad and I

have done a ton of talking the past week — real talking, about my mom and what happened two years ago when she left. And how he's changed as a person and a father, etcetera, etcetera, and how he wished he could make every one of my dreams come true, but sometimes, he just won't be able, that life will step in or whatever, and that all he can do is be there, always."

"That sounds good to me, Mia. Right and good."

She nodded. "Yeah. I guess I get it. I feel better about everything, anyway. Oh — do you know who has turned out be a really good boyfriend? Daniel. Even though his parents are happily married, he really helped me understand some stuff."

Maybe that's why Daniel Dressler had been in Holly's dream. "Sounds like a keeper."

Mia brightened and followed Holly into the kitchen, where she put down her backpack and tied on her apron. "He's awesome. Oh, hey, I never did get to show you a picture from the Fall Ball. Do you want to see one?"

"I've been waiting and waiting," Holly said, tapping Mia's nose.

Mia smiled and reached into the front section of her backpack, pulling out a soft photo album. She flipped through several photos of herself solo, of her and her dad, and a few of her parents during their two weeks of . . . discovery, Holly had come to think of it, and then Mia pulled out one of herself and Daniel in front of the trees outside her house. Mia looked so beautiful in her lavender dress, her hair slightly curled in long tousles, the beaded earrings glinting in the setting sun. Daniel, a very good-looking kid with alternative rocker hair, wore a suit and tie with black Converse sneakers.

Holly grinned. "You look great together."

"Talking about us?" Tamara asked as she and Simon walked into the kitchen, hand in hand with matching we're so-in-love goofy smiles.

Mia's mouth dropped open. "Omigod, are you two a couple now? That's so cool! When did *that* happen?"

"Well, we were actually both standing in the pasta aisle of the supermarket — I was reaching for penne and Tamara for fettucine and we both realized who we were at the same time, and I said something about always overcooking the penne, and Tamara invited me over to her place for a penne-slash-fettucine cookathon, and yadda, yadda, yadda, we're a couple."

"You yadda yadda yadda-ed over the best part," Tamara said and they burst into laughter.

"Uh, am I missing something?" Mia asked, glancing at everyone. "Is this about sex?"

"Old *Seinfeld* TV show reference," Holly said, handing Tamara and Simon aprons.

"Is everyone over thirty this weird?" Mia asked.

Simon dramatically dipped Tamara as though they'd been dancing the tango. "Yes."

"So I guess it's just us four," Tamara said as Simon pulled her up. "Did you know that Juliet went home with her husband, Mia?"

"No, but I'm really happy to hear it. I hope she won't be so sad anymore."

"That goes double for all of us," Holly said. "Well, we've got some osso buco and risotto alla Milanese to make. The kitchen awaits."

"So, are you and my dad in love or what?" Mia asked as she unwrapped the veal shanks that Holly had bought from her favorite butcher in Portland.

"We're taking things slow," Holly said. "One day at a time. Getting to know each other."

Simon shook flour onto a large plate.

"That's smart."

Tamara checked the recipe, then seasoned the flour with salt and pepper and dredged the veal in the flour, laying each shank on a clean plate. "I love that Simon and I got to know each other as friends first instead of going on a bunch of awkward dates. Our first kiss was so natural, like an extension of our friendship, but with firecrackers and a marching band."

"Do you really hear a marching band when you kiss?" Mia asked, raising an eyebrow as she carefully crushed a clove of garlic.

Simon leaned over and dipped Tamara in a kiss, getting flour all over his apron. "The answer is yes."

"Really?" Mia asked, turning toward Tamara. "You too?"

"Yup," Tamara confirmed.

"So it's like that for everyone?" Mia asked. "Even adults who are used to kissing? The first time Daniel kissed me — on the lips — I heard the roaring of the ocean. I almost fainted. And then every time after, it's like my iPod has turned on and a song just comes on, even if we're standing in that alcove between locker banks and the only sounds are people yakking and the principal droning announcements over the loudspeaker."

"Old people fall in love too," Simon said. "Even, gasp, old people over thirty, like me. And I'm thirty-*four.*"

"So's my dad," Mia said. "He hears his iPod too?"

Tamara flipped the veal shanks at the stove. "I'll bet he does." She slid a smile at Holly.

"My eighty-two-year-old grandparents hear music when they kiss," Simon said. "Love strikes at any age. And you know what? When your heart is full of gooey, mushy love, sad memories get pushed really far back in there. So since the ossco buco calls for a sad memory, I'll put into this sizzling skillet having to leave Tamara last night because my neighbor called and said her crazy cat had crawled from her little terrace onto mine and into my window and wouldn't be coaxed out even with leftover salmon that she put on her terrace. So I go home to free the cat, and guess who used my living room as a litter box?"

Mia laughed. "Not all cats can be as cool as Antonio."

They all glanced at the cat, sitting on his carpeted window perch, licking his paw and swiping his face with it.

Holly smiled as she peeled a lemon and

394

placed the rind on the plate with the orange rind. "Into this gremolata of lemon and orange rind and crushed garlic, I put my sad memory of how Antonio hated me when I first moved here. He wouldn't come near me. But now he loves me. Don't you, Tony?" she cooed, going over to his perch and scooping him up for a kiss on the head. And instead of desperately trying to get away, as he did in September and early October, Antonio rubbed against her chin, purring.

"My sad memory, Mr. Veal Shank," Tamara said into the sauté pan, "is seeing the bridesmaid dress my sister expects me to wear at her wedding." She removed the browned veal and placed it on a large plate, then added the vegetables and wine to the pan and turned up the heat, re-adding the veal. "My perfect younger sister of the *usually* good taste chooses a taffeta dress with a big honking bow on the butt. Why? The one time I wish my mother would overrule her, and of course she loves it too."

Everyone laughed, then oohed and ahhed at the delicious smell of the osso buco as it mingled with the garlic and oil. Mia reported that the broth was simmering (Holly was using the easy version of the risotto recipe, which used canned broth instead of marrow), and poured the oil and arborio rice into a butter-coated pan, and when the pan began to sizzle, Mia added the saffron threads, turning the rice a beautiful golden yellow. She was careful, per the recipe, to slowly add the broth, watching over the rice as it absorbed the liquid, adding, stirring, adding, stirring, until the consistency was just right, slightly firm yet tender. What a student — apprentice — she'd turned out to be. The risotto called for both a wish and a sad memory, and Holly wondered what Mia would say.

"I wish I'll forget the sad memory of telling Holly I hated her because it's really not true," Mia said, looking from the pot to Holly and back again. "I was just so mad. I'm still a little weirded out about my father having girlfriends but if he's going to like someone besides my mom, I'm glad it's you." She stared at Holly for a moment and it seemed she wanted to say something else, but she just took a deep breath and smiled.

Holly pulled Mia into a hug. "Thank you."

And then Mia poured the gremolata over the osso buco, Simon ladled the almost-perfect risotto, and they sat down to eat, everyone declaring the sad memories among the most delicious yet.

■ ■ ■ ■

At ten o'clock that night, Holly's cell phone rang. She'd been too wired to attempt sleep, and so she was trying to hang her new fancy curtain rods for the velvet drapes she'd bought. The rod looked slightly higher on the right. Huh. Who knew she'd need a carpenter — or maybe a hot architect — to put up something as simple as a curtain rod.

She rushed to the phone. Liam, of course.

"I'd like to take you on another official date," Liam said. "But this time one that does involve food."

She smiled and moved over to the window, looking out at the stars, at the almost full moon. From her bedroom window she could see the treetops that lined Cove Road. She could almost see the bay, a sliver of it. "Does it involve a rowboat in November?"

"Nope. Feel free to dress up too."

A dress-up date. She left the slightly crooked curtain rod and slid under the covers and turned off the lamp, wondering if he was planning on a restaurant or a fancy picnic in the woods. She slowly drifted off to sleep with visions of herself in a ball gown and Liam in a tux, spinning around in a wooded clearing full of wildflowers.

■ ■ ■ ■

Holly's dressiest dress was a red wrap dress that made her look curvier than she actually was, so she went with that, pairing it with simple, sexy, black high heels. She dusted on some makeup, fluffed her hair, and spritzed on a bit of her grandmother's Italian perfume. And when she looked in the floor mirror in the corner of her bedroom, the woman staring in disbelief at her was not the same brokenhearted woman who'd taken the red-eye from California, clutching all her possessions in a pathetic duffel and a plastic bag.

Holly rarely thought of John Reardon these days, but she did often think about Lizzie. She could only hope the administrative assistant was a lovely, kind person.

At seven the doorbell rang, and there was Liam, looking gorgeous in charcoal gray pants and a black wool overcoat. Where were they going?

He stared at her for a moment. "You look beautiful, Holly."

Her heart tingled. "Thank you. You too. Do I get to know where we're going now?"

"Nope. It's a surprise." He took her hand and led her to his car, and they sped off toward Portland.

The lights of the city always filled Holly with excitement. Portland was small, but a sophisticated little city full of a world-renowned museum, five-star restaurants, galleries, theaters, and beautiful parks. "Well, the only thing I know for sure is that you're taking me somewhere indoors."

He turned to her and smiled. "Actually, outdoors."

Outdoors. In mid November. Granted, it was in the high fifties, flip-flops weather for hearty Mainers, but it wasn't exactly beach weather.

She let herself just enjoy the drive as Liam took back roads into downtown Portland, the Arts District, where Holly and her grandmother had spent much time over the years at the museum and the art galleries Camilla loved to walk through. Liam parked on the street in front of the thirty-story new Portland Lights Hotel. Was he taking her on a tryst? Did being naked and ordering room service and making mad, passionate love all night require getting dressed up? Oh wait, she thought. Their date was outdoors.

She raised an eyebrow, and he laughed, then took her hand, and led her inside the beautiful art deco–inspired hotel, her heels clicking on the marble floor. He nodded at the concierge, who nodded back, Holly noticed, and stopped in front of the elevator marked RTG.

What was he up to? "RTG?" Holly asked. "You'll see."

Because the elevator had only one destination, the RTG, Holly had no idea what floor they were going to. Up, up, up they went and finally the light pinged and the doors opened into a foyer with a huge Renaissance oil painting of a man and a woman, a wrought-iron stand holding dozens of red roses underneath it.

To the left was a door, and Liam held it open for her, and when Holly stepped through, she gasped. It was a rooftop garden (duh on the RTG), with one elegantly set table for two with a bottle of champagne in an ice bucket, two glasses, and two menus. High above, heat lights glowed down, and it was so warm that Holly took off her coat and wasn't the slightest bit cold. A waiter appeared, opened the champagne, poured, then bowed and disappeared.

Liam handed her a glass and they clinked and both took a sip, then he set both glasses down and pulled her close against him.

"Alone at last," he said, his arms at her waist.

Holly clasped her hands around his neck.

"This is pretty romantic. And wonderful."

"As are you," he whispered. "I've put you through a lot, and I just wanted to say thank you, for sticking by both me and Mia. We haven't been the easiest people to care about."

"Yeah, you both have," she said.

She didn't think the rowboat could be topped, but this seriously rivaled it.

TWENTY-TWO

The next afternoon, as Holly was working on a new pasta salad involving three different kinds of olives for Fandagos Café, her number one client, the bells jangled and Holly headed into the entryway and stopped in her tracks. A very thin, glamorous woman wearing sunglasses and a silk scarf wrapped around her head like she was Audrey Hepburn in a convertible was peering into the refrigerated case at the pastas and sauces.

"I do love a good Bolognese," the woman said. "Do you offer a trial taste? I'm quite particular about my Bolognese."

Holly stood behind the counter for support. Whoa. Whoa. Whoa. She'd know those dark modelesque bangs and collagen-enhanced pouty lips anywhere. This was Mia's mother, Veronica.

"Um, sure," Holly said. "Let me just go get a little cup and spoon."

"Oh, hell, I was going to pretend to be a

customer interested in the sauce to sort of spy on you, but I should just introduce myself." She took off her sunglasses and slid them into her huge purse. "I'm Veronica Feroux, Mia's mother."

Holly appreciated the honesty. "I recognize you from the photos Mia showed me. She carries her photo album in her backpack. I'm Holly Maguire. It's very nice to meet you." Holly held out her hand.

Veronica gave her hand a brief shake. "So I hear from my daughter that you're the greatest thing since sliced bread and apparently my ex-husband likes you too."

Holly laughed. This woman was Mia's mother, all right.

Veronica smiled. "I just wanted to come in and say hi, get any awkwardness out of the way since I live here now, well, not on the island, but Portland. I closed on my house so it's officially official. I'm here for good."

"I'm so glad, Veronica. That means the world to Mia."

She turned away for a moment. "I know. I've . . . made a lot of mistakes. Leaving Mia being the biggest. I'm working on some . . . issues."

Holly stared at her. "I'm glad to hear that."

"I can only imagine what you must think

of me," she said, glancing at Holly.

Holly held her gaze for a moment. "I'm just glad you're back in Mia's life on a daily basis, Veronica. Would you like some lunch? I could heat up one of my famous spaghetti Bologneses. And I have such a craving for bruschetta."

Her expression, part insecure-fragile, I-don't-know-what-I'm-doing and part glamorous I-rule-the-world, morphed into relief. "I'm starving. And I don't know Bolognese from Tuscanese, if there is such a thing. I've been to Tuscany, though. Oh, well, I guess the sauce would be Tuscan, then."

"I don't think there's a sauce called Tuscan, but there should be," Holly said, taking out the pasta and sauce, then leading Veronica into the kitchen, where she handed her a Camilla's Cucinotta apron. Holly scooped out the pasta and sauce into two pots and set the burner on low, then grabbed an eggplant, two tomatoes, and the rest of the ciabatta bread. Holly asked Veronica to slice the bread and then lay it on a baking sheet. She put Veronica on tomato chopping duty while she sliced the eggplant.

"He was smart not to fall for everything I was saying," Veronica said, doing a fine job on the tomato. "After he told me he didn't

404

love me that way anymore, I realized it's not really him or our marriage I wanted back. Just the security, you know? The idea of family. I thought I could just come back to Maine when things between me and my husband went so sour, and move right in with Liam and Mia, then move out to my own house when I was ready and find my soul mate. God, that sounds awful, doesn't it."

Yeah, it did. "What I've been learning is that mistakes can bring you where you need to be," Holly said as she stirred the Bolognese sauce.

Veronica wiped her hands on her apron. "I know I'm where I need to be. I just have to figure out *how* to be. But I've made a vow to myself and to Mia to stay in her life. To be the mother she deserves. And I'm not just saying all this like I'm on *Dr. Phil* or something. None of this feels good. But it feels *right.* For once, putting Mia ahead of myself feels right."

"Good," Holly said, pouring the Bolognese over the steaming spaghetti. She used oven mitts to slide out the tray of toasted ciabatta bread and explained to Veronica how to brush the bread with olive oil and then top it with the tomatoes, eggplant, some minced basil, and a sprinkle of Parmesan, then broil it for just a couple of minutes.

"Thanks for being so nice to me," Veronica said, her pretty blue eyes sincere.

"Thanks for being so nice to *me,*" Holly said.

They dug into the food, Veronica declaring it delicious, and talked about France, where Holly had never been, and after a while Holly didn't feel so weird sitting there having lunch with Liam's former wife.

When Veronica left, offering an invitation for Holly to drop in at her house in the university district any time, Holly sat down on the sofa in the living room, exhausted. She liked Veronica on a certain level, but the woman was so needy, so fragile behind all that glamour, that Holly felt she had to walk and talk on eggshells. She'd been relieved to hear that Veronica had found a good therapist and saw her twice a week.

And she could see how easy it had been for Liam to be pulled back in. Veronica was completely disarming. And under all that me, me, me was a heart. She was the type of person who could get people to do what she wanted and needed and, hopefully, she'd now start to rely on herself. If she wanted to earn back Mia's trust in the same way she'd never lost her love, she'd have to. Veronica had insisted on washing all the dishes and the gooey pots and pans, and finally Holly had relented. Now she was glad she didn't have that mess left to herself. She needed to get out, go for a drive to clear her head.

She thought about going to visit the gorgeous lighthouse in Cape Elizabeth or just walking around Portland's Old Port neighborhood and browsing the one-of-a-kind shops and stopping at Whole Foods for some exotic vegetables she wanted to try. But when she got in her car and started driving, she found herself heading toward Portland's Deering Oaks Park, a beautiful oasis in the middle of the city with its duck pond and walking bridge, and then realized the cemetery where her grandmother and grandfather were buried was just minutes away. She'd been heading there all along and hadn't realized it.

Holly stopped at a florist and bought a bouquet of white roses, her grandmother's favorite flowers, and drove to the cemetery. The November wind whipped her long hair around. It was still warm for the season, but Holly shivered in her wool coat anyway. Cemeteries always made her shiver. She followed the path until she saw the markers for the area in which Camilla and Armando were buried. They were shaded in spring, summer, and fall under the leaves of a stately oak. Holly liked the idea of the tree's life, its protective branches, reaching out over the graves, the red, orange, and yellow leaves scattering like sweet offerings. Her grandmother had loved the season of fall most of all.

The two curved headstones were so close, as her grandmother had wanted. Holly wished she could have known her grandfather, the amazing Italian man with butter-colored hair and Adriatic Sea–colored eyes. She sat down beside Camilla's stone and laid down the roses among the brilliantly hued leaves.

CAMILLA CONSTANTINA,
BELOVED WIFE, MOTHER,
GRANDMOTHER, FRIEND.
RIPOSI IN PACE

"Rest in peace, Nonna," Holly said to the sky and closed her eyes. And indeed it was peace that Holly felt come over her.

The hour she'd spent in the cemetery, telling her grandmother everything, about mastering the risotto, getting the catering job, teaching the class, and about Liam and Mia and even the romantic date in the rooftop garden, had her longing to spend some time listening to her grandmother. And so she drove home and drew a bath, using her grandmother's lavender salts. She brought up a pot of Earl Grey tea and a chocolate-dipped biscotti and settled into the hot soapy water with the last of her grandmother's diaries. She turned to the final entry, dated the day before she died.

Dear Diary,

It's been a long time since I've written. Decades. But my dear girl is here. My Holly. And I have to write about how happy I am, how blessed.

I'm dying. I can feel the breath leave my body in the smallest of ways, just one extra intake of breath to reach for a tomato, to pour olive oil into the pan. It's time, finally, for me to join my Armando. My heart is at peace.

How glad I am that my Holly is here, in this house, where I know she belongs, where I know she is meant to be. Of course, I can't tell her that; it won't make sense to her yet. But one day it will.

She asked last night about her fortune, the one I gave her when she was just sixteen years old. I tried to explain as best I could. That the fortune didn't come from me, just through me, that I held my stones and closed my eyes, and the notion that her great love would like *sa cordula* was what came out of my mouth. I didn't make up the words; they just came. I didn't know why. I don't know what man could like *sa cordula,* especially if Armando didn't, and Armando liked everything, even sweetbreads.

Holly has always been afraid it meant there would be no great love in her life, and I tried to explain that it didn't mean that at all. She's had love in her life, and each one was great, starting with the smallest, first flicker in elementary school. A broken heart doesn't negate the love. Doesn't make it any less large.

"You'll understand when you need to, Holly," I told her. "That's the only thing I know for certain."

"Okay, Nonna," she said and held my hand and brought it up to her cheek. And then I brought both our hands down to my heart, where I held it until I began to nod off. Holly helped me up to my room and said good night, Nonna, then stopped at the door, turned around, and came back, leaning over to press a kiss to my forehead. I smiled at her and said, *"Ti amo, nipote."*

I know I will not wake in the morning. But I also know I will be with Holly for the rest of her days and that she will find herself — and more — in this apricot-colored bungalow at the edge of Blue Crab Island. She has come home.

Tears streaming down her cheeks, Holly turned the page, but that was it. Except for a recipe.

Sa cordula, with its final ingredient of one fervent wish.

The fortune *had* to mean something. Holly wasn't sure what, but it meant something. If she made *sa cordula* for Liam and he took one bite and politely said, "Um, Holly, you can have the rest if you want," she wouldn't discount him as her great love. He could certainly be her great love. Stewed lamb guts wouldn't decide that. They would. Life would.

For the last class, Holly was holding a Camilla's Cucinotta Italian cooking class potluck party the Sunday afternoon before. Everyone was to bring their favorite dish they'd made in class. And everyone could invite someone. Mia invited Daniel, since she knew she could count on Holly to invite her father. Tamara invited her sister. Simon invited his daughter, and even though it wasn't his weekend to have her, her mother gave special permission.

She would not make the *sa cordula* for Liam. Because when you had great love, you knew it.

Did she know it? Could you ever know it? She'd thought John Reardon her great love. Though she'd had to ignore months of warning signs. And bury her head in the sand.

Perhaps it was better to know, after all. To be forewarned and forearmed, as they said.

Holly got out of the bath and put on jeans, a sweater, and her coat and drove to Portland, to one of the last old-world butchers.

"Do you have lamb intestines?" Holly asked the butcher, a short, fifty-something man with surprisingly large biceps, as though she were asking for some shanks.

He stared at her. "Uh, I have them, yes."

It was meant to be. "I'll take enough to make an old-word Italian dish for two."

He shrugged and nodded. "You're the second person this month who's come in for lamb intestines. It's a rare request, trust me."

"This month?" Holly repeated.

"Yeah, just a couple of weeks ago. An elderly woman came in for some."

"Do you mean a couple of months ago?" she asked. "My grandmother was likely a regular customer."

"Who is your grandmother?"

"Camilla Constantina?"

"Oh, yes! I know Camilla. Knew her, I should say. I heard she passed. Beautiful woman."

Holly smiled. Yes, she was.

"The woman who came in wasn't Camilla," the butcher said. "She had a big wart on her face. Heh. Like a witch. And she had long, jet-black hair, even though she must have been seventy."

Huh. A witch had come in for the making of *sa cordula*. Perhaps Holly shouldn't make it after all.

He wrapped up the package. "I will tell you what I told her. Clean them well. I'm not even sure I'm supposed to sell them."

Holly nodded and took her lamb guts home. Not sure if she'd make the *sa cordula* or not.

TWENTY-THREE

Holly woke at midnight, the remnants of a bad dream clawing at her. Liam had been standing amid nothing, just a grayish air with no background, and he had no face, though she knew it was him. He wore his leather jacket, his hands shoved into his jeans pocket. And there was his gorgeous, thick, sexy dark hair. But no face.

She sat up, unsettled, and went downstairs for a glass of iced tea. Antonio was on his perch, watching her. She glanced up at the wall of little paintings by the window, of Antonio, of this house, of the three Po River stones, and of her grandmother, in her blue day dress, sitting in a wrought-iron chair by the tomato plants, a Mona Lisa smile on her stunning face.

She took the binder of recipes and searched for *sa cordula,* and there it was, between the chicken cacciatore and the chicken costoletta, the same recipe that

Holly had found in the diary.

Sa cordula.
Lamb intestines.
Peas.
Onions.
Butter.
Oil.
One fervent wish.

It was simple to make, a matter of rinsing the intestines well and letting them dry and then braiding them so they looked less like swirling guts and more like . . . Holly didn't know. Once again she thought it looked like exactly what it was. She sautéed the lamb with the peas and onions and set it on a plate.

She took a tiny bite. It wasn't *so* bad, really, if you took a bite with the peas and onions. So the peas did help, after all. She took another tiny bite. If she didn't know what it was, she would even like it. Maybe because she used twice the salt called for.

Maybe that made her her own great love. Maybe that had been her grandmother's point?

The great love of your life will be one of the few people on earth to like sa cordula.

So was this what her grandmother had

been trying to tell her? That she needed to be the love of her own life? Perhaps her grandmother had known that Holly would one day find her way back to her kitchen, back to herself. And she'd find the meaning of great love in the process.

The *sa cordula* was a mystery like her grandmother had been. And should remain.

With that, she took the plate and dumped it in the trash. A bit stuck to the plate, so she set it down for Antonio. The old gray cat waddled over and sniffed it, then his mouth curled as if in utter distaste and he waddled away and jumped back up on his perch.

Ha. Even an old-world cat didn't like *sa cordula.* "Antonio, you may not be my great love, but I do love you. So there, fortune."

The weather held for the party. Sunny and sixty-one glorious degrees, Holly moved the gathering into the backyard, setting up the large outdoor table as a buffet. Antonio lay half-napping in a patch of sunlight by the withering tomatoes. Holly made a mental note to read up on Gardening 101 that night. If she could make an incredible risotto alla Milanese, she could grow a tomato.

At one o'clock, she set out her dishes on

warming trays, her saffron risotto and her spinach and three cheese ravioli, two of her new pasta salads and a large platter of antipasto. Mia, her adorable boyfriend, and her handsome father were the first to arrive. Mia brought the chicken alla Milanese. Liam made his favorite penne in vodka sauce, and Daniel Dressler came fullhanded with tiramisu that his mother made for the occasion.

As Liam and Daniel went into the little garage for the extra warming trays, a beaming Mia said, "Isn't he so cute?"

"Very," Holly said. Mia and Daniel made an adorable couple.

"And guess what? I made a new friend. A new potential best friend. She just moved to Portland, right across the bridge, so we can even walk to each other's houses, and her dad has custody of her too. We have so much in common. And we totally have the same taste in boys. Not that she'd ever go after Daniel, but she has a major crush on a guy who's kind of a loner and into music just like Daniel is."

"I had a feeling things would work out fine," Holly said, popping an olive into her mouth.

The boy in question and Liam came back out, their arms full of warming trays, which

Liam set up. Simon and his daughter were next to arrive with the spaghetti and meatballs they'd worked on together that morning. And then Tamara and Francesca arrived, one with minestrone and one with Italian wedding soup.

Holly laughed. "Perfect."

After introductions and oohing and ahhing at the trays of delicious-looking and -smelling Italian food, everyone sat down, their plates full of a little of this, a little of that. Holly loved Mia's chicken alla Milanese. And Liam's penne was as overcooked as Holly's used to be, but the vodka sauce wasn't bad at all. In fact, Holly had a feeling he'd used a quart he'd bought from her a few days before.

"Oh, and I brought something else," Mia said, reaching under her seat for a foil-wrapped plate. She peeled back the foil.

Holly gasped. It was *sa cordula*. She stood up, her mind going blank, her legs feeling like rubber. She sat back down. What the —

"Dad, try some," Mia said, forking a bite and holding it up to him. "Don't worry about not liking it — you won't hurt my feelings. I didn't make it. I'm just curious to see what you'll think of it."

It was like slow motion as Liam smiled

and leaned forward to take the bite with his lips.

No. No. No. Holly didn't want to know.

Liam glanced at the fork Mia held before him. "Oh, it's that dish you served me a couple of weeks ago. What did you say it was called again?"

Mia grinned at Holly. "Just an old-world dish that Holly's *nonna* used to make."

He slid the fork into his mouth. Chewed. Swallowed. "I like it," Liam said. "I still can't quite figure out what it is, but I like it. To Holly's nonna, then," he added, holding up his bottle of beer.

He liked it.

Liam Geller liked *sa cordula.* One of the few people on earth.

Holly stared from him to Mia. What had just happened? And how?

Everyone raised their cup and sipped, and Holly managed to raise hers as well, and then Daniel got up and took over the iPod dock, a Killers' song playing. When Liam's attention was taken by Simon, Tamara came over to sit between Mia and Holly.

"Mia," Tamara whispered, "you kind of took a big chance there. What if your dad hadn't liked it? Holly would have felt terrible."

Mia shook her head. "No chance of that. I

had it made for him two weeks ago, after he told me he wasn't getting back with my mom and that he had feelings for Holly. I hired the Italian cafeteria lady at school to make it for me. I had to give her *fifty* bucks. I wanted to prove that my dad was wrong, that he *wasn't* Holly's great love, but he liked it. I couldn't deal at all."

Holly gasped again. She didn't need to ask if the cafeteria lady had a big wart on her face.

"That's why I freaked out so bad, Holly. My dad *is* your great love. Just like your grandmother's fortune said. It took me a while to tell you. Well, show you. Good thing I kept the *sa cordula* in the freezer, huh?"

"Oh, Mia," Holly said, putting her arm around her.

"So, this is kind of my way of saying I'm sorry again. For everything. And my way of saying thanks for teaching me how to cook — even if I didn't make that *sa cordula* thing myself." She leaned in. "I mean, *hello* — gross."

Holly squeezed Mia into a hug. There were some wonderful highs and some terrible lows to come, Holly figured. But they'd muddle through. And they'd come through fine.

According to her decades-old fortune, Holly had found her great love. But as her grandmother had said, "You knew it when you had it." And when you knew it, you didn't have to test it.

Liam went back to his seat and picked up his plate, taking another bite of the *sa cordula*. "I really haven't ever tasted anything quite like this. And the peas are interesting in it."

Mia rolled her eyes and shook her head with a smile. "Love Goddess," she whispered to Holly.

CAMILLA'S CUCINOTTA
RECIPES

Chicken alla Milanese
Serves 4

4 pieces skinless, boneless chicken breast
1 cup instant polenta
3/4 cup grated parmigiano-reggiano cheese
2 cups flour
1 large egg
1 tablespoon olive oil
Juice of 1 lemon
Salt and pepper to taste
1 wish

Pound chicken breasts between 2 sheets of plastic wrap. On a plate, combine polenta with half the cheese. Fill another plate with flour. In bowl, beat egg with splash of water. Season chicken with salt and pepper. Coat each breast in flour, then egg, then polenta/ cheese. Add 1 wish. Heat oil in large skillet over medium-high heat. Add chicken and cook, turning once, 6 minutes or until golden.

Risotto alla Milanese (quick version)
Serves 4

3 cups chicken broth
1 cup water
1 medium onion, finely chopped
3 tablespoons unsalted butter
1 1/2 cups arborio rice
1/4 cup freshly grated Parmesan
1/4 teaspoon crumbled saffron threads
1 wish

In heavy saucepan, cook onion in 2 tablespoons butter over moderate heat, stirring occasionally, until soft. Add rice and stir. Separately, bring broth and water to simmer and add 1 cup of mixture to rice, stirring constantly. Simmer until absorbed. Add 1 wish. Continue simmering and adding broth mixture, 1/4 cup at a time, until absorbed, 20 minutes or so in total. Done when rice is creamy, about 20 minutes. Stir in Parmesan, saffron, remaining butter, and salt and pepper to taste. Cook over low heat for a few minutes until heated.

Holly's Heartbreak Pasta Salad

Serves 4

3 cups uncooked rotini pasta
1 pound Italian sausage, cut into bite-size pieces
4 sliced garlic cloves
1/2 cup balsamic vinaigrette
1 cup diced onion
salt and pepper
2 (15-ounce) cans sliced tomatoes (undrained)
1/2 cup parmesan cheese
1 true statement

Cook pasta per package. In skillet, cook sausage on medium-high heat, 8 minutes or until cooked through. Drain and return to skillet. Add tomatoes in liquid, garlic, pepper/salt, onion and balsamic vinaigrette. Cook 5 minutes or until onions are tender. Add 1 true statement. Drain pasta. Toss with the sausage mixture and cheese.

Camilla's Cucinotta Tiramisu

Serves 4

500 grams (1 pound) mascarpone cheese
6 pasteurized eggs
2 packages ladyfingers (*savoiardi*)

3 tablespoons sugar
2 shots (2 ounces) cognac or brandy
12 ounces espresso
4 tablespoons powdered unsweetened cocoa
1 memory

Pour espresso into shallow, flat-bottomed bowl. Add one shot of cognac, one teaspoon cocoa, and allow to cool to room temperature. Separate egg yolks and whites. Beat egg yolks and sugar until creamy white. Add mascarpone and 1 shot of cognac and mix until blended. In another bowl, beat eggs whites until fluffy and fold beaten egg whites into mascarpone mixture. Mix enough to blend. Dip a *savoiardi* in the espresso. Place each finger in pan, sugar side down to fit. Spoon a layer of egg/mascarpone mixture across the layer of *savoiardi*. Add 1 memory. Use about 1/2 of the mascarpone mix. Dip another layer of *savoiardi* and lay them on the mascarpone mix, sugar side down. Spoon a second layer of egg/mascarpone mixture across the second layer of *savoiardi*. Use the remaining mascarpone mix. Sift cocoa on top of the second mascarpone layer. Refrigerate for at least 5 hours before serving.

READERS GROUP GUIDE

BOOK SUMMARY
Thirty-year-old Holly Maguire returns to a small island off the coast of Maine when she inherits her grandmother's cooking school. In the proud tradition of her Italian grandmother, known for her fortune-telling abilities as well as her amazing cuisine, Holly begins teaching a cooking class. The class changes the lives of its students: a grieving mother, a newly separated father, a chronically single thirtysomething woman, and a twelve-year-old girl from a broken home. Can this neophyte chef keep the business afloat and possibly find love in the process?

QUESTIONS FOR DISCUSSION
1. Holly arrives on Blue Crab Island after a devastating breakup. Two weeks later, her beloved grandmother passes away in her sleep. Now Holly is charged with keeping

her grandmother's cucinotta going, despite her marginal knowledge of the business. Was there ever a time in your life when you were as down on your luck as poor Holly? How did you make it through and what did you learn from the experience?

2. Holly returns to Blue Crab Island because of the special bond she shares with her grandmother and the safety and comfort the island represents. Where is that special place of comfort for you?

3. Why do you think Luciana did not share Holly's enthusiasm and love for the island? How does reading Camilla's diary give Holly a clearer picture of her mother's early life? How does their relationship change over the course of the story?

4. Each of Holly's four students is struggling with a personal hardship: Juliet, with the loss of her child; Simon, with his recent divorce; Tamara, with her family's concern over her being single; and Mia, trying to rid her dad of his awful girlfriend. How does the cooking class help each of them? How can cooking be therapeutic?

Do you think great cuisine can be considered an art form?

5. Romance was never easy for Holly: "She'd let her relationships take center stage of her heart, mind, and soul. Maybe because she'd never found her niche" (page 49). How did her attitude toward romance change after her breakup with John Reardon and her arrival in Maine?

6. She may not have the "knowing" like Camilla, but how does Holly reach out and help her students with their problems?

7. Camilla Constantina is known for her fortune-telling abilities, at least "for being right 70 percent of the time." Would you ever want to possess a gift like this? Have you ever had your fortune told?

8. Were you surprised at the disappearance of the infamous white binder full of recipes? Do you agree with the way Holly handled the situation? How did it make her grow as a chef in her own right?

9. Liam's ex-wife Veronica shows up unexpectedly and throws a wrench into his burgeoning romance with Holly. Do you

think Liam handled the situation tactfully? What about Holly?

10. What did you think of Mia's risky plan to make the *sa cordula* for her father, to disprove Camilla's prophecy?

11. Lenora Windemere branded Camilla Constantina a witch, which made life in the small island community very difficult for a woman on her own. How does Holly face similar treatment when she first arrives?

12. Holly might not have been the original "Love Goddess" her grandmother was, but she played matchmaker for two of her students, however inadvertently, and also managed to find love herself. Were you satisfied with the ending?

13. Melissa Senate's writing, especially the descriptions of the food and its preparation, is so vivid. Did it inspire you to attempt a risotto or to enroll in a cooking class?

ENHANCE YOUR BOOK CLUB

1. Make your book club night a potluck Italian dinner, with each member making and

bringing her own Italian favorites. *Sa cordula,* anyone?

2. Exchange recipes with your book group, slightly tailored the Camilla Constantina way. Make sure each recipe includes one key ingredient such as "one fervent wish" or "one sad memory," and each member can discuss what she chose and why.

3. Check out the author's website at www .melissasenate.com for her informative blog and interviews with other authors.

A CONVERSATION WITH MELISSA SENATE

1. Where did the inspiration for *The Love Goddess' Cooking School* come from?

I'd been thinking a lot about my own grandmother, who died a few years ago, and how much she meant to me, how much comfort she was to me during my childhood. It's very likely impossible for anyone to think of her grandmother without thinking of food. Now, my grandmother was not Italian, not 70 percent psychic, not a cook, not *anything* like Camilla Constantina, but to me, as a young girl, she *was* magical, the queen of Queens Boulevard in New York City, where I spent weekend after weekend in her kind company. I suppose *The Love Goddess' Cooking School* came out of my wanting to honor her memory, my enchantment with all things Italian — and a determination to learn to cook Italian food — and the wonderful way that cooking brings people together. My son, who's eight, loves to cook with me, and I've noticed that he'll tell me his secrets as he's scrambling eggs or stirring brownie batter. As long as I don't *ask*.

2. You live on the coast of Maine. Is Blue Crab Island a real place or just based on one of the many beautiful islands off the coast? How important is the setting of a story for you?
Blue Crab Island is fictitious and based on two nearby-tome islands — one, the island off my town (Yarmouth), which is reached via a beautiful bridge but is strictly residential, and the other, the amazing Peaks Island, accessible only by ferry but its own little world with schools and shopping and inns. Island life is so magical. And setting is everything to me — I moved to Maine from New York City in the summer of 2004, and as I set my novels here, I discover how much the state has become a part of me.

3. Poor Holly loses her boyfriend, her job, and then her beloved grandmother. Have you ever been at a simi-

lar crossroads in your life? How did you deal with the inevitable change that comes from these milestone moments?

I've been through some of life's whoppers, and I think what has gotten me through are three things: (1) I'm an optimist (which helps *a lot*); (2) I'm very motivated by *possibility.* It's one of my favorite words; (3) my motto is: *Just do it.* if you put those three things together, you can get through some trying times (including change, which has always been very hard on me).

4. You were an editor at a publishing house before becoming a full-time writer. Is it easier or more difficult being on the other side of the desk?

I loved being an editor (though I must say I hated contract negotiations), but it's tough stuff — you have to keep so many balls up in the air, put out fires, be creative on demand, be all business, be, be, be. You're the author's advocate, the publishing house's advocate. It's a very demanding job, but it's the best job in the world if you love books, love the business, love the process. Being an author isn't easy — from the words that won't come to the waits to the crushing disappointments, but it's so incredibly fulfilling. I make up stories, tell them in my own voice, work out my big and small life questions through characters and themes. Writing is a joy. I liked working for a corporation, liked every boss I've ever had (strange, but true), loved having coworkers and lunch buddies and office holiday parties, but I love nothing more than being my boss at a job so personally rewarding and making my own hours, especially since I'm a single mother.

5. Did you always want to write a novel where cooking was a major theme? What is it about cooking and good food that seems to be so cathartic? Is food central to your life?
I'm thinking about food right now. About spaghetti carbonara, which I wish I didn't love quite so much. I find cooking so satisfying — following the steps, improvising, allowing yourself to experiment, to make a recipe a bit of your own. And then you get to eat! It's so much fun to cook with others — especially with my son, who loves to help in the kitchen. It's impossible not to talk while you're cooking with someone. The whole process is about sharing — and then you get to share the results of your labor of love. I always knew

I wanted to write about cooking, but I wasn't sure in what way, until I started thinking about what would happen if a group of slightly lost strangers took a cooking class . . . how they'd form friendships, open up, how their lives would change because of the class, because of one another. I also wanted to learn to cook classic Italian . . . and did through Holly and her students. My chicken alla Milanese has gotten pretty darn good.

6. You have a knack for making the reader extremely hungry with mouthwatering descriptions of the Italian cuisine. Are you a cook yourself? What are the meals you go to for comfort?

Oh, thank you so much for that! It took me longer than it did Holly to make decent versions of the recipes I included in the book. I wish I were a great cook. I try so hard. But it's not my talent. My favorite cuisines are Italian, Indian, and Mexican, but my comfort meals are very classic American: meat loaf and mashed potatoes. A BLT. A good hamburger with ketchup and tomato and lettuce. Chicken soup. The perfect grilled cheese. And a caramel apple.

7. How long does it take you to complete a novel, from start to finish? How much research do you do for each book?

From start to finish, around nine months. I need to do a lot of writing in my head before I can start; I have to have the core of the story in my heart to understand what I'm doing. That can take me a while. But once I have it, the pages come quickly. I like to write a very clean first draft, revising as I go, so that when I get to the end, I basically have a third draft that needs only a solid edit and then a few rounds of polishing. *The Love Goddess' Cooking School* required a lot of research — about Italian cooking, which I'm fascinated by, about Camilla Constantina's era (for her diary entries). I read so many autobiographies and memoirs — from Marcella Hazan's to Julia Child's to Anthony Bourdain's. Food and cooking were my life for the writing of this book, and I loved every minute of it. Even the very bad attempts at risotto and tiramisu.

8. You've written young adult novels as well as women's fiction. Which proves to be more of a challenge?

Young Adult is *way* more challenging for me. To write a modern teenage main character with authenticity *and* not use one dated word, like "bogus." Emotional issues facing teens may be timeless, but capturing the voice is very difficult. It's funny that in two reviews of my last YA, one by a teenager said: "There was no cursing — *so* not realistic." The other, by a librarian, said: "There was no cursing, so refreshing!"

9. Holly is such a relatable and real character. Do you ever base your characters on people you know or are they pure fiction?

Thank you! I never base my characters, main or secondary or the most minor, on anyone in real life. I'm not even quite sure where the characters come from, how they form in my mind, how they evolve. Camilla was likely started by my memory of a tiny, beautiful, elderly cook in a restaurant in Milan, Italy, but she was a very hazy image; I had to imprint Camilla on her. Mia, though, came steamrolling in my head, fully formed from the get-go. I think all my characters deal with issues or emotions that are brewing for me, so the characters always feel so real to me. It's very hard to say good-bye to the characters and their world when the end is really The End.

10. Your novel *See Jane Date* was made into a TV movie with Charisma Carpenter. If *The Love Goddess' Cooking School* were to be made into a film, who would you cast in the lead roles?
Oooh, such a fun question. My dream cast: for Holly, Kate Winslet. For Liam, Robert Downey Jr. For Mia, Dakota Fanning. For Simon: Ryan Gosling. For Juliet: Vera Farmiga. For Tamara, Emily Blunt. (Colin Firth or Mark Ruffalo can substitute for Robert Downey Jr. if he's too busy with *Iron Man 3*.

11. When you begin a novel, do you have a clear picture of where you want to end up, or do you just see where the characters take you?
I need that clear picture. I always write to a last line, emotionally speaking. I write very detailed synopses — major emotional points, major plot points, and the major connectors — and then I use that synopsis to structure the novel by breaking the major points into chapters. Things shift, of course, but not the foundation. I need it strong and sound and supportive before I can write a word. When I first started writing *The Love Goddess' Cooking School,*

Simon was a young (childless) married couple (there was a Susannah, too). But as I wrote and his voice emerged, he let me know he was a lonely scientist trying to navigate single fatherhood. Camilla's diary entries didn't exist in the synopsis at all, but as I wrote, I realized Holly needed her grandmother's parallel story in Camilla's own voice to help her understand her mother. I never follow the synopsis to a *T*; the story needs to live and breathe and evolve on its own.

12. Your website is a treasure trove of information on authors and writing. How did you come to interview other authors about the process of writing? Who are some of your favorite authors?

I've long belonged to a great group of female authors who blog about one another's new releases (in a wonderful show of support), and I'll just ask authors whose work I admire if they'd like to participate in a Q&A for my blog. I love showcasing authors and reading about their writing processes and favorite books. As for my own favorite authors, I have so many. I'm crazy about Elinor Lipman, Anne Tyler, Richard Russo, and Jennifer Crusie (to name just a few), and right now I'm reading everything Elizabeth Berg has ever written. I love memoirs, too. I'll also generally buy any book that has half a woman on the cover. I love women's fiction.

13. What would you like readers to take away from *The Love Goddess' Cooking School?*

That fate and fortunes are a funny thing, that no matter what may seem predestined for you, *you* are the captain of your own little ship.

14. What are you working on next?

As of this writing, I'm putting the finishing touches on the first few chapters of a new novel about family, love, and the magic of movies.

The employees of Thorndike Press hope you have enjoyed this Large Print book. All our Thorndike, Wheeler, and Kennebec Large Print titles are designed for easy reading, and all our books are made to last. Other Thorndike Press Large Print books are available at your library, through selected bookstores, or directly from us.

For information about titles, please call:
  (800) 223-1244

or visit our Web site at:
  http://gale.cengage.com/thorndike

To share your comments, please write:
  Publisher
  Thorndike Press
  295 Kennedy Memorial Drive
  Waterville, ME 04901